THE
Midnight Hour

DON'T MISS THESE OTHER NOVELS BY BESTSELLING AUTHOR BRENDA JACKSON

THE MADARIS FAMILY NOVELS
Taste of Passion
Slow Burn
Unfinished Business

PLAYERS SERIES
What a Woman Wants
No More Playas
The Playa's Handbook

STAND-ALONE NOVELS
Her Little Black Book
The Savvy Sistahs
Ties That Bind
A Family Reunion

SHORT STORY COLLECTION
Some Like It Hot

ANTHOLOGIES
Mr. Satisfaction
An All Night Man
Let's Get It On
The Best Man
Welcome to Leo's

THE
Midnight Hour

BRENDA JACKSON

St. Martin's Griffin
New York

This is a work of fiction. All of the characters, organizations, and events portrayed in this novel are either products of the author's imagination or are used fictitiously.

Published in the United States by St. Martin's Griffin, an imprint of St. Martin's Publishing Group

THE MIDNIGHT HOUR. Copyright © 2004 by Brenda Jackson. All rights reserved. Printed in the United States of America. For information, address St. Martin's Publishing Group, 120 Broadway, New York, NY 10271.

www.stmartins.com

ISBN 978-0-312-98997-2 (mass market paperback)
ISBN 978-1-250-04212-5 (trade paperback)
ISBN 978-1-4299-0578-7 (ebook)
ISBN 978-1-250-62379-9 (trade paperback)

Our books may be purchased in bulk for promotional, educational, or business use. Please contact your local bookseller or the Macmillan Corporate and Premium Sales Department at 1-800-221-7945, extension 5442, or by email at MacmillanSpecialMarkets@macmillan.com.

First St. Martin's Griffin Edition: December 2019

10 9 8 7 6 5 4 3 2 1

DEDICATION

This book is dedicated to all the faithful readers of my Madaris and Friends Series who waited patiently for Sir Drake's story. I appreciate all of you and I thank you from the bottom of my heart.

To my hero, husband and best friend, Gerald Jackson, Sr.

To my good friends, Pat and Cleve Warren. Sir Drake's story is especially for you.

To my editor, Monique Patterson. Thank you for giving me the opportunity to continue the Madaris and Friends Series.

And to my Heavenly Father who makes all things possible.

THE MADARIS FAMILY

Milton Madaris, Sr. and Felicia Laverne Lee Madaris

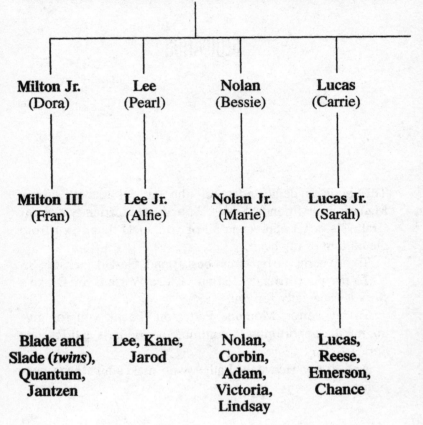

Milton Jr. (Dora)	Lee (Pearl)	Nolan (Bessie)	Lucas (Carrie)
Milton III (Fran)	Lee Jr. (Alfie)	Nolan Jr. (Marie)	Lucas Jr. (Sarah)
Blade and Slade (*twins*), Quantum, Jantzen	Lee, Kane, Jarod	Nolan, Corbin, Adam, Victoria, Lindsay	Lucas, Reese, Emerson, Chance

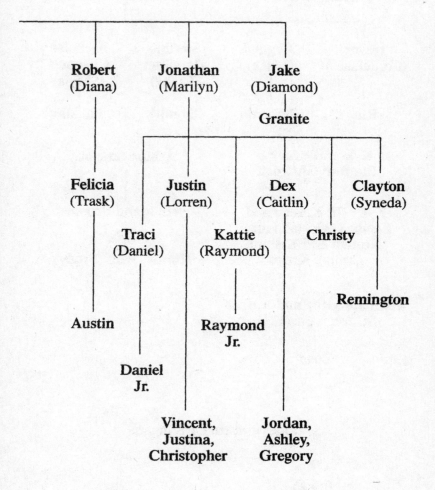

Robert
(Diana)

Jonathan
(Marilyn)

Jake
(Diamond)

Granite

Felicia
(Trask)

Justin
(Lorren)

Dex
(Caitlin)

Clayton
(Syneda)

Traci
(Daniel)

Kattie
(Raymond)

Christy

Remington

Austin

Raymond
Jr.

Daniel
Jr.

Vincent,
Justina,
Christopher

Jordan,
Ashley,
Gregory

FRIENDS OF THE MADARIS FAMILY

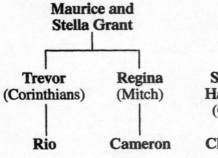

Maurice and Stella Grant

- Trevor (Corinthians)
  - Rio
- Regina (Mitch)
  - Cameron

Angelique Hamilton Chenault

- Sterling Hamilton (Colby)
  - Chandler
- Nicholas Chenault (Shayla)
  - Paladin

Kyle and Kimara Stafford Garwood

Kyle, VI; Kareen and Keisha (*twins*); Kamry; Keenan and Kellum (*twins*); Kenya

Ashton Sinclair

Netherland Brooms

Hunter, Wolf, Brody

Trent Jordache and Brenna St. Johns Jordache

Zane

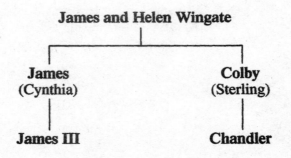

James and Helen Wingate

- James (Cynthia)
  - James III
- Colby (Sterling)
  - Chandler

**Paul Dunlap
and Callie Foster**

Jolene Maxwell Thomas

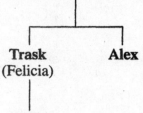

Shayla Kirkland
(Nicholas)

Trask
(Felicia)

Alex

Paladin

Austin

Drake Warren

**Ernest and Nadine
Kalloren**

Howard Reeves

Rainey Gilford

**Paris, Belgium,
Netherland Brooms,
Rome** (Jada), **Dakota**

**Reverend Nathan
and Maudlin** Avery

Senator
Nedwyn Lansing

**Joshua,
Corinthians** (Trevor)

Syntel Remington and Janeda Walters

Syneda
(Clayton)

Remington

For affliction does not come from the dust, nor does trouble sprout from the ground; but man is born to trouble as the sparks fly upward.

—JOB 5:6–7

THE
Midnight Hour

PROLOGUE

It was the midnight hour when a lone figure emerged out of the shadows and materialized into the halls of the Bethesda Naval Hospital. All was quiet and the few staff members on duty didn't pay any attention to the individual who was clutching a patient's medical chart, giving the appearance of a doctor making rounds, checking on patients.

The lone figure turned down a semi-darkened hall. Holding the medical chart firmly in hand and inhaling deep, determined breaths, the individual dressed in a doctor's white coat quickly continued toward their destination.

Marine Colonel Ashton Sinclair drew in a ragged breath as he stood by the side of the hospital bed and gazed down at his friend, Drake Warren, a man barely recognizable amidst all the tubes connected to his body. Lying there lifeless, Drake looked a lot older than his thirty-five years. He looked like a man who'd had a rough life and was making a smooth entry into the arms of death.

According to the doctor Ashton had spoken with when he'd first arrived that day, all five bullets had been removed, but due to extensive blood loss, there was a slim chance that

Drake would survive another night. The doctor was surprised he was still holding on for this long.

Ashton was also surprised.

It was well known among those who really knew Sir Drake, as he was fondly called, that for the past five years he'd been walking a fine line between life and death, usually tottering on the edge of the latter. Although he had existed, Sir Drake's life had basically ended in Haiti five years ago when the woman he loved, Marine Captain Sandy Carroll, had gotten killed. Since then Drake had been a walking time bomb, taking unnecessary risks; a man who constantly played Russian roulette with his life. A man who had a death wish.

Ashton, Sir Drake, and another one of their close friends by the name of Trevor Grant, had been marine captains and part of the marines' elite Special Forces, the Force Recon Unit. Trained to survive in difficult situations, each had a specialty. Trevor was the man to have at your back when it came to surviving in the jungles or any other unusual or dangerous environment; Sir Drake was a whiz at weapons and explosives and Ashton was a pathfinder, a tracker. He had the ability to locate anyone or anything in thick woods, jungles, forest, and any type of uncivilized or impenetrable territory—including the deserts of Iraq. Ashton's skill was the reason Sir Drake was back in the United States. He had located him, left for dead, on the southern edge of Tikrit and had taken care of the critically wounded former marine who was now an undercover agent for the CIA.

Ashton's thoughts then shifted back to Sandy Carroll, the only woman he had known Drake to love. Sandy, known for her skills in martial arts and marksmanship, had been the only female marine who had come close to becoming a Recon. Ashton, Trevor, Sir Drake, and Sandy had often teamed up for various coveted missions and had become known among fellow Recons as the "Fearless Four."

The last time the four of them had been on a mission together was that time in Haiti. American dignitaries had gotten kidnapped and held for ransom by a drug cartel. No one had known the entire thing had been a setup, orchestrated by a drug lord and psychopath by the name of Solomon Cross. Cross's and Drake's paths had crossed two years earlier when the marines special force unit headed by Drake was sent to destroy Cross's laboratory compound. During the course of the fighting, Cross's wife Maria was killed. Solomon Cross blamed Drake for Maria's death and vowed to uphold his principle of "an eye for an eye" and destroy any woman whom Drake ever loved.

Cross kept good on his vow when he found out about Drake's love for Sandy and had made sure that she was killed on that mission in Haiti. Drake had never gotten over what had happened to Sandy and vowed to one day get the man who had been responsible. But now it seemed that Drake had given up the will to live, to fight, to survive. His love for Sandy had been strong, invincible and a part of Drake had died with her that day. The only thing that had kept him going was his need for revenge.

And now Drake was dying a slow, agonizing death. He had finally gotten his death wish, but Ashton refused to give up on his trusted friend, a man who had been there for him in some of the toughest times. A man who, on more than one occasion, had saved his life. He, Drake and Trevor were as close as any blood brothers could be.

Ashton checked his watch. Trevor had left to go take a shower and would return in about an hour or so. Both he and Trevor had decided that no matter what, they would remain with Sir Drake until the end. Knowing what doctors said about comatose patients retaining their ability to hear in

some situations, Ashton sat down in the chair next to the
bed and started off by talking in the only way he knew how
to the rough and tough former marine—straightforward,
blunt and to the point.

"Damn you, Sir Drake, you jaded ass, what the hell were
you trying to prove in Tikrit? You should have waited for
backup instead of doing your own thing. It's a wonder you
didn't get your damn head blown off instead of just a few
bullets in your hide. What if I hadn't had a vision and knew
just where to find you?" he asked harshly, thanking God for
the special gift he had inherited from his blend of Cherokee
Indian and African-American heritages.

Ashton's voice then softened. "If I didn't know better I'd
take things personal and believe you're trying to get out of
being godfather to my sons—trying to pass the responsibility off on Trev."

Ashton smiled when he thought of his wife Nettie who
was back in Houston and presently pregnant with triplets. It
had been two months since he'd left her to go to Iraq to join
the Special Forces. Instead of flying out of Baghdad to return to Texas, he had flown to D.C. to check on Drake.

"Nettie is doing fine with three more months before de-
livery time. You ought to see how beautiful and radiant she
is, pregnant with my sons. And she'll expect you at the
christening a couple of months after the babies are born, so
you'd better get yourself together."

He shifted in his seat. "I guess I'll bring you up to date
on all the babies that were born since we last spoke. Clayton
and Syneda had a daughter who they named Remington.
Jake and Diamond had a son who they named Granite. Kyle
and Kimara had what everyone hopes is their final child,
another son; and Dex and Caitlin had a son who they named
Gregory Jonathan Halston Madaris, which I thought was a
hell of a lot of names for one kid."

He smiled and shrugged. "Then I remembered Trev's son's—Rio Maurice Nathan Grant—is quite a mouthful. And speaking of Trev, he's also here. He went back to the hotel to shower, but will be back soon. Oh, and his sister Gina got back with her ex-husband Mitch, and *they're* expecting so Trev's parents are excited at the idea of becoming grandparents again. And I may as well hit you with this shocker," he said chuckling. "Corinthians's brother, yeah, Senator Joshua Avery, the pain in everybody's ass, finally did something right when he used his connections to have you flown immediately back to the States instead of being treated in an Iraqi hospital. So remember that bit of redeeming quality the next time you see Avery and want to beat the crap out of him. But that act of kindness doesn't change anything with Trev. Joshua is still on his shit list."

Ashton settled comfortably in the chair and continued talking, hoping that Sir Drake was listening and praying that somehow, he was being pulled back into the land of the living.

The mysterious figure hesitated just out of reach of Drake Warren's door, not expecting to find a marine sentry posted there. The marine quickly glanced at the name tag on the doctor's jacket and snapped to attention as he stepped aside. "Colonel Chadwick."

"At ease. I'm here to see the patient."

"Yes, Colonel, but he has a visitor."

Dr. Chadwick raised a brow. "At this hour?"

"Colonel Ashton Sinclair has been in the room for over four hours."

Colonel Ashton Sinclair? He was supposed to be in Baghdad! This bit of news didn't sit well, but the plans had to be carried out. Time was of the essence.

Dr. Chadwick nodded and slowly opened the hospital room door and went in.

Ashton sat there, listening to the rhythm of his friend's breathing.

Nothing he had said had caused even a twitch. When he heard the hospital door open, Ashton turned, thinking it was Trevor returning, but it was only another doctor. He stood and crossed the room, not wanting Drake to hear his conversation with the physician.

"I need to check on the patient," Dr. Chadwick said, looking over the chart.

Ashton raised a brow and noted this wasn't the same doctor he had spoken with when he'd first arrived earlier that day. "I'm Colonel Ashton Sinclair. Where is Dr. Waverly?"

Dr. Chadwick glanced up from the chart and met Ashton Sinclair's gaze. "I'm Dr. Chadwick, his replacement for tonight. Dr. Waverly was called away unexpectedly, but will return in the morning."

Ashton nodded. "I'll leave to get some coffee while you check him over. Is there any way we can talk afterwards about his condition?"

Dr. Chadwick looked back at the chart. "Are you family, Colonel?"

"No. Drake doesn't have family. However, Marine Captain Trevor Grant and I are listed on all of Drake Warren's official records as his next of kin."

Dr. Chadwick nodded. "All right, but any information will have to come from Dr. Waverly. I'm here to check Mr. Warren's vital signs and to make sure he continues to sleep peacefully through the night."

"All right." Then without saying another word, Ashton

turned and walked out of the room, unknowingly leaving the imposter alone with CIA agent Drake Warren.

Once the door closed, the lone figure moved quickly across the room to the hospital bed to where Drake Warren lay. CIA agent Victoria "Tori" Green fought back the deep pain that hit her full force when she looked down at the man who was not trying to fight for his life. Instead he appeared content to lie there and die. Struggling, she forced memories deep down inside of her, but because of them she refused to let him go without first trying to talk some sense into the only man she had ever loved.

She knew that he was still in love with the memory of the woman he had loved and lost, Sandy Carroll. And because he hadn't ever gotten over that loss, he took on assignments where the risks of dying far outweighed the chances of surviving. She had to convince him to reach for another chance at life, at happiness, and one day, at love.

Moving closer to the bed, she leaned closer and placed a kiss on his parched lips before whispering close to his ear. She noticed a small thin scar on the side of his face that hadn't been there before.

"Drake, please listen to me. It's not your time to go. You still have unfinished work to do. I'm someone who cares and I'm also someone who knew Sandy. I believe in my heart that she would want me to tell you to fight and not let go. If you loved her, you won't give up your will to live, but will continue to live life with the same passion that she always loved in you."

Tori momentarily closed her eyes as emotions flooded her and again she struggled to keep the memories at bay. She opened her tear-stained eyes and for the next ten minutes, in a whispered voice she kept talking, pleading, and begging in an attempt to convince Drake to live.

And she said a silent prayer that she was getting through to him.

Punta del Este, Uruguay
Solomon Cross glanced up from his meal when Miguel Toscana entered the room. Of all people, Miguel knew not to disturb him when he was eating. He gave the man a deadly look. "Is there a reason why I'm being disturbed?" he demanded without preamble. He saw the man swallow nervously. Fear. Stark fear. Cross smiled. He liked seeing fear in people; especially the people who worked for him.

"I have information that might interest you, sir."

Cross leaned back in his chair. "I hope for your sake it does."

Miguel swallowed again and Cross's smile widened. Miguel knew to take his implied threat seriously. "Drake Warren is dying, sir."

Cross's hand tightened on the fork he still held. He placed it gently on his plate and picked up his wineglass and took a leisurely sip, then calmly asked, "Is he dead or merely dying . . . again? Sometimes I think the bastard has nine thousand lives."

"My informants tell me he's close to death. He was shot up pretty bad during some special operation in Iraq. I thought the news might please you."

Cross began eating again. Moments later when he became tired of Miguel's nervous breathing, he lifted his head and pinned him with a look of pure hatred and said, "Had I wanted Warren dead, I would have killed him years ago. I'd rather enjoy seeing him live and suffer. Dying is too easy and I resent being forced to bring an end to my game." He sighed deeply. "Oh, well."

He then returned to his meal. Moments later he said, "You can leave, Miguel."

The man quickly left the room and as soon as the door closed behind him, Cross stood and threw his wineglass across the room, watching it shatter and the blood-red liquid splatter on the wall. "Damn." He had enjoyed seeing Drake suffer the same way Drake had forced him to suffer.

Taking a deep breath he glanced at the huge portrait hanging on the wall. Maria. His beautiful Maria.

She had been the only thing that had ever been right in his life. She'd been the only person he could completely trust. Her father had been a high-ranking government official who had been appointed to the South American Antidrug Commission; a commission that was working with the United States government to increase their war on illegal drugs. Unknown to her father, he and Maria had been involved in a secret affair and had planned to marry. One night she had overheard her father and other government officials' plan to raid the drug lord's stronghold. That night she had turned her back on the pampered life she had always lived to come to him and tell him of her father's plan which had saved Cross's life, although she'd known he would retaliate by finding her father and slitting the man's throat.

And they had loved each other with a passion that no other woman could match or replace. Even now after seven years he still ached for her. The young women his men would often bring to him were of no use. After screwing their eyeballs out, he would usually turn them over to his men to do with as they pleased. He laughed whenever he thought about how many girls his men had kidnapped and brought to him. More than anything he enjoyed the pain he would put them through when he thrust over and over into their young, virginal bodies; bodies that would wash up on shore days later.

He walked over to the window and looked out at the Atlantic Ocean. He was a man who strongly believed in the principle of "an eye for an eye." Since Warren had taken Maria away from him, he had executed a bombing in Haiti five years ago that had taken the woman Warren had loved away from him. Marine Captain Sandy Carroll's fate had been sealed the moment he had learned that she was Warren's love interest. After losing her, Warren had become a demented and tortured man, living life precariously and on the edge. Cross enjoyed the reports he would periodically receive on how Warren had barely missed death on some mission or another.

But no matter what, there was one thing that had remained constant over the last five years. Warren had never become interested in another woman. Oh, Cross knew about the times he would bed women to take care of his sexual needs. He wouldn't be much of a man if he didn't and Cross would at least give him that much. But the one thing he would not tolerate or accept was Warren falling in love again. The man was doomed to live a loveless life like him. And just like Sandy Carroll, the fate of any woman whom Warren showed more than a sexual interest in, was sealed.

Feeling agitated, Cross walked across the room to ring the bell for service. Miguel came quickly.

"Yes, sir."

"Bring me a woman," he snapped. "On second thought, bring me two."

He saw Miguel's smile before he quickly nodded. "Right away, sir." Then the man left.

Cross had understood Miguel's smile. He and his men enjoyed getting Cross's leftovers.

Two weeks later
Tori sat outside the office of Abram Hawk, her boss and the man who headed Night Shield, the covert branch of the CIA. She was ready for the reprimand she knew awaited her. Hawk was angry with her. Furious was a better word. Going to the hospital that night two weeks ago and pretending to be a doctor in order to see Drake Warren had been a possible breach in security. It was definitely an outright defiance of orders and she was prepared to face whatever punishment Hawk dished out. But deep inside she knew she would do it again if it meant prolonging the life of Drake Carswell Warren, and from the last report, he had come out of the coma within twenty-four hours of her visit and would make a full recovery.

She closed her eyes. There were few agents who didn't know or who hadn't heard of Special Agent "Sir Drake" Warren. He worked alone and his reputation among the agents, who did not know his name, was legendary.

Drake was known to volunteer for assignments no one else wanted and took risks that were often in violation of the Agency's standards and codes. Several times she'd heard that Hawk had come close to terminating Drake's association with the Agency, but everyone knew that Drake was too valuable an operative to let go.

His risky antics were tolerated because no matter how he went about carrying out his assignment, Drake produced results and was always successful in getting the job done—and that included the rescue of the vice president, who had gotten kidnapped last year while en route to Syria, right from under his secret servicemen's nose. The embarrassment of that folly was highly confidential and the government was determined that the people of the United States remain clueless about it. It had been Drake who single-handedly entered the Al Qaeda stronghold and rescued the vice president just moments before he was to be taken to another location for execution.

"Hawk will see you now, Victoria," Lucille Mitchell, Hawk's assistant, said in her soft, professional voice.

Victoria's eyes opened and her brows shot up. Everyone at the Agency called her Tori, so in her own way Lucille was giving her a heads-up that Hawk was not in a good mood. "Thanks."

Victoria opened the door and entered what other agents jokingly referred to as Hawk's den. Usually a visit meant one of two things. You were about to be briefed on a new assignment or he was about to rake you over the coals. The moment Tori closed the door behind her and met the gaze of the man who stood next to the huge oak desk, she knew that not only was she about to be raked over the coals, she was about to be put on a spit and roasted until she was well-done.

Abram Hawk, the head of special covert operations for the CIA, stood well over six feet tall and possessed a very commanding presence. She had thought that very same thing of him when she was a marine captain and he had been her colonel. He had left the Marine Corps for this job with the CIA at the same time she had begun going on covert missions for the marines. And she could never forget he was the reason she was now working for the CIA.

His hair, a mixture of silver gray and black, was cropped short and the look reminded her that no matter what job he commanded, he was still military through and through, which meant he expected whatever orders he gave to be obeyed. At fifty-six, he had an athletic physique that was probably due to all those hours he spent at the gym. He was a fair man and would be justified in whatever disciplinary actions he took regarding her outright defiance of his orders.

"Hawk," she tried to say in a casual yet respectful tone. It had been hard making the switch from calling him Colonel to Hawk now that they were no longer in the marines.

"Do you know what you've done, Tori?"

His voice was filled with anger to the umpteenth degree and his features reflected such. He also looked world-weary, which was probably one of the reasons he had decided to retire in three months and spend more time doing all the things he wanted to do.

She swallowed as she continued to hold his gaze. "Yes, sir."

He looked at her for a moment longer, and then shook his head. "No," he said slowly. "I don't think that you do."

Hawk eased his body into the chair behind his desk and motioned for Tori to take the chair across from him. When he had gotten word of the bizarre incident at the Bethesda Naval Hospital a few weeks ago and quickly put two and two together, he knew that Tori had been the person posing as the doctor. Unfortunately, she had been on an assignment in Madrid when he'd gotten wind of it and hadn't been available for questioning. And now that he knew all the facts and had time to piece everything together, he knew without a doubt that it had been Special Agent Victoria Green who had risked everything he had carefully kept top-secret for the last five years, just for the chance to see Drake Warren.

Hawk by no means considered himself a heartless man and he knew the trauma Tori would go through when he'd first received word of Drake's condition. Unfortunately, Hawk had been vacationing in Barbados when word had spread to the other agents. Had he been here he would have made sure she didn't do anything rash, like going to the hospital to see the man. But he hadn't been here and she had gone.

Now everyone was wondering who was the woman who had slipped past security and paid Drake a visit, imparting upon him the will to live. Within twenty-four hours, Drake had come out of his coma and only remembered bits and pieces of his late-night visitor. He assumed what he'd had was an out-of-body experience with an angel, of all things.

But there had been two people who had actually seen "Drake's angel" to know the woman had been real flesh and blood. Now enough people were wondering who she was and what was her purpose in visiting Drake under the pretense of being a doctor? But most importantly, the big question was how had she pulled him back into the land of the living?

The two individuals who had actually spoken to "Dr. Chadwick" had been the marine sentry posted outside Drake's room and Marine Colonel Ashton Sinclair. The sentry's description of Tori was vague, but Colonel Sinclair's description was a whole lot sharper. He was a man trained to be observant, to notice any detail, no matter how minor and indicated he would definitely recognize the woman if he were to see her again.

In Abram Hawk's book that didn't bode well.

Everyone believed that Sandy Carroll had died during that mission in Haiti. Instead she had been left for dead, her body burned almost beyond recognition. Even with extensive injuries, she had managed to roll her critically injured body from the burning building before it exploded, only to be buried under flying debris. Because of the extent of her injuries, as well as the secrecy of the mission, she had been immediately secreted away to a private hospital under another name. And because Cross and his group had immediately claimed responsibility for the bombing, and Hawk knew the man would retaliate and try again if word got out that Sandy had lived, a decision was made that, in addition to the reconstructive surgery that she desperately needed, that she would also be given a new identity. In a way to protect both Drake and Sandy, such drastic measures had to be taken. Cross was already something of a crazed lunatic before his wife had gotten killed and her death had only pushed him more over the edge.

Besides Hawk, the only other person who knew CIA Agent Victoria Green was former Marine Captain Sandy Carroll was the highly skilled doctor who had performed the surgery, Stephen Hunt. By the time Sandy had regained consciousness well over three months later, she had awakened with a new face and a new identity with the understanding that Sandy Carroll had died in that explosion in Haiti and was gone forever. That meant establishing a new life and giving up anything and everything that had been connected to her past, including Drake Warren. There was no way they could ever let Drake know that Sandy had not died in that bombing. Cross's hatred for Drake was well-known and he wouldn't hesitate using Tori again to settle an old score.

When Drake began working for the Agency a year after Tori had come on board, it was also decided that their paths could never cross. Since Hawk was the boss of both of them, he had worked hard to assure that their assignments took them to different parts of the world, which hadn't been a hard thing to do since Drake Warren was such a loner. Besides, if they had run into each other, Tori would have recognized Drake, but there was no way Drake would have recognized Tori. Her facial features were totally different from those of Sandy Carroll. And because of the extensive nasal and throat surgery she had undergone due to scarred tissue, even her voice was different. Only her eyes had remained a dark chocolate brown. When Hawk had first seen her after the extensive cosmetic surgery, he had been satisfied that there was nothing about her features to indicate who she'd once been. Her mannerisms had been another story and she had undergone an entire year of in-depth training for the once right-handed person to become left-handed. That had taken a lot of hard work on Tori's part and in the end she had again mastered her skills in martial arts and marksmanship.

Unfortunately, no matter how successful they had been with Tori's makeover, the one thing they hadn't been able to replace was her heart. Since Hawk at one time had been both her and Drake's marine colonel, he had been one of the first to detect the blossoming romance between them, although Drake had fought it like hell. Tori had been more accepting and Hawk would never forget how, following her rescue, Drake had been the one person she had constantly cried out for during all the pain she'd endured from the trauma of the fire and explosion before lapsing into unconsciousness for those three weeks.

"I had to go see him, Hawk."

Tori's soft voice sounded defeated, filled with grief, loss, but held no remorse. He knew if this situation happened again she would risk everything for the man she still loved.

"By going to see Drake you outright disobeyed my orders, Tori. Sandy Carroll doesn't exist anymore. You know that as well as I do. She died in that explosion and for over five years now I've asked you to get on with your life."

Tori sighed deeply and wondered how she could get Hawk or anyone else to understand that she had tried getting on with her life and most of the time she succeeded. But there were those days when she wasn't consumed with work, when she suffered from bouts of depression, and she couldn't help but think about the man she had lost forever.

She fully understood that to let Drake know she was still alive would be a terrible risk, especially if Solomon Cross found out. The man was a cold-blooded killer and would hunt her down and kill her just because he would have felt he'd been cheated out of her death. Cross had eluded the DEA and CIA's clutches for more than eight years and was one of the most wanted men in the war on drugs. He had been in hiding for the past five years and for a while everyone thought he was dead, taken out by his own cartel. But recent reports that had been confirmed through several different governmental agencies indicated the man was still very much alive. But no matter the risk, she could not have stood silently by and watched Drake give up the will to live.

Struggling with a mix of emotions, Tori stood and walked over to the window and looked out at the Atlantic Ocean. To anyone looking in, this particular building, nestled on the ocean in Hilton Head, South Carolina, was a private vacation resort. Very few knew that the people who came to stay under the exclusive roof of the Diamond Bay Resort were CIA agents working on assignments that could take them anywhere in the country. Diamond Bay gave them the cover they needed to be linked as professionals to the outside world while camouflaging the true nature of their work.

The resort's proximity to the ocean made it easy when agents had assignments where exiting the island by boat was the safest and most surreptitious way to do so.

After a few moments, Tori turned and faced Hawk. "I know I disobeyed orders, Hawk, and maybe now is a good time for me to resign. I did something a good agent shouldn't do, which is to let my emotions dictate my actions. All it took was for me to hear Drake had been critically injured to kick me into action; especially when I heard he was dying."

Hawk's mouth tightened momentarily. He agreed that Tori needed time away from the Agency but he wasn't sure quitting was the answer. She had skills the Agency needed and was considered one of the best female agents they had. But still, with his retirement coming up in three months, he wouldn't be around to look out for her as he'd done in the past. In order to keep her alive he would have to tell his successor her history and he wasn't sure he could do that, especially if they brought in Ronald Casey to replace him. Casey had a reputation of being an opportunist, someone with his eye on the brass ring. Bringing in Cross would be at the top of Casey's agenda and if Hawk wasn't certain that Tori could do it, he wouldn't use her to accomplish his goal. So he had made the decision that if Casey was his replacement, he would not share Tori's history with the man, which meant after Hawk retired, there was a chance that, if Drake returned to work, Tori and Drake could be teamed up together on an assignment.

"What about that agent that I heard you were seeing in Chisholm's operations? Didn't things work out?"

Tori shook her head when she thought of Tom Crowley. They had dated a couple of times then wished they hadn't. The man had had an ego a mile long, and when on their second date he had hinted he was ready to move things to another level, namely the bedroom, she had quickly sent him packing.

"No, things didn't work out with me and Tom," she said with no regrets.

"And what about Daniel Horton? He's a nice enough guy and I understand the two of you were seeing each other last year."

Tori glanced away from him, wondering how she could explain that the reason things didn't work out between her and Daniel was because he was a nice guy. Knowing the danger her life would be in, always having to look over her shoulder, she had decided to remove herself from the relationship before it got too serious. "At the time I wasn't ready to get serious with anyone, Hawk."

For a long moment Hawk didn't say anything, then he asked, "Have you given thought to transferring to another operation within the Agency, Tori? Although I agree you should take some time off, I don't think leaving the Agency is the answer. Now that you know that Drake's condition has significantly improved, I want you to take the next six months off before making a decision about anything. Go somewhere on vacation and enjoy yourself."

And since he knew she didn't have any family, he added, "To be quite honest, I wasn't all that impressed when I heard you were seeing Crowley, considering what I've heard regarding his high level of arrogance, but I'm sure there are other men out there somewhere who're much more suited. Maybe now is the time you should seriously try to get out and meet someone and move your life forward."

Tori stared into her superior's cool dark eyes. "And if I refuse to voluntarily take the time off?" she asked, her jaw squared and her tone anything but respectful at the moment.

"You have no choice. I'm ordering you to take a six-month leave of absence from the Agency, and if after that time you feel you still want to resign, then I'm sure the person who'll replace me will have no trouble giving you what you want. However, if you resign now, I'll have no choice but to document your file that your resignation would be due to dishonorable conduct as an agent. I'm sure you don't want to leave the Agency with that on your record."

Tori tightened her fists at her sides. For the past five years the Agency had been her life. In a way it still was. Hawk was right. She needed time away to make decisions. She had purchased a little place in California, right off the bay. Six months was just the amount of time she needed to try and get herself together, rebuild her life, something she'd tried to do for the past five years. But she had only been fooling herself. Drake had been out of sight but not out of mind and definitely not out of her heart.

"All right, Hawk. I'll make arrangements to leave tomorrow." Without saying another word she walked out of his office.

Hissing a curse Abram Hawk stood and went to stand by the same window Tori had vacated earlier. Moments later, inhaling deeply, he walked back to his desk and picked up the phone. "Lucille, get Dr. Stephen Hunt on the line," he instructed his assistant with displeasure lining his voice. He wasn't sure what damage Tori had done by going to see Drake that night but he had to make sure all bases were covered.

CHAPTER 1

Five months later

Drake Warren stepped into the elegant lobby of the Diamond Bay Resort and removed his aviator-style sunglasses. The chandeliers overhead made him squint against the startling intensity of the lights' brightness. Glancing around he released a deep, ragged sigh.

After being on a six-month medical leave, he was back. The doctors had given him a clean bill of health and he was itching to return to the field. His experience with his "angel" had been his wake-up call and had assured him of one major thing. He still had work to do. After all, Solomon Cross was out there, wasn't he? And Drake intended to find the man and make him pay for all he'd cost him.

While lying in that hospital bed as pain racked his body, it had been so much easier to give up and escape a world that had been so cruel to him and caused him so much pain. But he'd been pulled back from the threshold of the dead, given another lease on life and he planned to take full advantage of it.

He smiled when he thought of Ashton and his friend's

thoughts of "Drake's angel." According to Ashton the woman had been real, flesh and blood. That thought didn't bother Drake any, but it had bothered Ashton and Trevor. Drake could only assume that neither of his good friends had taken the time to watch the television show *Touched By An Angel*. It was one of his favorites and whenever he was in one place long enough he made time to see it.

Everybody knew that an angel could take on many forms and if *his* angel had decided to be a doctor that night instead of just materializing in his room dressed in white, wearing a halo and showing off her wings, that was her business and he definitely wasn't going to question her mode of arrival. He was just glad she had shown up when she had and had talked some sense into him.

For the first time in years he felt like a blessed man. He had his health back, and years ago he had inherited a huge track of land in the Tennessee mountains from his grand-parents; land that kept him connected to his roots. Then there were the smart investments that he'd made over the years that had put him in a good financial position.

Checking his watch, he saw he had an entire hour to kill before his meeting with his new boss now that Hawk had re-tired. An unexpected encrypted message had been left on his computer that said he needed to report to Diamond Bay immediately for this urgent meeting. At the time he had been in Houston, visiting with Trevor, Ashton, and their families.

He couldn't help but smile. After he had gotten dis-charged from the hospital, Trevor's wife, Corinthians, and Ashton's wife, Nettie, had decided he would come to Hous-ton to recuperate. While he was there, Nettie had given birth to triplets, all boys, as Ashton had predicted. Babies and mother were doing well. He had attended the christening ceremony for Ashton's sons where he and Trevor had become their godfathers.

Deciding he needed a caffeine fix, Drake walked across the lobby to the coffee shop. After his purchase he took a seat at one of the tables that overlooked the beautiful Atlantic Ocean. He was about to raise the coffee cup to his lips when a woman, who entered through the revolving doors of Diamond Bay, caught his attention. From where he sat she could not see him, but he had an excellent view of her. His gaze moved over her tall, lithe, curvy figure in pure male appreciation.

His breath suddenly caught when she walked over to the check-in desk, tugging a piece of luggage behind her. There was something about her walk . . . that for a minute he couldn't move. Maybe it was the way her hips swayed with each step she took, or it could have been the way she held her head with such a proud tilt to it.

For a brief moment, she had reminded him of Sandy. He blinked and breathed in slowly, telling himself that Sandy was dead. In five years, this was the first woman who reminded him of her; not in her looks—she looked nothing like Sandy—but there was something about the way she moved . . .

She was wearing a pair of khaki shorts and a tank top and carried a cased tennis racket under her arm, giving an outsider the impression she was a vacationer who intended to play a few games of tennis. But he knew that the majority of the people who walked through Diamond Bay doors worked as operatives for the CIA under one operation or another. He wondered if she was an agent and if so, what department she worked for. He had never seen her before and could only assume she was a new recruit.

His eyes were drawn to her legs and he wanted to release

a slow whistle of admiration, but doing so would have drawn attention. She had a gorgeous pair of legs, the kind that had always driven him crazy on Sandy. He slowly shook his head, again not believing he was comparing this person to the woman he had loved almost to distraction.

His gaze slowly moved back to her face and when she removed her sunglasses, an odd sensation hit him right in the gut, almost knocking the air out of him. He couldn't understand the sudden jolt that went through his body, but her eyes were a gorgeous shade of dark brown . . . just like Sandy's had been. They were so dark it seemed they were creamy dark chocolate, and totally complemented her cocoa complexion and dark brown shoulder-length hair. Then there were her lips, full and luscious, and painted a sultry red. A total turn-on.

For the first time in five years, he had had such a powerful and immediate reaction to a woman, and he quickly decided his reaction to her was purely a male response to a beautiful woman and had nothing to do with the things about her that reminded him of Sandy.

He thought about the other women he'd been involved with over the past few years. He hadn't been celibate, but he had remained emotionally detached. Any woman he slept with had understood up front that whatever they shared in the bedroom stayed in the bedroom, and after a day or night of good mind-boggling sex, it didn't matter to him if their paths never crossed again. They'd scratched each other's itches.

And he didn't see that changing anytime soon. All he wanted now, all he had wanted for the past five years was to find Solomon Cross and personally put the bastard out of his misery. Drake knew Cross was out there somewhere and it would be just a matter of time before the agency or the boys over at DEA tracked him down. And when that happened he was determined to make sure Cross never lived to spend even one stinking day in jail. He would not be satisfied until he avenged Sandy's death.

Drake's hand tightened around the cup he held, trying to rid his body of the anger that seeped through his veins whenever he thought of Sandy and how she had perished in that explosion. For a long time he had blamed himself for allowing her to go on the mission and not keeping a closer eye on her. No amount of therapy and counseling the marines had mandated that he undergo had been able to erase the sounds of her screams in that burning building just moments before he'd been knocked out cold by a flying piece of wood when the place had exploded. They were screams that he could not erase from his mind no matter how he'd tried.

Afterwards, he hadn't wanted to see a therapist as Hawk had suggested. He hadn't wanted to talk to anyone about the tragic event and had faced his hell alone. There had been the nightmares that would leave his body drenched in sweat, and the hours he would spend awake, reliving every detail of that day and refusing to let anything or anyone break open the wall of grief that surrounded him. Instead of facing his emotions, he threw himself into his work, using that as a way to purge the unforgiving emotions that were eating him alive. He had witnessed such a horrendous amount of ugliness and brutality that it was hard to get a grip on how life could possibly be for him again.

Closing his eyes briefly as tension seeped through him, he slowly opened them moments later after he'd gotten his mind and thoughts back on track. It was then that he noticed the stunning-looking woman was gone. He was again flooded with an unfamiliar feeling. There was something about her that had piqued his interest and already he had marked her as someone he intended to get to know.

He would definitely make it his business to find out who she was.

Tori stepped into the elevator cautious and alert. Her senses were seldom off and for a few moments while standing in the lobby she had felt someone watching her, although when she had glanced around she had seen no one.

Because Diamond Bay was set up like an actual resort, the first five floors were exclusive-looking condos used as temporary housing for agents coming and going on assignments. The sixth through the tenth floors were where the administrative offices were located. Diamond Bay's sister resort, The Blue Topaz, was located on the West Coast right on the Pacific Ocean in San Diego. The two resorts also housed new recruits for training.

Tori wondered about the summons she had received to cut her vacation a month short and return immediately to Diamond Bay for this urgent meeting with her new boss, CIA Station Chief Ronald Casey. Casey was Hawk's replacement and she hoped he was at least half the man Hawk had been.

Hawk had known the agents who worked for him like the back of his hand and had always been open to their ideas and suggestions and oftentimes it seemed he had the ability to read their minds. He also understood the dangerous demands some missions could make on a person. Most of the senior agents who worked for him had once served under him while in the marines and although they knew he was tough, they'd always known he was fair.

From Tori's last conversation with Hawk when she had talked to him on the phone from her home in Stinson Beach, California, he had told her the Agency had decided to bring in Casey, a man who had headed up an operation on the

West Coast instead of going with Hawk's recommendation of the man who'd been second in command under him. That announcement hadn't set too well with Hawk but he felt that things would eventually work out.

He told her he would be retiring to a ranch he had purchased years ago in New Mexico and had given her his phone number just in case she ever needed him for anything. Finally, he told her that he had made a decision not to tell Casey about her past history and that she should consider his suggestion that she transfer to another operations so her and Drake's paths wouldn't cross.

When the elevator stopped on her floor she glanced at her watch. She would have time to shower and change clothes before she was due in Ronald Casey's office.

Ronald Casey released a long, mental sigh. It was obvious that the man standing across the room was madder than hell. It was just as well they cleared the air between them now so Drake Warren would know what Casey expected in the way of tolerated behavior. Everyone had warned him that working with Warren wouldn't be easy and that Abram Hawk had pretty much let the man do whatever the hell he pleased. But Warren was going to find out that he wasn't Abram Hawk and under no circumstances would he allow him run roughshod, which was something Hawk evidently had done if all the stories he'd heard about Warren were true. And looking at Warren he had no reason to believe they weren't.

News of Drake's daredevil antics had spread all the way to the West Coast. He was considered a modern-day Rambo among fellow agents. Hell, some of them even admired him for the risks he took. Personally, he thought the Agency could do without men of Warren's type. They were unpredictable, lived dangerously on the edge and were like a time bomb just waiting to go off.

Warren definitely had a commanding presence. He stood a tall six-foot-four inches and was muscular and well-built. There was a look about him that seemed dangerous and warned he wasn't a person to toy or trifle with. He had a hard look, one made of stone as if nothing and no one could move him or stir his frozen blood. His rock-solid jaw added to the granite look, and besides looking like he probably ate nails for breakfast, he also gave the appearance that he consumed snakes and snails for dinner. Casey was reminded of something else he'd also heard about Warren. Somehow and someway, he'd always gotten whatever man he went after . . . except for one, Solomon Cross.

Hawk had briefed Casey on Warren's history so he knew all about how he had suffered when he'd lost a team member on an assignment five years ago; a team member who'd also had been Warren's lover. According to Hawk, Warren still grieved for the woman. Warren's hunger for revenge was the driving force behind his determination to get the elusive Cross.

But Casey felt Warren's hunger would be quenched in good time since there was no one in the Agency who didn't want to bring Cross to justice, including him. However, Casey had a feeling Warren would want to dish out his own brand of punishment on Cross, which wouldn't be a pretty picture. In the meantime, Casey refused to let Warren continue to operate a one-man show, especially in this particular situation.

"Evidently I didn't make myself clear, Casey," Warren said, breaking into Casey's thoughts and reclaiming the man's attention. "But I don't do partners and never have. I work alone. Those were the terms I gave Hawk when I signed up. I stopped working in a team when I left the marines as a Recon five years ago. I'm surprised Hawk didn't tell you that."

Casey shook his head. "He told me but with this particular assignment I didn't take that into consideration. On this mission you'll need to take someone else along."

Drake's eyes turned cold, hard as steel. "Then get another agent because I'm not interested."

Casey flinched and sucked in his breath. Disrespect and insubordination were two things he would not tolerate. Coming to his feet he stared long and hard at the man standing in his office. He would have loved to tell Drake to get out of the office and never come back and that his days with the Agency were over, but Casey knew he couldn't do that when he had direct orders from the president himself. Apparently the vice president, who'd been impressed with Warren's rescue of him, had put a bug in the president's ear and the commander in chief wanted Warren on this particular assignment; no other agent would do.

"It doesn't matter if you're interested or not, Warren, you're going."

Evidently no one had ever told Warren what he would or would not do. He had just given the man a direct order and refusing to comply could mean him his job. However, it seemed that didn't mean a damn thing to Warren because he crossed his arms over his chest and said, "The hell I will."

Casey also crossed his arms over his chest and said, "And the hell you won't. The order comes directly from the president so to decline is not an option."

Drake unfolded his arms and lifted a surprised, dark brow. He cocked his head, zeroing in on what Casey had just said. "The president?"

"Yes. His niece was snatched off a beach in Costa Rica this morning by a group of revolutionaries. She was mistaken for one of the president's daughters, who luckily had

decided to skip the beach to stay inside the villa to read."
Casey sighed. "The reason we hadn't acted sooner was because we didn't know the exact location of where she was
taken. Now thanks to an informer, we do."

Anger consumed Drake like it always did whenever he
heard of a kidnapping. He remembered how a few years ago
Trevor's wife, Corinthians, had been a victim and how he,
Trevor, and Ashton had raced against time to find out her
whereabouts. "Where are they keeping her?"

"At a fortress-type house in the middle of the jungle. My
guess is they don't know they grabbed the wrong girl,
which is a good thing. From what I understand she's been
drugged and as long as she's unconscious she's okay. But if
she wakes up and starts talking, claiming she's not who
they think she is, she'll unknowingly place her life in danger since they won't have any use for her after that. There's
no telling what they will do then."

Drake nodded. He didn't want to think about that part of
it. Rebels were known to have fun with their female victims
before slitting their throat.

"When do you want me to leave?" Drake asked, already
gearing up to go. Adrenaline poured through his veins at the
thought of getting back into action.

Casey hitched a hip on the edge of his desk and narrowed
his eyes. "I meant what I said, Drake. You won't be going
alone. You're to team up with a partner in this assignment."

Drake sighed deeply, anger replacing the adrenaline.
"And I've told you I work alone. I know that area like the
back of my hand, Casey. Another agent will only slow me
down."

"And like you've been told, you have no choice. Since
we're talking about a kidnapped female and we don't know
what condition we may find her in, it was decided that you
need to team up with a female agent and—"

"A female agent! Forget it! That's out of the question!" Drake said at the top of his lungs, not letting Casey finish whatever he was about to say. His expression became murderous. "Under no circumstances will I work with a woman and—"

"Excuse me, but Lucille said for me to come right in."

Both men turned to stare at the woman who had entered the room. "Damn," Drake said, immediately recognizing her as the woman he'd been checking out earlier downstairs in the lobby.

"Victoria Green, I presume?" Casey said, standing and moving across the room to shake her hand. At her nod he said, "You're right on time. I was just briefing Drake Warren on what the two of your assignment will be."

"What!" they both exclaimed at the same time.

"What the hell do you mean by that?" Drake asked in a deep growl, reluctantly taking his eyes off the woman to look at Casey. "You're not pairing me up with a new recruit!"

Casey's lips turned into a frown. "She's not a new recruit. It's my understanding that Ms. Green has been with the Agency longer than you have, and like I said, Warren, for this mission you'll need a female partner and she is it."

Eyes narrowing, Drake said gruffly, "When hell freezes over."

Warmth crept up Tori's neck and into her face. She wasn't surprised by Drake's outburst; she expected no less since he had raised holy hell years ago when she'd gotten assigned to be a female part of the Recons. Trevor and Ashton had been okay with that decision but Drake had felt that when it came to down-in-the-trenches-type covert activities, a woman had no place amidst that kind of danger.

Tori had heard his raised voice before she had reached

Casey's office and had recognized Drake's immediately. At first she had almost staggered, lost her balance when she realized they were about to come face to face after all this time.

She had paused outside the door to get her bearings and probably would still be standing there if Lucille hadn't been watching her curiously before asking if something was wrong. With all the strength she could muster, she knew she had to play it cool and get through this somehow.

It seemed while walking upright and not lying flat on his back in a hospital bed, very little about Drake had changed, definitely not in the way he could throw his shoulders back so damn arrogantly, and tilt his head with such overbearing pride while looking at you with deep dark eyes that always had such an alluring effect. And then, just like now, there was so much power and masculine strength contained in his well-built body.

But she had to admit that there was a hardness about him now that wasn't there before and it was apparent in his features. Gone were the laugh lines beneath his eyes and there were no signs of a dimpled smile. Now she saw tension and anger.

She would always remember the first time he had approached her in boot camp. Instead of formally asking her out, he had merely informed her where he would be taking her that night, and had looked at her like she'd lost her mind when she had told him in a nice way that she wasn't going anywhere with him and that he could go to hell.

She had discovered early that the best way to handle Drake's brash attitude was to respond likewise. He hadn't been able to handle a cocky, smart-ass, streetwise woman who could hold her own with him; especially one who almost, and she meant almost, could best him in martial arts. And from the way he was now acting, it seemed she needed to bring him down a notch again.

She held Drake's gaze and her heart began beating furiously within her chest. She took a deep breath as she tried to calm her breathing as every emotion she possessed suddenly centered in the depth of her heart. Only someone who'd been as close to him as she had could read his emotions. There was curiosity in his gaze as well as the anger, but she also felt something else; it was something that made a heated sensation flow lower through her body.

Attraction.

She felt it deep in her bones. Drake Warren was attracted to her as a woman. She didn't misread the desire she saw in the dark depths of his eyes or the way his nostrils flared in heated lust. It only proved that he was still a man who appreciated what he perceived as an attractive woman. A part of her couldn't help but feel good about that but another part made her cautious.

Although he didn't recognize her physically, being in close proximity with him for any amount of time might trigger something where he would make mental comparisons between her and Sandy. Although she had worked on changing her mannerisms, she knew from experience that Drake was a very observant man.

"I don't understand what's going on," she finally said to both men. She watched out of the corner of her eye as Drake moved across the room to stand at the window. Instead of staring out of it, she felt the intensity of his gaze focused on her.

And for the first time in five years, her body was responding to the interest of a man.

For the next few minutes Drake listened as Casey briefed Victoria Green on the situation. Drake tried like hell to keep his expression neutral while doing a slow study of her.

While her full attention was on Casey, Drake's full attention was on her.

He leaned tensely against the windowsill and studied her. She was no longer wearing the khaki shorts, tank top and sandals, but had changed into a business-casual attire of dark brown dress slacks and a beige blouse. There was no doubt about it, the woman was stunning and up close she was more ethereal than real and her dark eyes were even more beautiful. Her dark brown hair flowed around her shoulders in a healthy, glossy glow and her lips were more than just full and luscious, they were also inviting.

His gaze slowly moved to her chest. She wasn't large-breasted, but she wasn't small either. In his opinion, the size of her breasts was just right and looked firm pressed against her blouse. There was something that was too graceful about her to be a CIA agent and he couldn't imagine her dodging bullets or roughing it. The thought of that shook him to the core. To him, she was more suited in some man's bed and not going on missions hunting down the bad guys.

He angered at the thought of her life being in danger and was amazed at his reaction to her and her well-being. But the one thing he knew for certain was that she would not be going with him on this mission, no matter what Casey said. The last thing he needed was a partner who was a woman . . . and an incredibly beautiful woman at that.

After Casey finished talking, Tori glanced at Drake and tried to ignore the flutter that went through her body when their eyes met. A warning went up in her mind. She had to convince Casey that she and Drake could not work together. Years of being Drake's lover gave her the ability to read him like a book and she knew what he was thinking. If he couldn't change Casey's mind about them teaming up to-gether, he would follow orders and take her along only to dump her somewhere while he went on the mission alone.

And there was no way she would let him dump her any-place. Why did Drake Warren have to be so damn hand-some? Why was he so damn self-assured and cocky?

"Before I get teamed up with Warren, sir," she said to Casey, "I want some kind of assurance that he won't go off half-cocked and try to be a superhero. I've heard about how he likes taking risks, and personally I like choosing the risks I take. I love my life and want to be around for retire-ment, so if you don't mind I'd prefer that you find another female agent to go with him."

Drake narrowed his eyes at Tori before saying, "And I prefer doing the mission alone."

Casey crossed his arms over his chest and met both of their gazes. "Unfortunately what the two of you want doesn't matter in this case. My only concern is the life of a young woman who happens to be the president's niece. Whatever problems you have in working together, I suggest you quickly get over them. There's going to be a boat docked out back to-night that will transport the both of you to a military ship that will carry you to Costa Rica. Members of the Marines Spe-cial Forces are standing by as your backup, but it will take the two of you working together to make your way through the jungle to rescue the woman safely."

Tori signed deeply. She knew Casey was right. A woman's life was at stake; somehow she would find a way to endure Drake's presence without giving anything away. "What's her name?" she decided to ask.

"Robin Thomas." Casey then switched his gaze to Drake. "Any questions?"

Drake glared. "No questions for you but a statement for Miss Green." He turned and gave a full-leveled stare. "You had better hold your own because I don't plan to slow down for you."

Tori narrowed her eyes. "And I don't plan to slow down

for you, Rambo." Ignoring the intense anger that was spreading to every one of Drake's features, she turned to Casey. "When do we leave?"

Casey looked at the mutinous expressions on the two agents' faces. Although they had come highly recommended, he wondered if perhaps he'd made a grave mistake by teaming them together. It was too late to make any changes now. They were on their own and he hoped they didn't kill each other before things were over. "You leave out during the midnight hour."

Solomon Cross's hands tightened into fists in his lap as he sat at the conference table and met the stares of the seven men looking back at him. They were the heads of the ASI cartel, the kingpin and his six drug lords. He had requested this meeting with them. He was tired of keeping a low profile. It had been five years and he was ready to return to his place among them.

"Your request has been denied, Solomon."

He glanced slightly to his right. Manteo Pella had spoken. He and Pella had never seen eye to eye on anything and it left a bad taste in Cross's mouth that of all people it was Pella who had delivered the cartel's decision.

"May I ask why?"

It was the kingpin, José Delgado, who spoke. "This cartel is still cleaning up the messes you've made, Cross. You're too quick to let emotions get in the way of sound thinking. The only reason you're still with this cartel is out of respect for your stepfather who gave all of us our start. But don't push your luck as to how far our gratitude to him goes. Because of you the organization had to decentralize into several smaller groups, which is a risky way for us to operate. But as long as we have the CIA and DEA breathing down our necks we can't function any other way. That incident in Haiti was inexcusable."

Cross leaned forward. Inexcusable, hell! He had needed to get revenge for what had been taken away from him. Didn't they know that? Didn't they understand the principle of "an eye for an eye"? He sighed deeply. Evidently they didn't. "That was five years ago."

"Yes, but the United States government is yet to get over it, and there has been a price on your head since," Delgado said angrily. "They would just love to get their hands on you. In the meantime, this cartel has had to make adjustments."

Cross slowly stood. Rage flowed through him but he refused to let it show. "Is that your final answer?"

Delgado met his gaze. "Yes, and the cartel wants you to continue to keep a low profile. Hopefully, within another year we can take a look at your request again."

Cross nodded then turned and walked out of the room. Damn Delgado and his stinking lords. What they didn't know was that over the past five years he had kept a low profile and at the same time he'd slowly been clipping away at their safety net. When they met again in a year, they would discover they didn't have control over anything. He would. He had more South American government officials, DEA and CIA agents in his pockets than they could ever imagine. And he'd held several secret meetings with Martino, the head of the Uruguay rebels.

Yes, in less than a year he would be in full control and the first thing he intended to do was to put bullets in each of their damn heads.

CHAPTER 2

It was a few minutes past midnight when two black-clad bodies slipped aboard the sleek and elegant-looking yacht that would carry them out further into the Atlantic where a huge military ship was waiting.

Automatically, Drake and Tori went to opposite sides of the boat, each needing distance from each other for totally different reasons; each feeling the frustrations and anger of having been sent on a mission together.

As Tori removed her jacket and knelt down to straighten her gear, she stole a quick glance in Drake's direction. With his thunderous expression it was easy to see that he was still angry about being partnered with her. She knew after leaving Casey's office that Drake had stayed behind to convince Casey that he worked better alone. A part of her had hoped he'd been able to do so and had waited for Casey's phone call saying her part in the mission was cancelled. But a phone call never came and as instructed, she'd been packed, ready and waiting at the docks at midnight. So had Drake and he hadn't said a single word to her since. The moment she'd arrived and he had stepped out of the shadows, she had been fully aware of him as a man.

She still was.

Tori straightened her body and leaned against the railing

of the boat and looked out into the night. The lights from shore were fading, which meant they were heading deeper and deeper out into the Atlantic and closer toward their mission. She had to put all personal turmoil in dealing with Drake out of her mind and concentrate on Robin Thomas, a woman who was depending on them to bring an end to her nightmare. She just hoped Miss Thomas was still drugged or at best, wouldn't let her abductors know she wasn't one of the president's daughters.

Tori checked her watch. They would connect with the military boat in a few hours and then it would take a few more before they arrived on the shores of Costa Rica. She eased her body down on a bench, trying to think of anything but the man standing across the boat from her. A man who still had her heart.

Drake leaned against the rail and watched Tori as she sat down on the bench. Anger boiling, muscles tensed, his gaze raked over her. His attraction to her had risen another notch and there didn't seem to be a damn thing he could do about it. Even while the two of them had been in Casey's office, he'd had a major fight on his hand every time he'd felt himself getting aroused, something that had never happened to him before, especially while conducting business. In his life there was work and there was play. Ever since he had lost Sandy, all women he'd associated with had been labeled for play but now it seemed the two would be intertwined, although he was determined to keep things separate. Tori Green was the kind of woman a man had sex with, not one to go off on dangerous missions taking risks. They would be placing their lives in each other's hands. He much preferred placing something else of hers in his hands, like the pair of firm breasts pressing against her black shirt. There was enough light from the moon to illuminate her body and what he saw he found mouthwatering.

He swallowed deeply. His jaw tensed. His eyes narrowed. Now was not the time to get horny. Maybe he should have made it a point to get laid after he'd recovered but the opportunity had never presented itself while he had been in Texas. Surrounded by Ashton and his family, as well as Trevor's and his, not to mention all those Madarises, there hadn't been time to slip away and do much of anything. All of them had decided what he needed was rest and plenty of rest was what he'd gotten. Thanks to them he felt fit as an ox, well-adjusted and alert. Too alert. He couldn't dismiss the woman sitting across the boat from his mind.

After Tori had left Casey's office, he had hung back to talk to the man, trying to get him to understand his need to go solo on missions. But Casey refused to budge on this particular assignment. He and Casey had ended up having a lot of words, some that were still burning his ears, but in the end he had walked out of Casey's office with the same orders intact. He and Tori Green would work together on this mission and would leave out at midnight.

After leaving Casey's office and checking into his room, he had racked his brain trying to discover what there was about Tori Green that held his attraction and for the life of him he still didn't have a clue other than she was a good-looking woman. He'd come up against good-looking women before and after a good night spent in their bed or his, he had dismissed them from his mind without blinking. But through the rest of the afternoon, including the short nap he'd taken, this one particular woman had invaded his thoughts.

He had a feeling that Tori Green wouldn't easily get dismissed from his mind or any man's. For the second time he wondered why their paths had never crossed if she had been with the Agency for as long as Casey claimed. When he posed that question to Casey, the man only shrugged and said he assumed for no particular reason they never had, and moved on to something else like that was the end of it. But as far as Drake was concerned, that was not the end of it. The both of them had worked for Hawk so it would have made sense that at some point, he would have run into her. She'd been a surprise and he didn't like surprises.

Trying to take his mind off her, he glanced around the boat. From the moon's light he could see that this particular yacht was a beauty, from the gleaming floors to the sparkling walls, not to mention the leather benches. The government intended to give the impression this boat was owned by some wealthy person while docked next to the Diamond Bay Resort, and it did. Drake loved boats. In fact he owned one and couldn't remember the last time he had taken it out to do some fishing. While in Texas, he, Ashton, Trevor, the Madaris brothers, along with Trevor's brother-in-law Mitch, had spent some time in a cabin on the Madaris brothers' uncle Jake Madaris's ranch. For four days they had fished to their hearts' content and for him those days had provided some very relaxing and soothing moments.

So much for taking his mind off Tori Green, he thought when his gaze wandered back to her. A bevy of small flutters began moving around in his stomach and he decided this wouldn't do. He was determined to find out what there was about her that attracted him. Without making a sound he eased over toward her.

She must have been in deep thought about something because she hadn't heard his approach and when he slipped into the seat beside her, Tori quickly turned, her round eyes looked startled, just moments before she caught him off-guard, and in a martial arts maneuver that was faster than anything he'd ever seen, she flipped him off the bench. He lay on his back staring up at her in total amazement.

Two things hit him at once. The first was that she was good and quick, and the second was that he knew of no other person, man or woman, who mastered ninjutsu, a particular style of martial arts other than Sandy. But he had to admit that she was a tad better than Sandy and to his amazement, she was left-handed, which had to have added a greater degree of challenge for her.

"Sorry," she said apologetically, with more than a tinge of anger in her voice as she reached out her hand to help him up. "I didn't know it was you. What the hell were you thinking about sneaking up on me like that? You could have gotten hurt."

Ignoring her outstretched hand, Drake got back to his feet without her help. His lips tightened at the thought that she was operating under the illusion that she could have physically hurt him. He gave her a measured look. Besides being an expert in martial arts, according to Casey, she was also one hell of a sharpshooter who could easily take out her target. A cloud of unease raced through him when he remembered that those two things had also been Sandy's specialties but in the end they hadn't saved her life. But then neither had he. He had given her a direct order not to go back inside that warehouse but she had been lured by the sound of an infant crying. In the end it had been a setup, a tape recording, and she had fallen for it just like Solomon Cross had planned. He sighed deeply. He didn't give a damn just how good Tori Green was. In the end she could die just like Sandy had. Guilt over being responsible for the loss of one woman's life was bad enough. He didn't want to deal with two.

As he looked at her, he tried not to notice just how beautiful she was. She had pulled her hair back in a ponytail, yet the glow from the moon picked up its gloss as well as her startling features. She was annoyed with him, highly upset, deeply pissed and was giving him a look that spoke volumes.

He glanced around to make sure the boat's crew was not around and decided to have his say. "When we get to shore and make it into the jungle, I want you to hang back and let me handle things from there." Drake could immediately tell that his comment only angered her more.

"Forget it, Drake. Whether you like it or not, we're a team and you will not dump me in the jungle to twiddle my thumbs while you go off and play soldier alone. You heard what Casey said and you know what rebels are quick to do with female prisoners. Robin Thomas might need me and I intend to be there if she does."

A growl automatically erupted from deep within Drake's throat. Instead of taking a step back like any person with good sense would have done, Tori Green merely placed her arms across her chest and stood her ground. He frowned. Even Sandy had known when to back off and leave well enough alone.

"You'll do as I say, Tori."

"If you think that then you have another thought coming. We'll work together as a team and that's final. I'm not someone you can push around."

He could see that. His frown deepened and he tried to use another approach. Like Sandy she had a huge amount of self-confidence but unlike Sandy, Tori was displaying an inner strength that almost matched his own. The woman was tough but still, she wouldn't be tough enough. "I've worked this area before. I know the terrain and I know the minds of those revolutionaries."

Tori rolled her eyes in frustration at the powerfully built man standing in front of her. "Why do you think you're the only agent who knows anything about dealing with the bad guys? What make you think you're all-knowing and all-doing and that no other operative can measure up to you?"

"I never said that!"

"You don't have to because you're insinuating it and I resent it. Whether you choose to believe it or not I don't care, but I can hold my own against anyone, including you. Knowing the importance of this mission, do you for one minute think Casey would have sent me if he didn't believe I wouldn't be useful?"

Drake tightened his lips. He wanted so bad to tell her that he thought she could be useful all right, plenty useful in some man's bedroom but he didn't think she would appreciate hearing that right now,

Tori saw Drake's face darken and recognized his facade for what it was. He was trying to scare her off, at the least intimidate her with his boorish attitude. But what he didn't know was that she wasn't easily scared or intimidated. Besides, she knew that hidden behind his mean and rough demeanor was a man with a sensitivity that would astound most people considering everyone thought there was nothing soft about him. But she happened to know another side of him. He was loyal and dedicated to those he loved and at one point in her past life she had been one of those individuals. Although she knew that losing Sandy had taken away some of his warmth and kindness, she refused to believe that part of him was eradicated completely. A part of her had to believe the human side of Drake Warren still existed even if he thought that it didn't.

"Look, Tori," Drake said, interrupting her thoughts. "I have nothing against you personally, and to be quite honest a part of me does believe that you can hold your own, but I prefer doing the solo act for reasons I prefer not to share. I don't like having a partner, especially one who's a woman."

"Because of Sandy Carroll?"

Stunned, taken aback by her question, Drake's eyes darkened. He took a step closer. "What do you know about Sandy Carroll?"

Tori forced herself not to squirm under the intensity of Drake's gaze and the hard sound of his voice. She had thrown out the question before thinking about it. But now that it was out there, she had to answer it and tread carefully while doing so. The last thing she wanted was to raise his suspicions about anything.

"Only what I heard."

"And just what did you hear?" he asked, taking a step closer to her, his face almost turning to stone.

"I heard that the two of you were close. Some say you were engaged to be married. I never met Captain Carroll although we were in the marines about the same time but I did know of her. Most female marines credit her with proving that a woman can hold her own against any man as a Recon."

He lifted a brow. "Sandy was never a Recon."

"No, but she very well could have been since she accompanied a lot of Recons on missions and proved how good she was."

Drake stared at her for a moment, then asked, "Did you do basic training in South Carolina?"

Tori wondered if he was trying to make some sort of connection between her and Sandy. "No, I did all my training in California at Camp Pendleton, which is probably one of the reasons my and Carroll's paths never crossed."

When she saw Drake's slow nod, she breathed easier as she continued. "Because of your former relationship with Carroll, I can understand your reluctance to take on another female partner. Although I understand and can even sympathize with you, I still have to do my job, Drake. There's a woman whose life is depending on us working together to rescue her and I don't plan to let her down." She then gave him a challenging stare and asked, "Do you?"

Drake hesitated in responding, opening his mouth and then closing it. He turned and looked out into the night and for the longest time wasn't sure what he would say so he decided to remain quiet for a second to gather his thoughts. Tori Green had a way of throwing him curves. Sighing internally, he turned back around and met her gaze. "No, I don't plan to let her down nor do I plan to let you take unnecessary risks."

"Why . . ." Tori asked in a low voice, "can't you forget that I'm a female on this mission, Drake?"

A corner of his mouth flexed in anger. "Because that's not possible. You're too much woman for that," he said grumpily.

Caught off-guard by his offhanded compliment, Tori dropped her brows slightly as she tried to ignore the ache she felt in her heart. During her last year as Sandy Carroll, Drake had become her whole life. After her grandfather's death, she had joined the marines. It had been her rough-and-tough Granddad who had taught her how to fight and shoot. He had retired as a marine and had been proud to serve in that branch of the military. When her parents had gotten killed in a train wreck when she was four, it had been her grandfather who'd taken her in and given her a home. His wife, her grandmother, had died just a year before his only son and when Sandy had arrived, the old man had been shrouded in loneliness. He had needed her as much as she had needed him and together the two of them had made a wonderful team. He had loved her and she had loved him.

Then after joining the marines and meeting Drake, she had fallen in love with him. Setting his arrogance aside, his rough-and-tough exterior had reminded her so much of

Grampa Kenny. During his time in the marines, her grand-father had tried several times to be a Recon and had never made it. And a part of her felt he'd been disappointed that her father, his only child, hadn't been interested enough to join any branch of military. But she had, and he had died unexpectedly of a heart attack a week after she had gradu-ated from high school. She hadn't had time to tell him of her decision to enlist.

Bringing her thoughts back to the present, she met Drake's stare and tried not to remember that before her stood the only man she had ever slept with and the only man she had ever loved. Even now she could vividly recall his kisses and especially how his strong, hard body felt on top of hers, inside of her, while sending her soaring in unadul-terated pleasure.

She lowered her gaze as a sharp pain of despair tore through her and she felt instant regret for everything she had lost in her lifetime that had meant so much to her—her grandfather, her true identity, the right to still claim the man she loved.

"What's wrong, Tori?"

Lifting her gaze back to his, she asked softly, "What?"

"There was a look in your face that . . ."

When he didn't complete the sentence, she lifted a brow. "That what?" He didn't answer quickly enough and she de-manded again impertinently, "That what?"

For just a moment, Drake allowed his gaze to take in everything about her; every angle of her face, every feature, before saying, "That was filled with sadness and pain. It seems that I'm not the only one who's lost someone that they care deeply about, Tori."

For just one millisecond, there was a softness in Drake's gaze that touched her deeply. "Yes, I've lost someone," she said quietly. "The man I had planned on marrying one day."

Drake nodded. "Was he also an agent?"

Tori sadly shook her head. "No, it was years ago and he was in the marines."

Drake nodded, hearing the pain in her voice while thinking that the two of them had something in common. They both had lost the people they had loved who'd been marines. He was about to say something, just what he wasn't sure, when the sound of one of the boat's crewmen interrupted him.

"Cut the motor," the man called out.

For just a moment, Drake and Tori's gazes locked. Moments later they turned to look out into the night. Looming ahead in the darkness was the military ship that would carry them to their final destination.

Tori turned back and met Drake's deep stare. Adrenaline flowed through them and they both felt it. Pending danger was just as much her element as it was his and she knew he'd finally realized that. But realizing and accepting were two different things. "I can take care of myself, Drake," she said as she began nervously fiddling with the ammunition belt around her waist.

She heard his quick intake of breath and looked up. It was then that she remembered those had been the last words Sandy had spoken to him that ill-fated day moments before disobeying his order. Without saying anything, he turned and walked away.

CHAPTER 3

For the past three hours, Drake and Tori had silently made their way through the jungle when Drake swore under his breath just seconds before quickly pulling Tori beneath a bevy of large low-hanging trees. The smell of smoke was in the air and up ahead voices could be heard, which meant they had come upon a camp.

"Don't say anything, let alone breathe," Drake whispered close to her ear as he eased their bodies into the huge hollowed indention of a tree trunk to shield them from view. It was pitch-dark with very little light. The only thing they'd had to depend on since setting foot onshore was the gear they'd brought along and the ammunition strapped around their waists.

Tori nodded, her signal that she understood the danger they'd almost walked into. Even in this life-threatening situation, she thought his voice sounded low and sensuous and instead of thinking of revolutionaries with guns, she had a momentary vision of naked bodies underneath satin sheets.

When they heard footsteps, probably from a night watchman, her thoughts were snatched back to the present. Drake pulled her closer to him and tried to ease more into the tree trunk to keep them from being discovered.

"Shh," he whispered and held her tightly to him, embracing her closely.

A shiver coursed through Tori at the feel of being pressed so close to his body. His chest was squashed against her spine and she felt the lower portion of his front compressed right up to her bottom. One of his hands was around her waist, holding her tight and the other, she knew, held up a pistol, aimed and ready to shoot at a moment's notice. She also held a Beretta 9mm, cocked, aimed and ready to fire.

Tori wondered how she could think of the sensuality of their positions when their lives were so dangerously close to coming to an end if they were discovered. Yet, she couldn't put out of her mind the feel of Drake's hot breath against her skin, and the way his hand was wrapped around her waist and the feel of the way his groin area was cradling her backside.

She tried forcing away the thoughts of how they'd once made love in the jungle when they'd been almost out of their minds with sexual need, and the only private time they could find was sneaking off from camp and finding a secluded spot under the low-hanging branches of tree limbs. Drake had captured her scream in his mouth when she had come apart while her body had responded to his deep, hard and unyielding thrusts.

The passion they'd always shared was strong, uncompromising, and profound. It was only during those times that they'd been truly unguarded and in some ways reckless. In the past, his gaze across a campfire had a tendency to be burning, seductive, hypnotic, and the lovemaking that eventually followed whenever they made eye contact would end up being scorching. They'd satisfied each other tremendously sexually; it was all those other times that he'd wanted to play leader and she his follower that would drive her crazy.

"I think the way is clear now," Drake whispered a short while later. "We need to hang east and be on the lookout for more revolutionaries mulling about."

She nodded and felt immediately lost when he dropped his hand from her waist and eased them out of the indentation of the tree trunk. Tori turned and watched as he sheathed his gun back into the holster at his waist before she did likewise with her own revolver.

"Do you think you can cover another five miles tonight?" he asked, searching her face for signs of fatigue.

Tori frowned. If he still had ideas about leaving her behind, he might as well toss them out. They had already covered a lot of ground and she knew it would be better to catch the revolutionaries off-guard at night. That meant they needed to keep pressing forward before daybreak. When dawn hit, their plan was to have gotten Robin Thomas safety onboard the military ship that was waiting offshore for them.

An hour later they continued pressing forward to their destination. Occasionally, they would crouch for cover when they heard voices. The trees, shrubs, and other natural plants served as their cover, protecting them from being seen. The route they were taking had been one the informant had given them and the same one naval intelligence had advised as the best one to use. The house where Robin Thomas was being held was reported to be the home of the head honcho in charge and was located in a clearing at the foot of a private tropic-like beach.

Parts of Drake and Tori's gear contained tracking devices so the military ship, along with several Recons stationed around the small island knew their location at all times. The moonlight was bright and they knew they worked against time if they wanted to rescue Robin before the crack of dawn.

Once they reached the fortress and got over on the other side, they would sheath their hands in gloves. They didn't want to leave behind any fingerprints that could later be identified. If things went smoothly according to plan, their informant who was planted inside the villa was to slip every guard in charge of watching Robin Thomas a drug that would render them unconscious for a while. It was the same drug that had been used on Robin Thomas, which meant the men would be getting a taste of their own medicine. The informant had also stripped some of the alarm wires to that section of the house to neutralize the alarm system for that particular floor.

The informant, a native of Costa Rica, had been planted within this group and working with the CIA for over a year, feeding the Agency valuable information. He had confirmed that the revolutionaries' activities had been funded through Al Qaeda's network. After his bold stint of drugging some of the guards, it would be time for him to leave before his true identity was revealed. His asylum in the United States had already been worked out with the State Department.

When they reached the barbwire fence that surrounded the fortress-like villa, Drake and Tori knew they had reached their mark. The informant had relayed information as to exactly where Robin was being held. Tori and Drake just hoped that she hadn't been moved for any reason.

Tori inwardly sighed. Even with drugged guards and a semi-neutralized alarm system, getting the young woman out without any trouble wouldn't be easy, but she felt confident that together she and Drake could do it. She glanced over at him, more aware of him than ever before because of the danger that surrounded them. He was busy pulling out the special clippers he needed to cut the wire. Chances were high that an alarm system was connected to it and the last thing they wanted to do was to alert anyone of their presence.

Also, there was the possibility of hidden cameras being stationed both inside and outside. If this was the home of the head man in charge, then he would take whatever measures necessary to be protected against any outside elements, especially unwanted intruders.

Silently, she watched as Drake worked quickly and methodically, cutting away at the wire. Not far away Tori could see an outline of the sea that was shimmering beneath the moonlight. Since they had been tracked, she was well aware that marine boats were somewhere out there, standing by, waiting to give them backup if they needed it. Drake had verified their location with them less than an hour ago and she'd heard the eagerness in the voice of the lieutenant he had communicated with. As usual, the marines were ready for action. Tori couldn't help but smile as she remembered those days.

"Happy thoughts, Tori?"

Tori, surprised by Drake's question, glanced at him. Although the majority of their faces were smeared with camouflage paint, she could see the intensity of his gaze. "Yes, one or two. Doesn't pay not to have them at a time like this."

"Ditto," he said going back to what he was doing, letting the job of cutting through the barbwire take his full concentration. While he was busy doing that, she decided to check their state-of-the-art night detector that could identify any areas on the grounds that was wired to the alarm system, lasers or spotlights. They would need to avoid stepping on anything in those areas. The last thing they wanted was to trip anything to set off the alarm.

"All right, that should do it," Drake whispered, and Tori saw relief wash over him as well as grim satisfaction. He had cut a sufficient section of the secured gate out to allow their passage. "Ready?"

She nodded and fed off the adrenaline that she felt flowing through him. Ever since Sandy's death, danger had become Drake's life, the full extent of his element, and she was about to see firsthand just how he toyed with it. After quickly putting on her gloves, she placed her gloved hand on his. There was a lot she wanted to say, and even more that she wished she could say, but the main thing now was the both of their safety as well as the safety of Robin Thomas. "We follow the rules, Drake. No deviations unless absolutely necessary, all right?" She watched as his dark eyes glittered before he winked at her.

"Don't worry, Tori, you'll get your piece of the action. Just stay safe."

She nodded. "You stay safe, too."

After gaining entrance inside the building through a side door the informant had left unlocked, Drake and Tori were crouched down between the crevices of a wall and had been for over twenty minutes. They had heard voices; loud, angered and raised voices being spoken in rapid Spanish, but not too rapid for Drake to decipher what was being said.

"Damn," he muttered and behind him, pressed close to him, Tori could feel his muscles tense. Being this close to him, with her face nearly plastered to his back, she felt his muscles, tight and hard. Somehow heat was penetrating through the protective vests they were both wearing. She also inhaled the manly scent of him and it made her feel warm inside, heated, and for a brief moment she was able to shift her concentration off her muscles that were aching from being in the same position for so long, to the man whose back was braced against her chest.

"What is it?" she asked, her voice barely a whisper. Even

with her fluency of Spanish, she hadn't been able to fully translate what was being said.

"We've got to move fast," Drake whispered back. "Someone just called to say they think the wrong girl was taken, but orders were given for them to sit tight until they find out for sure. We need to have her out of here before they get another call."

Tori nodded. Time was not on their side. When footsteps sounded in their direction they held their breath then let it back out when the sound went away. Drake moved his body just a fraction, as much as their tight position could allow, and looked over his shoulder for his gaze to meet hers. "Let's do it."

But seconds ticked by and he didn't move as their gazes locked. He merely met her gaze. Then slowly he reached up and touched the side of her mouth with his fingers. Tori sucked in a deep breath when his gloved hand slipped away and he bent and lowered his head and whispered against her ear. At the same time she felt the casual brush of his hand against her thigh. "As much as I didn't want one, you make one hell of a partner, Tori."

She met his eyes, almost drowning in their dark depth. "Thanks."

Tori's heart stopped beating and for one earthshaking moment she wondered if he would kiss her and felt a tinge of disappointment when he pulled back and slowly stood, straightening his tall form. Tension grabbed her stomach tight when she also stood, coming to her feet beside him.

"Let's get this show on the road," he muttered low, somewhat angrily to her ears.

They moved together in well-orchestrated silence, two black-clad figures whose senses were keen, minds were alert, and sight sharp. Adrenaline flowed through their veins as they tensed for action, braced for danger. They backed up against a wall when they heard noise coming from a room at the top of the stairs that was followed by the sound of doors opening and closing. Tori knew that everything about this rescue had to be perfectly timed, especially the drugging of the men guarding Robin.

Tori couldn't help but admire Drake's outwardly calm demeanor. He had gone into his remote mode and she knew that the only thing on his mind, his total concentration was in getting the job done.

Seconds ticked by and then it was quiet again. Drake and Tori moved slowly, cautiously up the stairs. According to their information, Robin Thomas was being held in a room at the end of a hall.

Tori's nostrils flared with the scent of Drake every time she drew her breath. It was a masculine scent, robust, hot, sweaty, and she shivered in reflex to it. Her body was silently, provocatively responding to the only male it recognized as its mate. She bit down on her lips. Somehow, some way, she had to control her need for him but her body was reminding her that five years had been a long time.

When they reached the top of the stairs, she glanced around him, straining her eyesight to see into the darkness. At the far end of the hall they made out moonlight that was filtering in through a small window, deciding that some light was better than none. After taking a few steps Drake paused and she felt his warm, gloved hand on her thigh. "It's the last room," he whispered. "Stay behind me and protect my back."

She nodded. Although she would protect his back, he would be stationed in front of her, using his body as a shield to protect her as well. If something went wrong and there was gunfire, he would take the bullet instead of her. She just hoped and prayed the protective vests they were wearing did their jobs.

Outside they could hear the wind beginning to howl, indicating the possibility of a coming storm. Sudden and unexpected thunderstorms in this area were not unusual but unwelcome, especially tonight. Tori's only consolation was in knowing that no matter the weather, a group of Recons were stationed nearby, ready, on alert, poised for action, if things went wrong. And if things went right, that same army of men would be there, strategically placed in the jungle, waiting to get word that Robin had been rescued before moving in for an attack.

Barely breathing, Drake moved forward knowing Tori was right behind him. His dark eyes focused, his ears sharpened when he got closer to the room and heard the sound of a woman moaning. His mouth tightened. Had they gotten here too late? Had those bastards already . . .

Tightening his grip on the pistol he held in his hand he tried to get his mind in check. The one thing he could not tolerate was the violation of a woman. Through the small window he could see lightning flash. *Damn.* Either way it would be a rather messy night, he thought, easing into the semi-darkened room.

The room was dirty and cluttered. Guards, who'd been drinking, probably celebrating what they thought was a victory to kidnap the president's daughter, were sprawled everywhere, unconscious from the combination of both alcohol and the drug they'd been given.

Behind Drake, Tori heard the sound of a woman's gasp when Robin saw what she perceived as a huge, giant of a man walk into the room. Tori quickly moved from behind Drake to ease the young woman's fears. "Shh, we're here to help you," she said in a soothing voice, releasing a deep sigh when she saw the woman was still fully clothed. Although it was apparent she was shaken up pretty badly, there was no signs that she'd been raped. Evidently the rebels had been given orders that she remain untouched until their leader arrived.

She sat huddled in a dark corner of the room on the floor, with tape over her mouth and with her hands and feet tied; obviously frightened, confused, scared out of her wits. The effects of the drug were wearing off, leaving her disoriented, woozy.

Not knowing if the young woman would resort to hysteria if they removed the tape off her mouth, Tori began talking. She needed to make her understand they were there to help her.

"We've come to take you home. Robin, are you injured in any way?"

The woman shook her head that she was not. Satisfied with that response, Tori then asked. "Can you walk?"

Tears burned the woman's eyes when she nodded that she could walk. "Good. We're going to release you but—"

"No time," Drake said, crouching down beside them. "The storm is about to break. Besides, it will be easier for me to carry her out the way she is. And keeping her gagged will assure she doesn't go into a state of hysteria and alert anyone of our presence. I heard the phone ring downstairs just now. Chances are that's the call to tell them they nabbed the wrong woman so we need to move out."

Tori nodded, knowing Drake was right. She took Robin Thomas's hand in hers soothingly, to assure the young woman that everything would be all right. "We're going to have to carry you out, so don't panic. We need you to continue to be brave for us, okay?"

Tori smiled when Robin nodded again, knowing she was fighting hard for control of her emotions. After Robin's ordeal, she would need plenty of tender, loving care when she got back home. Tori then quickly moved aside. Shakily, Robin looked at Drake when he crouched down and lifted her effortlessly into his strong arms.

"Let's go. We have less than two minutes to get out of here," Drake said, leading the way out of the room. When they reentered the room where the unconscious guards were sprawled about, Tori noted it appeared one was slowly coming around. Before she could say anything, Drake had taken the butt of his revolver and hit the man on the head. After a hash grunt, the man lost consciousness again.

They inched into the hallway and silently eased back down the stairs. Tension tightened Tori's stomach when the sound of pounding feet met their ears. Robin twisted frantically in Drake's arms and Tori was glad for Drake's decision to keep the young woman gagged. Robin was frightened and would have probably screamed at the thought that her captors were returning for her.

As soon as they made it down the stairs, Drake pulled Tori into a small and darkened alcove beneath the bottom of the stairs just seconds before an army of men came around the corner and ran up the stairs. A violent curse erupted and the loud sound of several doors opening and closing permeated the building.

"Let's move out," Drake whispered harshly against her ear and she nodded. Knowing they couldn't leave the same way they'd come, Drake quickly led the way out the back while they ignored the gunfire that was going off upstairs. Evidently the leader, angered with the unconscious men for failing to do what they were ordered to do, had decided to put an end to their lives while they were still knocked out cold. When it came to revolutionaries who thought they were fighting for what they considered a just cause, they could be merciless, even to their own kind.

When they made it out of the building the first thing they noticed was that dawn was fast approaching; the second thing was that it was about to storm. When the spotlights suddenly came on and a siren sounded, Tori knew they would have to make a run for it.

"All systems are go," she heard Drake bark into the transmission radio he had pulled from his belt, alerting the Recons they had rescued Miss Thomas.

It would be too dangerous to attempt to get out back through the barbwire so Drake led the way around the side of the building. They dodged the spotlight every time it scanned the area where they were. When Drake motioned to a small area near the back end of the building, he turned and mouthed the word "grenade" just moments before pulling one from his belt and tossing the explosive. It was then that Tori remembered Drake's specialty while a Recon. He was a weapons and explosives expert. The best.

As soon as the smoke settled the way was cleared. Drake had effectively made a passage for their escape. Unfortunately, he had also brought attention to that area and the spotlight shone brightly. A couple of revolutionaries rounded the corner with their pistols ready to open fire. "Now it's time to show your stuff, Green," Drake said smiling at her.

She smiled back and nodded. As more revolutionaries came running around the corner, Tori smoothly, and with accurate precision, picked them off, shot after shot. Suddenly, it began to rain; a turbulent downpour, and Drake pulled her forward, while adjusting the weight of Robin in his arms. "Let's make a run for it. Now."

Dodging the enemies' fire they sprinted across the lit yard, running toward the passage Drake had blown open for them. The sound of gunfire surrounded them and they heard men scrambling about trying to get back their hostage and take down the individuals who'd had the audacity to invade their stronghold.

Tori's heart began soaring in triumph as they ran farther and farther away from the building. Although they weren't out of the woods yet, and were heading deep into the jungle with men fast and furious at their heels, a part of her knew they would survive. The most dangerous part of the mission, rescuing Robin, was over. Rain poured down, slashing violently into their faces and eyes as they ran deeper into the jungle where the trees swallowed them up. She felt exhausted and knew Drake had to feel the same way, doubly so since he was carrying additional weight. But they couldn't slow down to talk. They had to keep moving.

Drake cradled Robin in his arms, holding on to her tightly as he and Tori raced deeper into the jungle. At some point they would stop running and find a place to sit and wait, but not yet. Danger was still lurking all around them. He'd heard the sound of a jeep's motor and knew some of the revolutionaries were chasing them in a jeep, so they needed to run into an area where a vehicle couldn't go. He heard the sound of a man shouting and then gunfire behind them. He wished there was some way to wipe the rain from his face, but knew he couldn't, at least not while holding Miss Thomas. He looked around. They couldn't be far from the area the military had pinpointed to be their holding position. There he would find food and more ammunition. It would be a place they would stay until the Recon showed up to escort them back to the ship.

When he suddenly heard an exchange of gunfire, he knew the Recon had arrived and the revolutionaries had to forgo their search for the missing hostage to deal with the

United States Marines. Drake smiled. He already knew who
would be the victor.

Less than six hours later, Tori stepped out of the shower onboard the military ship. She had needed the deep cleansing
the hot water had given her. Her body ached tremendously
and her throat felt somewhat raw. But still, the mission had
been a success. Robin had gotten checked by a naval doctor
onboard ship and was sleeping soundly.

The Recon had attacked the fortress, taking the leader as
well as his comrades into custody. The president had been
notified that his niece was safe and in good health.

Tori heard a knock on her cabin door and tightened the
sash of her robe. She moved slowly, stiffly, wondering if
something had gone wrong. As far as she knew, the ship
was headed for the military base in Guatemala where a private plane would be picking up Robin. A military aircraft
was scheduled to fly Tori to California and she'd heard from
a member of the ship's crew that Drake would be departing
for El Salvador.

She opened the door and suddenly felt the aches leave
her strained muscles. Drake stood in the doorway. From the
dim lights in the hallway their gazes met in the shadows.
This was the first time she had seen him since they had
boarded ship. He had immediately gone to brief the military officers on what had transpired during the mission and
she had left to accompany Robin down in the brigs to be
checked by the doctor.

A shiver went through her and her heart began pounding
fast and furious in her chest. Surprised, she watched as his
mouth quirked into a rare semblance of a smile. "I thought
I'd check on you before I left."

Left? She inhaled, as she struggled to ignore the panic

that gripped her with that one word. "I thought you were going as far as El Salvador," she said, trying to sound as casual as she could.

"That was before I got orders to go elsewhere. A chopper's on its way to take me to South America."

She lifted a brow. "South America?"

"Yes. I'm needed on another assignment."

"So soon?" she asked, not liking the thought that he was about to place his life in danger once again, escaping death by the skin of his teeth.

"Yes, it seems Santiago and his band of rebels are causing problems again."

She nodded, studying the depths of the dark eyes that had been in her heart and thoughts for the past five years. When a couple of sailors passed by in the hall, she decided that she needed to invite him in, if only for a short while. Licking her lips, she whispered nervously, "Would you like to come in for a second?"

He smiled again. "Yeah, just for a minute. The chopper is to arrive in a couple of hours."

When the door closed behind him, she glanced around. "I would offer you something to drink, but the strongest thing I have at the moment is bottled water."

He met her gaze. "No, thanks. I'm not thirsty."

Tori broke eye contact with him and noted he was dressed in black jeans and a black T-shirt, ready for action once again. She also noted how good he looked. Her gaze returned to his face and probed his eyes. He was watching her intently.

"How long do you think you'll be in South America?" she decided to ask. When he walked out that door, chances were their paths would never cross again. She hadn't told Casey yet, but she had decided to leave the Agency. She couldn't risk having to work with Drake on another mission.

"For at least four months."

She nodded. That was all the time she would need to disappear. When he returned from his mission she would have relocated elsewhere and started a new life. Since it was the Agency's policy not to give out the address of any of their agents—former or present—for fear of the data getting into the wrong hands, no information would be given out as to her whereabouts if Drake was to ask. It would be better that way. Her past was a secret she would have to carry to the grave with her. He would never know that the woman standing before him was the same woman he had planned to marry after that Haiti assignment. The same woman he had asked to share his life and have his children. The only woman he'd ever let steal a way into his heart.

He was a man who'd been known to be hard as steel in most situations, inhumanly controlled in combat and relentless of his pursuit of anyone who threatened the country he loved. But when it had come to Sandy Carroll, he had loved her with such an intensity, a tenderness that was so unlike the giant of a man that he was, that even now remembering those nights he'd held her in his arms after making love to her, Tori wanted to weep at the thought of all she'd lost. All they'd lost.

As natural as the breeze flowing beyond the cabin window on the sea, she took a step forward at the same time that he did, and he gently pulled her into his arms. Immediately she melted with his touch when he tilted her chin up, bringing her gaze level with his.

"I don't understand it, but something is going on between us and damn it, I don't like it," he whispered hoarsely, as the ferocity of his emotions began shattering his ironclad control. "I feel like I've met you before, but I know that's not possible. There's something about you that reminds me of someone that I—"

Before he could finish what he was about to say, Tori placed her arms around his neck and brought his mouth down to hers, silencing his words. She knew that she shouldn't, but for just this one time she wanted to taste him again, love him again. She wanted to know how it felt to be held in his arms once more, making love with him. The heat of his body caused a slow sizzle to radiate up her spine and a stirring of desire ran rampant through her when she remembered how making love with him used to be. And how it felt when he would lower her to the bed and ease his hot body into hers.

At this moment, she wanted take what she could get and have her memories to add to all the others. Her mind turned to full concentration on his kiss and was lulled into a state of total awareness of him. Her senses came fully alive under the intense onslaught of his mouth as her body trembled from the pleasure he was giving her.

She arched shamelessly against him and heard the animal growl that emitted from deep within his throat. She wanted to breathe in the scent of him; she wanted to forever know the taste of him on her lips. And she wanted to pretend that time meant nothing and there hadn't been five years that had invaded their lives, keeping them apart. She knew at that moment she loved him with a ferociousness that had not faded. If anything, knowing about him, with him *not* knowing about her, only increased the amount of love and desire she felt for him.

Slowly, he broke off their kiss, pulled back and looked deeply into her eyes. She fought the urge to tell him the truth, to let him know who she was but knew that as long as Solomon Cross lived, Drake could never know. She fought the tears she was holding back and prayed that he didn't see them. She couldn't let him know what this moment meant to her, the beauty of them being together again this way, something she never thought would be possible.

"That was just a taste," he said almost in a growl. "I want more, Tori."

She felt herself being pulled closer into his arms and could feel the deep hardening of his body against her. The thought that she could still bring him to such an aroused state almost made her breathless. Special memories from the past claimed her senses when they had kissed, but she desperately needed to make new memories; memories to keep long after he walked out of that door. She had missed him so much and hadn't been aware just how much until this very moment.

She lifted her chin and met his gaze, and her body stirred even more from the dark desire she saw in his eyes. A sigh rippled from her throat just moments before the words flowed from them. "I want more, too, Drake."

As if he'd been holding his breath for those very words, he lowered his mouth to hers at the same time he wrapped his hands around her waist and lifted her into his arms. Moments later he broke off the kiss and his face found the side of her neck. She felt the heated moisture on his breath moments before his lips gently caressed her there.

She felt him move with her in his arms to the bed. It was small and had cotton sheets instead of the satin she had envisioned, but at the moment she didn't care. The only thing she could concentrate on was the ache consuming her to be touched by him again. It had been five years since she had been intimate with any man and the last time Drake had been that man.

As soon as her back touched the bed she pulled him down with her, needing the contact of his mouth on hers once again. And he gave it to her. She sensed a need in him as well. His mouth settled provocatively on hers, taking everything she offered and giving everything she wanted.

More than one strangled sound emerged from her lips while he had total control of her mouth.

And then she felt his hand sliding downward to open the folds of her robe and she knew at that moment there was no turning back, no retreat and no calling a halt to what they were doing. Tonight was meant to be. This was more than just a weakening of the flesh; this was about appreciating your blessings. This man was to have been her husband; the very person she was to share her life with, and to have him back in her arms, if only for a little while, meant the world to her. Nothing had ever felt so right in her life.

Drake continued to kiss Tori, stroking her tongue torridly with his while sliding his hand underneath the folds of her robe. Her skin felt hot, soft, and his hand trembled as his palms traveled hungrily over her bare skin, skimming around her breasts, which seemed to fit perfectly in his hands.

He pulled back and had to take a look at her. When he saw her naked breasts, a primal hunger welled up deep inside of him and his fingers pushed the rest of the robe aside, needing, wanting, and desiring to see all of her.

The beauty of her nakedness almost made him groan and a desire to make love to her flickered through him with every passing second. He stood and quickly pulled the shirt over his head and his hand immediately went to the waistband of his jeans. Tugging them down his legs, he hurriedly stepped out of them along with his underwear, standing before her completely unclothed and totally naked.

When he moved closer to the bed she eased up and unexpectedly leaned against him, letting her face cover his stomach as if she needed to have the scent of him in her nostrils. He sucked in a deep breath when he felt her hot tongue boldly explore the muscular planes of his stomach as if she not only needed his scent but also his taste.

"Oh, hell." The words were torn from Drake's lips. He couldn't take any more. He needed her now. He knew there was something he needed to do before joining his body with hers but whatever it was evaporated from his mind when he toppled her onto her back and quickly covered her body with his.

He reached down and slipped his hands between her legs needing to know she was ready for him and just as hot as he was. Her slick wetness touched his fingers and he began stroking her, not ready to move his hand from her just yet. He felt her fingernails digging into his shoulders and heard the way she was gasping for air. Whatever sensations were tearing through her were also ripping their way inside of him, and without moving his hand from her, he leaned down and kissed her again, long and hard.

When he finally pulled back and looked down at her, what he saw almost took his breath away. Lying beneath him was a woman whose features were swirling in the heated lust he had encased her in. She was shamelessly and immodestly revealing just how much she wanted him. It was there in the way she was breathing, the way the nipples on her breasts had darkened and hardened, the deep hunger in the eyes staring at him and the amount of wetness her femininity was generating. He thought that no woman was more prepared or willing to take on a man, to make love to a man, to share in the passion that awaited them both.

He was suddenly consumed with a desire to mate with her so thick it was like a fog surrounding him and the only way to breathe through it was to be inside of her, sharing what she was offering. As she widened her legs for him, he eased his turgid flesh into her, his nostrils flared as he sank deep into her, inch by inch, as breath whooshed from his lungs.

The deeper he sheathed himself inside of her, the more

delirious with need and desire he became. He couldn't think. The only thing he could do was mate with her with every strength of his being. He'd never been so intense with making love to a woman and in the back recesses of his mind he knew that had included Sandy. Most of the times they'd made love had been stolen moments on missions. Rarely had they been able to just sleep together under normal situations like regular people. Their lives were filled with danger and their lovemaking had been no different.

But for now he could push all thoughts of danger aside and concentrate on this, a mating of a lifetime. Bracing his hands on either side of her shoulders he began thrusting in and out of her, the rhythm fast and furious, her soft moans of pleasure music to his ears. He was determined to take them over the brink of ecstasy and for some strange reason a part of him felt a connection of mind, heart, and soul with her.

And then everything exploded when he felt her body jerk in a climax that shook him to the core. He clenched his teeth when he felt her nails dig deeper into his shoulder and with his arms straining, he continued to rock into her over and over again. Then moments later, he threw his head back when a powerful explosion ripped through him and he grasped the hips she automatically lifted, needing to go deeper and knowing that for the first time he was totally out of control.

Needing the taste of her, he leaned over and kissed her long and hard while scaling the crest of passion as they rode out the climax that simultaneously ripped through them.

Long moments later he buried his face against her neck and held her while his body eased back down from heaven and returned to earth. Nothing had prepared him for such prolific and profound lovemaking. Slowly, reluctantly, he eased his weight from her and pulled her into his arms, still needing the contact. And when he had her in the position where he wanted her, snuggled close against him, he closed his eyes. For the first time in five years, he felt totally at peace.

Drake came fully awake and glanced down at the woman still sleeping beside him as emotions stronger than he'd ever encountered before knotted his stomach. Their mating had been wild, uncontrollable, and intense and afterwards, mindless with exhaustion, they had succumbed to sleep.

Since Sandy, he had never felt a gnawing hunger to take a woman more than once and he'd certainly never entertained the idea of waking up beside one in bed. But he didn't have any qualms about waking up Tori to make love to her again, and the thought that he had drifted asleep beside her didn't bother him the way it should have.

He leaned on his elbows and continued to study her, wondering what there was about her that had attracted him from the first, pulled him in like a moth to a flame. Although he couldn't understand it, their lovemaking had felt like he had come home. The sense of completeness he experienced when he was buried deep inside of her took his breath away.

And then there was the way Tori seemed to know the exact moment he was about to come; how she lifted her hips, tightened her legs around him and used her inner muscles to clench him, drain the very essence of his release from him like she was entitled to it. She even had Sandy's intimate scent. It was a special scent that used to send his hormones into overdrive and would make him want her right then and there, no matter where they were.

Drake rubbed a hand over his face, thinking he was going insane. How could two women be so much alike and then so different physically? It seemed his mind evidently refused to let go of the past. Instead it had driven him to a woman he was unconsciously and unintentionally using as Sandy's substitute and that was the last thing he wanted. Tori deserved better than that. A part of him felt the emotions he was experiencing were because of Tori and had nothing to do with her similarities to Sandy. But then another part felt the only reason he'd been drawn to Tori from the first was because of those similarities. He closed his eyes and for long moments he felt confused, torn in two halves and incomplete. He was struggling with the conflicting emotions that battled inside of him.

Eyes closed, features tense, emotions in turmoil, he knew he owed it to Tori to be completely honest with her and not to use her in any way. He owed her that much.

He opened his eyes when he felt her shift next to him. Their gazes met and immediately he felt his body get hard. The woman definitely packed a lot of feminine power, he thought, as a jolt of need ripped through him, sending urgent pulses throughout his body. He wanted her again, but this time in a different way. He wanted her to tantalize his taste buds.

Still holding her gaze he tossed the cover off of her, exposing her nakedness. Then he reached out and let his fingers gently stroke all over her, beginning with her breasts, liking the way the areola on her nipple darkened, hardened with his touch. Knowing he couldn't move another inch until he tasted this part of her, he leaned over, caught the nipple between his teeth and licked. "Umm, good."

He then moved to the other breast and gave it the same torment, liking the way the tiny bud fit into his mouth. He noted the change in her breathing when he lifted his head and his attentive hands moved lower, and his questing and eager fingers aimlessly yet thoroughly touched her everywhere, taking his time to sample the taste of her along the way.

"Open your legs for me, Tori," he leaned down and whispered when his hand had moved down below her waist, his mouth, mere inches from her lips.

Without hesitating to do what he'd asked, he watched as her thighs parted and breathed in deeply at the lush sight of her. She was wet already, nearly drenched, and when his fingers gently touched her, invaded her, she moaned like a woman in heat, calling out to her mate.

"I want to taste you," he whispered just seconds before he eased his body downward in the bed. And when his mouth touched her in such an intimate kiss, she cried out his name. Drake's hungry tongue went to work on her, while acknowledging he had never performed this special art of lovemaking but on two women, her and Sandy. He closed his eyes and again he felt a deep familiarity with Tori. It was like he had done this to her before when he knew there was no way that he had.

And when she began shuddering beneath his mouth, coming apart as the force of her tremors began shaking her to the core, he continued to feast on her, feeling immense male pride that he could make her come this way.

Moments later he edged up her body, settled between her legs and with one single thrust was planted inside of her. He began mating with her, fast and furious, as another series of orgasms ripped through her, making her cry out again and again. And then he came, joining her in reckless abandonment, gut-deep exhilaration, pure sexual pleasure of the most primitive kind. He was on the highest of highs. And as he slowly began floating back down to earth, a low moan escaped his lips as he collapsed, then rolled to his side with their bodies still locked.

For the second time that night he drifted off into a peaceful sleep.

When the beeper went off in the pants he'd tossed on the floor, Drake reluctantly eased from Tori's side. It was only when he reached into the pockets of his jeans to turn off the beeper did he remember what he'd forgotten. Condoms. He knew he should be worried about the possible consequences of his screwup, but his mind was still filled with thoughts of what they had shared. Still, he needed to let her know.

He went back over to the bed and gently pulled her into his arms. "The chopper is here," he said softly, regretfully, while raking his hands through the strands of her hair that had come undone during their lovemaking and now hung loosely around her shoulders. She looked even more beautiful than before because somehow he felt he had branded her as his over the course of the night.

"Yes, I know," she said, body still filled to overflowing with all the ways he had made her feel. Even now the way he was touching her was sending shivers through parts of her body.

He pulled her closer into his arms. His expression suddenly turned serious. "There's another thing you need to know; something I need to apologize for. I didn't use a condom."

A hint of surprise flashed in her dark eyes and he knew she hadn't thought of protection either, and for a moment she seemed at a loss for words. Then finally she said, "It isn't the right time of the month, so I should be okay."

He studied her features, intently. "You sure?"

Unfortunately, she wasn't sure, but she wouldn't tell

him that. She took a deep breath and answered, "Yes, I'm positive."

He pulled her back into his arms. "If your calculations are wrong, I want you to let me know. Casey will know how to contact me. Okay?"

She nodded. "Okay."

He then kissed her again, long, hard and filled with all the desire she had come to expect from him. Moments later he eased her from his arms and stood up. Picking his clothes off the floor, he proceeded to redress, all the while watching her.

When he finished he reached out his hand to her and she eased up off the bed and walked naked into his arms and he kissed her again. When he ended the kiss, for the longest time they stood staring at each other, then Drake lifted his hand and grazed her cheek with his finger before trailing a path down the side of her face.

A part of him was glad for what they had shared but then another part of him felt confused, disoriented. He needed to ask himself whether he'd been attracted to Tori for herself or if the attraction was because he'd found similarities between her and Sandy. The woman he had lost had forever forged a place in his heart that was hers and hers alone and as much as his lovemaking with Tori had touched him to the core, there was only one woman whom he would ever love in his lifetime and even in death, she still claimed his heart.

"It's time for me to go," he said quietly.

Tori nodded, as her gaze still held his. She fought back her tears and smiled weakly when she said, "Take care of yourself, Drake."

"And you do likewise. And you'll contact me if you're . . . ?"

"Yes," she said softly, knowing it was a lie even when she said it. The thought of having Drake's baby, a part she could have and love forever, filled her with such profound joy. It would be a miracle if she were to get pregnant after what they'd shared tonight and it was too much to hope for. The baby would be hers and hers alone. He would never know. As much as she would want to tell him, she would never be able to. Their fate had been sealed five years ago and it was an act of kindness of the Almighty for them to have shared this time together now.

"Good-bye, Tori." He took a step back and turned to leave, and then he swung back around and pulled her to him and captured her mouth hungrily, almost violently, as if he intended for her taste to be his good-luck charm. The unexpectedness of his kiss sent every sense within her skyrocketing.

Tearing his mouth from hers, he whispered the words, "Until we meet again," in her ear before finally walking out of the cabin without looking back.

Knowing they would never meet again, Tori couldn't contain her tears. She made it to the bed and flung herself across it, crying in earnest. Even through the passing of time, their forced separation, the trauma that had ripped them apart, she still loved him with a love that she knew would last forever. She thanked God for this special time that she was able to spend with Drake and prayed that he be kept safe.

By the time she was able to pull herself together, she glanced over at the clock near the bed. It was the midnight hour and the man she loved was lost to her forever once again.

CHAPTER 4

Two months later

"Welcome back," Lucille said with a smile as she rose from her chair.

Drake had just stepped off the elevator and took a deep, calming breath. He was glad to see a familiar face and the woman who was Hawk's assistant was just that. Unlike a lot of other people at the Agency, she had ignored his bark and over the years had gone above and beyond in tolerating his often-foul moods.

She rounded the desk and clasped her hand in his. Lucille was more than a mere assistant to the CIA director, she was often the lifeline to the agents as well. Short and buxom, in her early sixties with a head of gray hair and caring dark eyes, she easily reminded you of someone's grandmother. She had worked for the Agency well over forty years and was someone everyone depended on for everything from smoothing out ruffled feathers between agents and their bosses, to expertly editing the reports agents turned in at the end of an assignment, while threatening to give them a crash-course writing class.

"Before you go into Casey's office, Drake, I want to know how things went. I see the assignment was completed ahead of time. Are you okay?"

Another thing the agents liked about Lucille was that she genuinely cared about their well-being. "Yeah, we did what we were sent to do in less time than expected. We were able to drive Santiago and his rebels back into the hills at least for a while."

"And what about you personally? How are you?"

Drake couldn't stop the smile that stole into his roughened features. From the first time he had gotten off the elevator at Diamond Bay to take his first assignment, Lucille had gone out of her way to be more than kind to him, and for that he'd developed a soft spot for her. Like others, she had heard that he was the new agent, a former Marine Recon, who was suffering and grieving for the woman he'd loved and had lost on a mission. She had been able to read his wariness, his anger, and had known the times he had needed to lash out, be left alone and be handled carefully. And she had done all those things with loving-kindness.

But then on the flip side, Lucille expected respect and the one thing she would not put up with from any agent was a foul mouth and like some agents, he had a tendency to be rather colorful with his words at times, which Lucille would not tolerate. So everyone knew to be on your best behavior and to watch your mouth around her or run the risk of getting your ears boxed.

"So, Lucille, are you still sneaking off to the break room every day around lunchtime to watch your favorite soaps?" he asked, knowing she probably did.

"Don't try and dodge my question, Drake. How are you doing?"

As much as Drake wanted to say that all was fine with

him, he couldn't. Lucille had the ability to tell when he was
lying, so he decided to tell her the truth . . . as usual. "I'm
tired and feel like hell. I think I may have overdone things
after coming off medical leave by taking on those two assignments back-to-back. I'm going to ask Casey for some
time off before my next assignment, possibly as long as a
month."

Lucille nodded in understanding as concern clouded her
eyes. "I was worried about you taking on so much and so
soon. And I agree that you should ask Casey for time off.
He didn't change Hawk's policy about agents needing time
off after an assignment to relieve themselves of the stress
that went along with it. You won't have a problem getting
the time. There hasn't been a lot of activity around here
other than the usual."

Drake nodded. Hawk had operated with the belief that a
well-rested agent was more valuable to carry out whatever
mission he was called upon to do. A burnt-out agent, tired
and under tremendous stress, made mistakes that could end
up costing him his life.

Knowing Lucille kept up with just about every agent in
Casey's operation, he rubbed his jaw and decided to ask her
about the one person who had been on his mind constantly
over the past couple of months, Tori Green. Even now he
could vividly remember the lovemaking they had shared.
Just thinking about it stirred so many unwanted and unexpected emotions within. He still didn't understand how Tori
had done it. How she had been able to pull such strong feelings out of him and send them escalating through every part
of his body. He didn't understand, but was determined to
find out what was there about her that still touched him so.

He wanted to take her out to dinner, take her to a movie,
dancing. In other words, he wanted to get to know her better. It had been a long time since he'd gone out on a date and

in a way he was looking forward to actually spending time with Tori and seeing where things went from there. While in South America, he'd had time to think about a lot of things and he knew he'd been given another chance at life for a reason. Maybe it was time to finally put the past to rest and move on.

His attention was drawn back to Lucille when she walked back around to her desk. He tipped his head to the side and in a deep, rumbling voice said, "Since we finished the mission early and while I have some free time I'd like to check on a fellow agent; the one who partnered with me on that Costa Rica assignment, Tori Green. Is she expected back out of the field any time soon?"

Lucille halted what she was doing and a slight frown touched her features as she met Drake's eyes. The look in her gaze saddened. "Since you were in South America, I guess you didn't get the word about Tori."

Dread suddenly flared through Drake. He wondered what had happened. Had Tori been injured while on an assignment? Or even worse, had she gotten . . . ? He didn't want to think of that possibility.

He felt a deep tightening in his throat and forced himself to breathe deeply. He raised his chin and forced himself to meet Lucille's troubled eyes. "What about Tori?" he asked in a hoarse voice, one that sounded almost strangled.

"She left."

Drake stood there stunned but relieved that at least Tori was okay. But still, he needed more information. "What do you mean she left?"

Lucille studied Drake. She couldn't help but recall the first time she had seen him. He had stepped off the elevator guarded and uneasy and mad at the whole world. That first year had not been easy in dealing with him. He had wanted to present himself as being the meanest and orneriest agent she ever had the privilege of working with. And for a while she had begun to think he didn't have one gentle bone in his body.

But her old eyes had been able to see past his rough defenses and had seen the hurt and pain he carried around. She had seen fear, real fear, of getting too close to anyone for fear of losing them again. Other than those he always considered as friends, he hadn't intended to add any more to that number.

However, something just now had definitely caught her off-guard, had definitely thrown her off-balance. It was the look in his eyes when he'd asked about Tori. Maybe it was the look of male interest that had lighted his eyes or the softening of his lips when he had spoken her name. Then again, it could have been the deep look of anxiety when he'd thought something bad had happened to Tori.

Although she wouldn't give Drake any indication of what she was thinking, Lucille couldn't help but wonder if things had gotten pushed to another level between him and Tori during their three-day mission in the Costa Rica jungle.

"I mean she quit working here, Drake. She resigned right after you two completed your mission. She delivered her report and her resignation to Casey at the same time. Two weeks later she was out of here. She was one of the best female operatives we had and we hated losing her, but her mind was made up."

Drake suddenly felt shaky, unsettled. One of the things that had helped him get through his last assignment was the thought that at the end of it he would be returning to the States with definite plans to see Tori again.

"Any idea where she's gone?"

Lucille held his dark gaze. "Unfortunately no, but even if I did, Drake, I wouldn't be able to tell you. Company policy.

The only person able to make an exception to that rule is Casey."

Drake's jaw hardened in frustration. He understood Lucille's position, but he intended to find out Tori's whereabouts. He still didn't know if she was pregnant or not. He wasn't sure what was driving him to such determination, but it was there and there wasn't a damn thing he could do about it. There was something about her that had touched him in a way he hadn't been touched in a long time. Although he hadn't wanted to, he had enjoyed everything about her, even their sparring matches. He had discovered she was just as stubborn and strong-willed as he was and so many other things about her that intrigued him as well. The time they had spent together rescuing Robin Thomas would forever be branded in his memory. They had worked well together, like two halves that formed a whole. He had felt the same way when they had made love.

He gave Lucille a long look then said, "Then I guess I need to see Casey." Without waiting for her to announce him, he turned on his heel and marched into Casey's office.

Lucille sat there for a moment thinking how sad it was that now that Drake was finally interested in a woman, that woman was no longer available to him.

"Hi, beautiful."

Lucille's thoughts were interrupted and she glanced up into the smiling face of another agent whom she was fond of, Tom Crowley. "Oh, hi, Tom, glad you're back. How was your assignment?" she asked, accepting his report.

"Bloody."

She shuddered at the thought. For the past year, Tom and a number of other operatives had been working to keep a lid on the things that were going on in Argentina.

"I see the 'Man Wonder' is back," Tom said, looking at the closed door to Casey's office.

Lucille grinned, knowing that was what some of the agents called Drake—behind his back, of course. "Yes, Drake returned today and I had to deliver him some bad news."

Tom's interest was piqued. "What?"

"That Tori Green had left the agency while he was away on assignment."

Tom lifted a curious brow. "Why would Green's departure bother Warren? It's not like they had a thing going on . . . or did they?"

Lucille shrugged, thinking she had possibly said too much, especially since she knew that Tom had also been interested in Tori at one time. "I need to get back to work. Thanks for the report, Tom."

Tom nodded when it became apparent Lucille had no plans to answer his question. He returned her smile. "Yeah, I'll see you later."

Drake turned from looking out of the window and gave Casey a look of pure, unadulterated anger. "You don't have to quote agency policies to me, Casey. All I want to know is where Tori went. You don't even have to give me an address. Just name the city, or the state, and I'll find her."

Casey sat behind his desk, his interest piqued. Warren's temper was in rare form today. This was only his second meeting with the man after becoming his boss and all he could see was his attitude was getting worse. He had barged into his office and before he could ask Warren how the assignment in South America had gone, the man had asked for the whereabouts of Victoria Green. Hearing she had resigned from the Agency hadn't been good enough for him. He had wanted her address, which was information he couldn't provide. However, Warren wasn't letting the matter go. "I can't do that," Casey said, his lips tightening in frustration.

"Yes, you can," Drake all but snapped. "You can make an exception and tell me what I want to know."

Casey raised his eyebrows. "But why should I do that, Warren? If I remember correctly, the last time you and Ms. Green were together in my office, you were all but eating nails at the thought of going on that assignment with her. What changed?"

Drake scowled. "Nothing changed. There's just some unfinished business between us."

Casey nodded. He then slowly stood, his voice tight. "Well, that's unfortunate because there is nothing I can tell you. Victoria Green made a point of requesting that we not tell anyone of her whereabouts. I reminded her that that was Agency policy anyway and she went on to let me know she expected that policy to be followed. I distinctively got the impression that she wants to put her job with the CIA behind her and start a new life. After giving this agency five years of hard work and dedicated service, I think she deserves that and I would hope you would feel the same way."

Casey released a ragged breath before continuing. "I don't know what unfinished business you feel is between you, but evidently she doesn't feel the same way, otherwise you would know where she is. So my advice to you, Warren, is to move on with your life. If you still want that thirty-day leave, then I suggest you take it. We can discuss future assignments when you get back."

Drake glared at him, not liking the way Casey was so easily dismissing him. Fine, if he couldn't get Tori's address from him then he'd use other means to get it.

Without saying another word, he turned and walked out of Casey's office.

. . .

"You have a phone call, sir."

Solomon Cross glanced up from the papers he'd been read-ing and took the phone that Miguel was handing to him.

"Yes?"

"Cross, this is Red Hunter."

Cross smiled. Red Hunter was the code name for one of the CIA agents he had on staff, a rather nice way of saying "in his pocket." "Yes, Red Hunter, and to what do I owe the pleasure of your call?"

"I found out some information that might interest you about Drake Warren."

Cross leaned back in his chair. "What about Warren? Is he dying again?" he asked in an embittered chuckle. The man had been near death eight months ago and had some-how miraculously survived. If Cross was a religious man he would begin to think that someone up there really gave a damn about Warren.

"No, he isn't dying but he might have a love interest."

That definitely got Cross's attention. "A love interest or a bedmate?"

"I'd say a love interest since word is out that he's ob-sessed in finding her. It seems he's been asking around about her, trying to find out where she's gone." The Red Hunter then relayed the information that he'd heard earlier that day.

"Interesting," Cross said moments later, dragging out the word as he rubbed his chin. "It's very unusual for Warren to show more than a passing interest in a woman." Then mo-ments later he said, "I want her."

"Excuse me?"

The very thought that Red Hunter acted like he didn't

understand him irritated the hell out of Cross. "I said that I want her. Find her before he does and bring her to me."

There was silence on the other end of the phone. The Red Hunter asked, "Why?"

Rage built up inside of Cross. "Don't ever question my orders. Just do it!" He then slammed the phone down.

Moments later he stood and walked over to the window. At any other time the sight of the ocean would calm whatever raged inside of him but not today.

There was a woman in Drake Warren's life?

Cross wanted to laugh. So he did. After nearly five years the man had finally found a woman to make him forget Sandy Carroll. If that was true, then unfortunately her fate was definitely sealed. He sighed deeply. The Red Hunter would follow his order and deliver Victoria Green to him. He needed to know what there was about her that had Drake Warren coming back for more. He would diligently find out and have fun with her for a while, and then he would save Warren the trouble of finding her when Cross shipped her body to him in a box. He grinned. At least he would ship only parts of her to Warren; the parts he hadn't fed to the sharks.

The thought of ruining Warren's life for a second time sent a burst of pleasure through him. He couldn't wait for the arrival of his houseguest.

Stinson Beach, California

Tori took several deep breaths, trying to remain calm after reading the article that had appeared in this morning's paper. It was about Rico Santiago's rebels and how the South American government had been successful in defeating them. What the paper hadn't told and what most Americans didn't know was that the CIA had been behind the scenes in helping South America keep the rebels under control. There had been an unspoken agreement between the two countries that the U.S. would assist them in their fight with the rebels if they kept our country abreast of any drug shipments headed our way.

Tori reread the section that said the only casualties had come from the rebels and although she knew it would never be put in print if there had been a CIA casualty, a part of her felt that Drake was alive and safe. For some reason she was almost certain of it.

She tenderly rubbed her stomach, smiled and whispered softly, "Your daddy is safe, little one."

She had found out last month that she was pregnant, and had cried so hard in the doctor's office, the staff hadn't been sure if she was shedding tears of happiness or sorrow. She had been quick to tell them they were definitely tears of joy. More than anything she wanted this baby; her and Drake's baby.

Her heart started to pound just thinking about it and she stood up from the chair on her porch. The home she had purchased over a year ago faced the beach and instead of having a green, landscaped lawn, she had sugar-white sand that led to the waters of the Pacific Ocean.

She loved it here and was glad for the wise investments she had made over the years. She had fallen in love with the West Coast after Hawk had given her a week's vacation as a gift two Christmases ago. Even during the winter months she had found Stinson Beach to be one of the most beautiful beaches in the world and during her travels she had seen plenty. It was more than just the sugar-white sands, it was also the beautiful blue-green hue of the waters that seemed to have calming and healing powers.

She threw up her hands in a wave when one of her neighbors jogged by and acknowledged her with a greeting. Because she had been away from home most of the time while an agent, her neighbors believed the story she had fabricated for their benefit. She'd told them that she was a teacher who worked for the federal government and that her job was to travel to different countries to teach the children of U.S. soldiers who lived abroad on military bases.

She knew Amanda Guyton, her closest neighbor who lived half a mile down the beach, believed her story. The older woman of seventy-four had always enjoyed the trinkets Tori would bring back for her from whatever country she had been to in exchange for keeping an eye on the house.

Her other neighbor, the one she had just seen jogging by a few minutes ago, Sarah Nelson, had moved into the beach house a few miles down the road three weeks ago. Sarah was single, friendly enough and pretty much kept to herself. Tori didn't have a problem with that since she was also a private person, too, and she wasn't quick to strike up friendships with anyone. However, she and Sarah often ran into each other while out shopping and once or twice they had enjoyed lunch together. Sarah was pretty tight-lipped about herself, but then so was she. As far as Tori was concerned, everyone had secrets and she appreciated a person's rights to keep those secrets.

Her thoughts again drifted to Drake. The memory of their lovemaking, which had resulted in this tiny life now inside her, still sent a flow of warmth through her. Having a baby would add such meaning to her life. Over the past five years even Hawk hadn't known about the turmoil or anguish she had endured. No one knew about the many nights she went to bed aching to be held in Drake's arms, desperately needing the physical contact with the man she loved. In the jungles of Costa Rica, her past had caught up with her, and she had been more afraid of Drake discovering who she was than she ever had been of the revolutionaries.

She had seen the world she had established for herself over the past five years unravel and she knew another chance assignment with Drake would have destroyed all Hawk's carefully laid plans. For Drake to find out her true identity would mean they would go into the protection program, or else Cross, the sick psycho that he was known to be, would hunt them down for the rest of their lives until he was satisfied he had gotten his revenge.

She stared out at the ocean and her thoughts switched to Hawk. He had gotten news of her retirement and had called to give her words of encouragement. He was the only person who knew how to contact her and he called her from time to time to see how she was doing. Whenever he would call, she would assure him she was doing fine enjoying her life of retirement, just like she knew he was doing. Again she appreciated her wise investments and because of them she didn't have to work, but would do so anyway after the baby was born to assure her child's future.

She hadn't told Hawk that she was pregnant. It was her secret and hers alone. Her grandfather's death had left her with no living relatives, at least none she'd known about. Eventually the people in the community where she lived would find out she was about to become a single parent, but that was fine with her. She would not be the first and definitely not the last. She would give her baby all the love any one child could ever receive.

Tori had turned to go into the house when she heard the phone ring. She raised a brow. There weren't many who knew her phone number. She had spoken with Hawk last week and chances were he wouldn't be calling her again until next month.

When she walked back inside she took a quick glance

around, appreciating the coziness of her home. Her furnishings were simple but nice and she had enjoyed decorating the place. In the corner of her room sat her Motown collection that included all her favorite Marvin Gaye tunes as well as those of the Temptations. A lump formed in her throat when she remembered that was the one thing she and Drake had immediately discovered they had in common, their love for soul music and many of the same rhythm and blues artists.

She reached the phone and glanced at the caller ID. The fact that the caller's phone number was blocked was the first thing she noticed when she picked it up. "Hello."

After a few seconds she frowned when the person on the other end didn't answer. All she heard was dead air. Then there was a click in her ear when the person finally released the line.

She hung up the phone and tried to force the knot forming in her stomach to ease, and her heart from thumping so hard in her chest. She shook herself and took a deep breath. She was an ex-marine and an ex-CIA agent. She would probably be looking over her shoulder and viewing strange phone calls with suspicion for a while yet. Such things were to be expected. You couldn't live the life of an ex-agent without feeling paranoid every once in a while.

Slipping out of her sandals, she padded through her carpeted house, liking the way it felt beneath her bare feet. She had toyed with the idea of carpeting her home, knowing she would be spending a lot of time vacuuming up sand she would carry in from the beach. But in the end, the carpet had won out. She detested the feel of her bare feet touching a cold floor.

Once again thoughts of Drake filled her mind. She wondered if he was back in the States or if he had gone off on another assignment. He had just come off medical leave when the two of them had left on that assignment together, yet he had acted as if he were fit as a bull. Even when they had made love his stamina had been unrelenting. Had he pushed himself too hard? Was he still pushing himself too hard? Was he taking care of himself like he should?

She frowned. Knowing Drake like she did, she knew that he probably was doing no such thing and couldn't help but worry about him. She would always worry about him.

When she made it to her bedroom, she changed out of her sundress and put on a pair of shorts and a tank top to go walking along the beach. Later, she would drive into San Francisco for dinner.

There was a Denzel movie that was coming on television later and she intended to watch it. Life was good and she could definitely get used to this.

CHAPTER 5

Trevor Grant glanced over at the man sitting on the sofa holding his son, Rio, and wondered why he'd been surprised when he had opened his door last night to find Sir Drake standing there, like dropping in at three in the morning was a normal thing. Doing the unexpected was synonymous with Sir Drake.

Sir Drake.

He couldn't help but grin as he remembered when he and Ashton had given their friend that nickname. According to English definition, a knight was generally a man of noble birth who served well before ceremoniously being inducted into knighthood by his superior. A knight swore to be brave, loyal, and courteous and to protect the defenseless. Drake had been all of those things, although to say he was always courteous would be stretching it a bit. But after saving both his and Ashton's lives a number of times, they had decided that even with that shortcoming Drake had deserved the title of Sir Drake.

Trevor knew the extent of pain his friend had carried around inside of him for five years and how he had suffered and grieved over a loss that could never be replaced. For a quick moment his mind dwelled on how he would handle it if something were to happen to his wife, Corinthians, and stark fear almost snatched his next breath. Even from their less than amiable beginning, the woman he had married meant everything to him and he didn't like to remember the time when a crazed kidnapper had almost snatched her away. It was a time he'd had to call on his friends, Sir Drake, Ashton, and the Madaris brothers, to help him get through and to do what was needed to get Corinthians back.

Now as he sat looking at Drake, a large part of him understood the bitterness that had pushed him the past five years. Sandy had been Drake's weakness. She had also been his strength.

From the first time he had met Drake at marine boot camp, Trevor had known he was a man who kept his carefully tended armor in check. Yet, Trevor and Ashton had been able to find that one chink that had forged a friendship for life. There wasn't anything he wouldn't do for Drake and Ashton, and he knew there wasn't anything they wouldn't do for him.

As Trevor took a sip of coffee, he studied Drake. He wondered what had driven Sir Drake to show up on his doorstep in Houston before daybreak. The way Trevor saw it, Sir Drake might as well spill his guts to him before Corinthians got back from shopping with his sister, Gina. A party was being planned for tomorrow to celebrate Rio's first birthday and Drake had shown up just in time for the festivities.

But still, knowing Corinthians and her overprotective nature when it came to Drake, she would demand answers of her own regardless of the perfect timing of Drake's arrival. The only reason she hadn't drilled Drake already was because by the time she realized he was there, he had already fallen asleep, or had pretended to if for no other reason than to give himself time before facing the likes of Corinthians

Avery Grant. When it came to people she cared about, she could be relentless in her pursuit of their happiness.

Trevor grinned when he thought about how Corinthians and Ashton's wife, Nettie, had managed to wiggle their way under Drake's tough shell—more than either Trevor or Ashton had seen Drake allow since Sandy's death.

"So who do you think Rio looks like?" Trevor decided to ask. The last time he'd asked Drake that question Rio had been a couple of months old and the answer Drake had given him had almost gotten him slaughtered.

Drake chuckled as he studied the face of the sleeping baby he held in his arms. His godson. The little future marine looked so much like Trevor it was ridiculous, although he would never admit that to his friend. He liked ruffling Trev's feathers by claiming that his son looked like his wife's brother. Joshua Avery was a brother-in-law that Trevor could very well do without. He doubted that either Trevor, Ashton or he would forget what a pain in the ass Joshua had been during that time a few years back when they had been frantically trying to rescue Corinthians from the clutches of a madman.

He glanced up at Trevor. "Do you want to know the truth?"

"Not if *your* truth will want to make me knock the hell out of you."

Drake smiled. "Then I have nothing to say." He then looked down at the baby again, fascinated with how peaceful he looked.

Moments later, Drake looked up and caught Trevor's inquiring gaze. He knew his friend had questions and intended to get answers. The concern in his eyes was genuine. Ashton was a man of few words. Trevor, on the other hand, always had a lot to say and had used his big mouth to badger Drake into doing what he needed to do.

There was an intense alertness in Trevor's eyes and Drake knew he didn't miss seeing much. It was what had made him such a damn good marine. "I think Rio will be more comfortable in his bed now," Drake said, cutting through the silence that had filled the room.

Nodding, Trevor stood and crossed the room, gently easing the child from Drake's arms. "When I get back, we're going to talk, Sir Drake."

Drake nodded. He'd known that they would.

When Trevor came back into the room a few moments later, he noticed the tension now lining Drake's features. Something had changed. There was a vulnerability there that he had never seen in Drake. What the hell had gone down to bring about such a reaction in Sir Drake of all people?

At the sound of the doorbell, he watched Drake glance up. "That's probably Ashton," Trevor said, making his way to the door after picking up his unfinished cup of coffee off the table. "It wouldn't surprise me if Corinthians contacted Nettie to let them know you're here."

Drake nodded and gave Trevor a half smile. "Just as well," he said, his voice low. "There's something I need to talk to you both about. I have a problem."

"A problem? What kind of problem?" Trevor asked, over his shoulder when he reached the door. He knew it couldn't be money problems since Drake owned that huge track of land in the Tennessee Mountains, not to mention a number of smart investment moves, thanks to Jake Madaris, who, besides being a wealthy rancher, was also an expert in investments and finance.

"Well," Drake hedged, "It's a woman problem."

A woman problem? Shocked, Trevor whirled around, almost dropping the half-empty cup of coffee from his hand.

He strengthened his hold on the cup at the last moment. He stared at Drake. "A woman?" he asked in disbelief. At Drake's slow nod, Trevor shook his head and studied Drake anew, ignoring the sound of the doorbell ringing again.

Had he finally found someone to love? And for him to feel the need to travel all the way to Texas to talk about it with him and Ashton meant it was pretty damn serious. Trevor blinked relief from his eyes and hoped fervently that this was a sign that Drake had finally put the past to rest and was embarking on a future.

Trevor smiled tentatively, not wanting to jump to any conclusions where Drake was concerned. He and Ashton would let him do the talking and they would definitely be listening.

"Time heals all pain," Corinthians Grant whispered to her husband as they stood watching Sir Drake. Their backyard was swarming with both kids and parents who had come out to help celebrate Rio's first birthday. Sir Drake was on the sidelines, reclining in one of their lawn chairs sipping a glass of lemonade while watching a clown paint the faces of the kids who stood still long enough for him to complete the task.

Trevor had told his wife about the conversation he and Ashton had had with Drake yesterday. He and Ashton had listened attentively while Drake told him about CIA agent, Tori Green. The crux of Drake's problem was that since returning to the States, he'd found out the woman had resigned and he had no way of getting in contact with her. He had questioned the two agents that he'd heard she had gone out with in the past. Both men claimed they hadn't known her whereabouts, and if they did, they hadn't talked. Drake had even called in contacts and so far no one had anything to report. The thought that he even wanted to find the woman was surprising to anyone who knew Drake. For the longest time it was obvious that Drake had pretty much accepted a future without a serious involvement with a woman, and now it seemed that this Tori Green had, for the short while they had spent together, more than piqued Drake's interest and had possibly given him a reason to hope again. Although Drake had insisted he merely wanted to see the woman again and that his interest didn't particularly mean anything, Trevor and Ashton knew better.

Trevor had noticed the gleam of hope in Sir Drake's eyes when he mentioned that a friend of the family, Alex Maxwell, who owned an investigating firm, was good at locating people and felt pretty sure the woman could be found. Alex would be attending the party later and Drake had plans to talk to him.

"Time may heal all pain, but I wouldn't go overboard and start planning the wedding yet," Trevor said, after hearing the hope and excitement in his wife's voice.

A soft smile tugged at Corinthians's mouth. "Yes, but it's a start."

"Yes, it is." Trevor smiled as he glanced across the yard at all the babies that had been born to his close friends over the past year. First, there were Ashton and Nettie's triplets; Clayton and Syneda Madaris's daughter; Jake and Diamond Madaris's son; Kyle and Kimara's son; Trent and Brenna Jordache's son; and Dex and Caitlin Madaris's son. No one was surprised when Trask and Felicia Maxwell had shown up with their six-year-old son Austin and announced they were having a baby in seven months. Now Felicia joined Trevor's sister Gina among the new list of pregnant women.

Trevor frowned when he noticed that his wife's brother, Joshua Avery, had arrived. A part of him had wished that

Joshua wouldn't show up today. Trevor inhaled deeply and wished there was some way that he could overlook Joshua's faults and decided the man had too many to dismiss. Besides, Joshua wouldn't know how to handle it if he were to suddenly start being nice to him so it was best to leave well enough alone.

He glanced around and smiled when he noticed that the Madaris brothers' youngest sister, twenty-one-year-old Christy, was busy organizing a game of kickball for the older kids, many of whom were her nieces and nephews. He smiled, thinking how Christy had grown up over the past few years. He could vividly recall when she'd been born. At the time Justin, Dex, and Clayton had been in their late teens and had long since become the most overprotective big brothers he had ever seen. Now that Christy was officially a young woman, he wondered how the brothers would continue to keep a tight rein on their sister when she appeared to have definitely developed a mind of her own.

Even with all the noise surrounding him, Drake managed to drop off to sleep. Once or twice he was awakened when one of the kids' balls landed near him, but otherwise he was able to tune everything out. With his arms covering his face, he stretched his body out in the lawn chair and dropped right off to sleep, secure in the knowledge that he would soon be one step closer to finding Tori.

She was in his thoughts now. He couldn't help but remember the first time he had seen her while sitting in the coffee shop, then how they had sparred off later in Casey's office. Then there was the mission and how well they had worked together. But nothing could top the memories of them making love. That moment in time would always be branded into his mind.

He opened his eyes and his gazed drifted to all the babies he saw. Why couldn't he let go the memory of him and Tori having unprotected sex? She had promised that she would contact him if their night together had resulted in a pregnancy and she hadn't so he could only assume she wasn't having his child. But for some reason he needed to hear her say it. He needed the confirmation to come from her lips.

"Warren, I'm glad to see you're still doing better."

Drake glanced to the side and saw Joshua Avery was standing next to his lawn chair. Months ago while in Trevor and Corinthians's home when he'd been recuperating, he had thanked the man for using his clout to get him out of Iraq. Having to thank Joshua Avery for anything had left a bad taste in his mouth but he'd felt compelled to do it. "Thanks," he said and closed his eyes, hoping Joshua would take the hint that he wanted to be left alone and move on.

He did.

When Drake reopened his eyes moments later, he noticed that Joshua was now talking to Jake Madaris. He hadn't wanted to stare before but Joshua, it seemed, had a little bit more hair on his head than before. Drake grinned. If he didn't know better he'd swear the man was trying to grow an Afro. He chuckled. Was Joshua Avery, the former staunch Republican senator, making an attempt to reconnect to his roots? Drake shook his head. If so, he still had a long way to go to do so.

Drake was about to close his eyes again when he saw that Alexander Maxwell had arrived. Alex at thirty was a former FBI agent who owned and operated Maxwell Security and Investigators. Drake had seen firsthand how competent Alex was when one of Nettie's employees at the restaurant had been kidnapped by her ex-husband last year. Filled with jealous rage, the man had broken out of prison, intent on teaching his wife a lesson. It had taken a team effort of Drake, Alex, Trevor, and Ashton to find the woman after Dex Madaris, a geologist, had pinpointed her location from a dirt sample. Also, Alex had successfully destroyed the plans of a demented person who'd been intent on killing wealthy rancher Jake Madaris a couple of years ago.

When Alex caught Drake's gaze he began walking toward him with a glass of lemonade in his hand. He was six-feet-four inches tall and was impeccably dressed in a pair of jeans, a chambray shirt, and western boots on his feet, giving the appearance of a Texan, through and through. Drake also knew that Alex was as sharp as he looked. He had obtained a bachelor's degree from Howard University and a master's degree from MIT.

"I saw you sleeping earlier and didn't want to wake you," Alex said to Drake. "How you manage to sleep with all the noise going on is beyond me."

Drake pulled himself into a sitting position as Alex took the patio chair across from him. Drake shrugged. "I'm used to snatching sleep where and when I can." He extended his hand to Alex and gave him a firm handshake. "It's good to see you again."

Alex smiled. "Same here, Drake, and I remember those days with the Bureau when sleep was a precious commodity you never got enough of." He then leaned back in his chair and took a sip of the lemonade Corinthians had placed in his hand the moment he had walked into the backyard. "Trevor told me you want me to find someone."

Drake inhaled deeply. "It's this woman I met, a former CIA agent by the name of Victoria Green. While I was out on an assignment she left the Agency and per Agency policies, no one can give me any information as to where she's gone. I tried using the contacts that I had but it seems like she's fallen off the face of the earth."

Alex nodded. "Finding a former agent who doesn't want to be found isn't easy although not impossible." He studied Drake for a moment then asked, "Why do you want to find Victoria Green?"

"It's a personal matter."

Alex's lips tightened and a few moments later he said, "You know usually I'd turn down a job like this. I respect any agent's desire to build another life for themselves and put the past behind them." He stared at Drake and Drake stared back, determination and sheer stubbornness firming his jaw. Alex sighed. "But in this case, I'll make an exception and get on it right away."

Drake let out a breath he hadn't realized he had been holding. "Thanks. I wouldn't ask if it wasn't important."

Alex's lips eased into a smile. "I believe that." He then took another sip of his lemonade and glanced around the bustling party. He went still as something—or someone—caught his attention. Out of curiosity, Drake followed his line of vision.

Christy Madaris.

The young woman was standing next to Corinthians near the grill and holding one of Kyle and Kimara Garwood's kids on her hip. She appeared to be in a happy mood and was laughing at whatever it was Corinthians was telling her, and seemed not to have noticed the attention she was getting from one particular person.

"That's the Madaris brothers' youngest sister, isn't it?" Drake asked when Alex just sat there, staring, not saying a single word.

"Yes, that's her."

"She's kind of pretty, don't you think?"

Just like he'd known he would, Alex tore his gaze away from Christy Madaris and looked at Drake. He gave him a tight smile before saying, "Yes, I think she's kind of pretty."

The harshness in Alex's tone of voice almost made Drake chuckle. Alex was acting like a male animal marking his territory and Drake wondered if he knew he was also courting danger. Anyone who knew Justin, Dex, and Clayton Madaris also knew that when it came to their baby sister, they had a tendency to be a little overprotective.

"So you think you'll have the information I want in a week?" Drake asked when he saw Alex's gaze had wandered back to Christy Madaris again. She had returned the little girl to the Garwoods and was standing off to the side talking to her three brothers.

"Although I assume Victoria Green will have covered her tracks well, I'm hoping it will take less time than that for me to find her. I have a knack for finding people, especially those who don't want to be found," was Alex's reply, without refocusing his gaze on Drake.

"Interesting," Drake murmured, as a small smile pulled at his mouth. And he wasn't talking about Alex's efficiency.

Christy Madaris shook her head as she met the glares of her brothers, Justin, Dex, and Clayton. "Hey, you guys, let up. I'll be turning twenty-two in a few months, not to mention that I'll be graduating from college in six weeks. Don't you think it's time to get over the overprotective kick the three of you have been on for the past twenty years?"

Justin leaned back against a huge oak tree. "All we want to know is who's the guy you're going out with tonight?"

"How old is he?" Clayton threw in.

"And who's his people?" Dex Madaris added.

Christy raised a brow at the third question. "Who's his people?"

Dex shrugged. "Yes. Who's his family?"

Christy gently pushed the reddish brown curls back from

her forehead. "No one you would know. David and his family moved here recently."

"Then we'd like to meet him," Justin said, smiling.

"And I'd like to meet *them*," Dex added, not smiling.

Christy frowned. "What the three of you mean is that you'd like the opportunity to scare David off but it won't work. I've already told him about the three of you and how you operate. He doesn't mind meeting you and in fact he's looking forward to it and found it rather amusing that you behave this way."

Dex crossed his arms over his chest and narrowed his gaze. "Since he finds it so funny maybe we ought to really give him something to laugh at."

Christy raised her eyes upward, totally exasperated. "You know there's going to come a time when the three of you will have to loosen the reins."

Clayton chuckled. "Why should we?"

Christy glared. "Mainly because you can't keep up with me forever. You have wives and children of your own. Don't you think you should be keeping up with them?"

"Yeah, but we have an obligation to keep up with you as well. Just think of how boring your life would be if we didn't," Clayton said, grinning.

Christy shook her head, wondering if they actually believed that. When she was younger she'd thought their overprotectiveness was rather cute, and it hadn't bothered her any since she'd always had a crush on Alex Maxwell, and had made up in her mind that she would one day grow up and marry him. But last year Alex had pretty much burst her bubble when he'd told her that he wasn't interested in her childhood fantasies and she needed to grow up and remove him from the picture.

So she had.

Seeing that she wasn't getting anywhere with her brothers, Christy turned to walk off, only to bump into a hard, solid chest. When she realized who it was, she took a step back. But it hadn't been quick enough. She had felt the heat from Alex Maxwell's body the moment they had touched, but she refused to let him know how strongly he affected her. "Alex."

"Christy."

She met his eyes and the look in them was dark, intense, like he was the hunter who had cornered his prey. She shook her head to clear her brain cells, thinking she was definitely imagining things. Alex had pretty much let her know he was way out of her league. Anger filled her every being at the very idea that at one time she'd thought her entire existence had revolved around this one man.

"I see the three of you have pissed Christy off again," he said to her brothers in a deep tone of his voice that she found slightly hypnotic. It reminded her of that one time he had lost control and kissed her.

It was a night she didn't want to remember but could not forget.

"She's upset because we cared enough to question her about her date," Clayton explained.

"Oh."

Christy's anger increased. They were discussing her like she wasn't standing there! She met Alex's gaze again and saw the hint of amusement that touched his lips. Unable to find anything remotely humorous about the situation, she angrily walked off, leaving the four men staring after her.

"California?" Solomon Cross murmured to the caller on the phone. The Red Hunter had called to report they had located Victoria Green. It seemed that she had purchased a place on the beach in California.

As far as Cross was concerned it had taken long enough to locate her. "What took you so long to find her?" he asked, annoyed. It had been almost two weeks.

"Someone in the Agency wanted to make sure she wasn't found. It wasn't easy breaking the code in the database and getting the information in a way that it couldn't be traced."

Cross sighed. He really didn't want to hear excuses. "How soon can you get her to me?" He'd been thinking about her a lot lately, anticipating her arrival.

"We have to plan this one well and not be too hasty," the Red Hunter was saying. "She's a former CIA agent and if she suddenly becomes missing, a lot of questions will be raised. We don't want anything to look suspicious or there will be an investigation that you don't want."

Cross shrugged. "And nothing will be linked back to me. How can it? Besides, I'm paying you enough to make sure that it doesn't."

CHAPTER 6

Tori's eyes suddenly flew open when she heard a sound. Struggling through the sleep that clouded her mind, she quickly sat up in bed; her heart was rapidly beating in her chest. She sat there, straining to hear whatever had awakened her.

There was nothing but the pound of the surf outside. She looked toward the window opposite her bed and didn't see anything, but still, her sixth sense had alerted her to danger. Goose bumps were forming on her arm and a shiver was running down her spine.

Moving quickly, she quietly eased out of bed and slipped into her robe. She automatically opened the nightstand drawer and pulled out the Beretta 9mm pistol she kept there. Flicking off the safety, she moved across the room and silently opened her bedroom door.

Narrowing her eyes to slits she searched the darkened living room and the entrances to the other two rooms. Her heart began racing wildly and she forced herself to calm down. Seconds passed before Tori eased from her position after detecting no further sound. But still, she knew for certain she had heard something. It hadn't been her imagination. First the suspicions last week and now this. She refused to believe she was just acting paranoid.

And then she heard a noise again and quickly crossed the room at the same time she heard the sound of running feet outside on the porch. With her gun raised, ready to fire, she snatched open the door and made out the silhouette of someone running down the beach.

"Freeze!" she said, taking aim but not pulling the trigger. She had to remember she was not in some hostile country, and the person who had tried entering her home could have been a teenager with nothing to do but get into trouble. She was a sharpshooter and the bullets in her gun were not intended to warn but to kill.

Before lowering her gun she glanced around, quickly checking the areas around her porch beyond the open door, just in case her trespasser had brought along an accomplice. Seconds passed and once she was satisfied there was no one else, she turned and looked beyond her porch, noticing the footprints in the sand that the moonlight revealed.

Breathing hard and taking precautions, she walked off the porch to examine the area. It was man's shoe and from all indication it looked to be about a size eleven. Tori glanced around and noticed the screen from the side window of her house lay on the ground. Raising her gun again, she quickly circled her house to see if anything else had been tampered with, her ears tuned to pick up any sound. When she returned to the porch she sighed deeply.

Someone had tried to get into the window of her guest bedroom and she had two questions. Who? And why?

Drake pulled the SUV he had rented into a hotel off of Interstate 580. He had caught a plane from Houston to Oakland, California, deciding to drive the rest of the way to Stinson Beach. But since it was night, he decided to check into a hotel and arrive on Tori's doorstep first thing in the morning.

It had taken less than seventy-two hours for Alex Maxwell to provide him with the information he needed. He had been both elated and somewhat nervous. If Alex could find Tori so easily, then so could anyone else. Although according to Alex, it hadn't been as easy as it seemed to find Tori since there were a lot of Victoria Greens living in the United States and she had apparently tried hiding her tracks. He had narrowed the list down to those who had changed residences within the last six months and then from there he had zeroed in on those who had recently searched the Internet for job opportunities. It seemed that a Victoria Green who lived in Stinson Beach, California was a new resident who had moved into the beach community recently, although she had owned the home for over a year.

After traveling for almost an entire day, Drake didn't know what he planned to say to Tori when he saw her. "Hey, I was passing through and thought I'd look you up" just didn't sound plausible. He then decided that "I need to know if you're pregnant" was better. However since she hadn't tried contacting him, he could only assume that she wasn't, and she might be quick to bring that fact to his attention.

A frown marred his brow as he pulled his overnight bag out of the SUV and carried it inside the hotel to register. He would get a good night's sleep and think things through before showing up at Tori's place unannounced.

A few moments later, after entering his hotel room and closing the door behind him, he unpacked his toiletries and placed them on the counter in the bathroom. Taking off his jacket, he removed the 9mm Beretta from his holster. He might travel light but he never went anywhere without his gun.

He didn't want to think that he had no right tracking Tori down the way he had, invading her privacy and interfering with the new life she had created for herself. He struggled with the thought that she would immediately think he was nothing but a selfish bastard, and he shrugged knowing basically that that was true. They had only been together that once, but there had been something about her that had driven him to this point; to where he couldn't let go of the memory of her compelling dark-brown eyes or the soft brown hair that framed her face and flowed over her shoulders, giving her features such an innocent look. Or the sassiness of her attitude—there was definitely nothing innocent about a woman who could take down a man twice her size with her bare hands, and who was surprisingly at home with just about any firearm he could think of.

And she seemed to be just his kind of woman.

As Drake began stripping off his clothes, hope sprang within him. Sandy would always hold a special place in his heart and he still intended to make sure Solomon Cross paid for what he did, but for the first time in a long time something other than revenge consumed him.

Over the past five years he had learned plenty about emotional pain and the benefit of hard work—being out in the field had helped. But nothing had prepared him for his response to Tori, both physically and emotionally. Just in the short time they had spent together, she had made him feel things he hadn't felt in years.

He still had to admit there were times when he had been with her that he had been reminded of Sandy, and he had accepted that he would always think of Sandy at some point in future days. But he also realized that his interest in Tori was because of who she was, her own unique vitality, and not because he was looking for a Sandy clone. Ashton and Trevor had asked him about that and now he was sure. It was Tori he wanted. And for the first time in five years, he felt the stirrings of anticipation, heated desire and longing flow through him.

And it was for that very reason that he knew he had to see Tori again to understand why.

"Do you understand what I'm saying, Tori? You need to leave right away."

Breathing raggedly, Tori tried to do all she could not to scream out in anger. Hawk had called to let her know that someone had broken into the CIA employee database and she was one of the agents whose confidential information had been retrieved.

After telling Hawk about the attempted break-in the night before, he had become insistent about her leaving Stinson Beach until he made sure the two incidents weren't connected.

She inhaled deeply. Why would anyone break into the database to find out where she had gone after leaving the Agency? She had tried covering her tracks but it seemed that someone had uncovered them anyway. "Do you know who may have done it?" she asked, not liking what she was hearing. Suddenly, everything started meshing together; that mysterious phone call and the attempted break-in.

"No. You've been involved in a lot of missions and it could be linked to any of them."

Tori nodded. "Do you think Drake would have done it? You said he contacted you and seemed obsessed with finding me."

"Yes, but Drake wouldn't operate that way. He would have no reason to try to terrorize you. He would have appeared on your doorstep like it would have been his damn right to be there. Besides, no matter how much Drake might have wanted to find you, he would never have violated Agency policy by deliberately breaking the code and going into confidential information. I think we have a mole within the organization."

Tori sighed. It wouldn't be the first time nor would it be the last. She had worked for the Agency long enough to know that there were moles; crooked agents who worked as informants for the other side, and who would sell their souls if the price was right. It was sad that for some people, corruption was a way of life and it wasn't safe to trust a fellow agent without question.

Another name came into her mind, a person she didn't want to think about but someone who'd had her looking over her shoulders for the past five years. "What about Solomon Cross, Hawk? Do you think any of this is connected to what happened in Haiti?" she asked quietly, feeling her muscles tightening and her nostrils quivering in anger. "Do you think there's a chance that he knows that Sandy Carroll didn't die in that explosion?" she asked, hating to do so but knowing she had to. She didn't want to think that her visit to Drake's hospital room could have alerted Solomon Cross that Sandy Carroll was still alive. There was no way he could have put two and two together and come up with that.

She heard Hawk's deep sigh. "Heaven help us all if he has, but I doubt very seriously that any of this is connected to Cross. I'm no longer with the Agency so I'm relying on the information I'm getting through my contacts and appreciate them letting me know what's going on. It seems Casey has his hands full explaining to the top brass how this happened. Your information wasn't the only data the person retrieved. Whether it was intentional or done to mislead I'm not sure. The one good thing is that your medical history was not on that file. It's somewhere else on a top-secret database that can't be decoded."

"Anything can be decoded, Hawk," Tori said bitterly. "A trained hacker could penetrate any system, even highly sensitive information."

"Yes, but we treated your medical history differently. Because of the secrecy surrounding your case, I decided not to store that information in the Agency's databank. It's somewhere in a vault and the disk will disintegrate the moment someone tries to decode it. But still, until we find out what's going on, and rule out Solomon Cross, I want you to leave Stinson Beach as discreetly as you can and make sure you aren't followed."

Tori opened her mouth then shut it after realizing that no matter what she said, Hawk would not change his mind if he felt she was in some kind of danger. If she had only herself to worry about then she would be stubborn and refuse to run away from trouble, but she had more to think about than herself. She had her baby—a baby she still hadn't told Hawk about. "All right, Hawk. I'll leave as soon as possible."

"Only pack what's necessary, Tori."

She tried to smile. Hawk used to get on her case about not being able to travel light. "Okay." After hanging up the phone, Tori proceeded to follow his instructions.

Hawk hung up the phone and immediately began pacing around in his living room. He didn't like coincidences, which was why he had told Tori to get lost for a while until he could determine if there was a connection to the decoding of the records at CIA headquarters and the attempted break-in at her place. Although he hadn't said as much to

Tori, there was a chance Cross had found out Sandy Carroll was still alive.

Tori had made a mistake going to the hospital to see Drake. If news of that visit had gotten into the wrong hands and someone interested enough had started doing some in-depth digging, a person's curiosity could have gotten piqued. And if they had been able to get the list of all the female agents who either knew Drake or had worked with him, Tori would be the least likely candidate. However, being the least likely could also make her the most suspicious, considering the circumstances. But still, to think that someone had connected Tori's hospital visit to Sandy Carroll was too big of a leap in logic and he wasn't buying it. Something else was going on and he intended to find out what.

His thoughts were interrupted when he heard the phone ring. He picked it up immediately. "Yes?"

"Hawk, this is Kent."

Hawk nodded. Kent Malloy had served with him in the Marine Corps, and like him had ventured into service with the CIA. Also, for a while Kent had been head of special operations for the FBI where he still maintained close contact.

Over the years they had shared vital information when necessary. Now retired, Kent was still considered computer-savvy, ultra-intelligent and could find out any information a person wanted within or not within reason. "Did you find out anything?"

"A couple of things that you might find interesting," Kent responded.

Hawk lifted a brow. "What?"

"First of all, over the past few weeks there have been a number of inquiries made in databases on Victoria Green, and it seems they aren't coming from any one source. I haven't been able to pinpoint where the majority of the inquiries are coming from but the person or persons definitely have the expertise to work the system so they aren't traced."

Senses on alert, Hawk sat on the edge of the desk that he had tucked in the corner of the room. "I'm sure Drake Warren is connected to a few of those inquiries since he wanted to locate Tori. He probably hired someone to find her, which would account for some . . . but not all of them."

"Drake Warren?" Kent asked, surprised. "Why would Drake Warren want to find Victoria Green?"

Hawk rubbed a hand across his unshaven chin. He had never shared information with Kent about Tori's past and wouldn't do so now unless it became extremely necessary. The less people knew the better. "He claims they have personal business to resolve."

"Oh," Kent said, chuckling. "One of those situations, huh?"

Hawk shook his head. Kent didn't know the half of it. "Evidently." He paused and then said, "I suggested to Tori that she go into hiding for a while until we find out something concrete."

Kent sighed deeply. "I hope she does what you've asked her to do."

"I hope so, too. Tori can be pretty damn stubborn at times." Which might be the reason she is presently in this mess, Hawk decided not to add. He had a gnawing feeling in his gut that he didn't like.

"I'll try to find out as much as I can. This is like a damn puzzle and I intend to put all the pieces in place," Kent said. "If we have a mole within the Agency, I intend to find out who he or she is. You know how I feel about informants, Hawk."

Yes, Hawk knew. Ken had blasted a few away in his day—literally. No one had wanted to squander time investigating who'd wasted a couple of corrupt agents. After ending the conversation with Kent, Hawk thought for a moment, then made a decision, one he had hoped he'd never have to make. He picked up the phone to call Drake Warren.

Drake jerked awake, his breathing ragged, his chest rising and falling rapidly. He glanced around the darkened hotel room, suddenly remembering where he was and why he was there.

He got out of bed as sweat clung to his body, needing a drink of cold water. It had been the nightmare again, but some things had been different this time.

He remembered how he, Trevor, Sandy, and Ashton had been crawling low on the ground, away from the warehouse when suddenly they had heard the sound of an infant crying. He had ordered everyone to stay down and not move, but when the sound of the infant grew louder, Sandy had been the one to defy his order by taking a chance and going back into the warehouse to save the child. The moment she had gone in, the warehouse had exploded into a ball of fire. It was only later that they discovered it had been a setup and the sound they'd heard hadn't been an actual baby but a recording to lure Sandy inside. Cross had known that Sandy would give in to maternal instincts before military orders.

Drake would always remember the sound of her screams right before a second explosion had erupted. But in tonight's nightmare, what had been different was the face he'd envisioned within the smoke, fire, and the flying debris; the face that went with the screams had been Tori's and not Sandy's.

Cursing softly, he poured himself a glass of cold water and took a long drink. Small ice particles eased down his throat, cooling his body but not his mind. Why had images of Tori and not Sandy formed in his mind when he'd relived the explosion?

After finishing off the last of the water, he rubbed his mouth with the back of his hand at the same time a funny feeling settled deep in his gut. Something had triggered anxiety inside of him and he wasn't sure just what it was.

At that moment his cell phone rang and he quickly padded barefoot across the carpeted floor to answer it. He figured it was either Trevor or Ashton calling to make sure he'd made it to California okay. "Yes."

"Drake, this is Hawk."

Drake raised a brow, surprised. The funny feeling deep in his gut flared to life again. "Hawk?"

He had spoken to the man a few weeks ago after returning from South America. When Casey had refused to give him any information on Tori, he had contacted Hawk to see if he knew her whereabouts. Hawk never said whether he'd known Tori's address or not. What he had said was basically the same thing Casey had said. Due to Agency policy, he was unable to give out any information on a former agent.

"Drake, I don't have time to explain and I need to make this quick. How far are you from San Francisco, California?"

Drake smiled faintly. "It just so happens that I'm right across the Bay. Why?"

Hawk sighed deeply. He didn't need to ask Drake why he was in California. Evidently like he'd told Kent, Drake had taken matters into his own hands and tracked Tori down himself. That thought didn't sit well with Hawk. If Drake could find her, so could someone else.

"Hawk?"

"Yes?"

"Why did you ask how close I was to Frisco? What's going on?"

There was a slight pause before Hawk said, "Tori Green might be in trouble."

Drake frowned, his attention alert and focused. "What kind of trouble?"

"I think someone has put a hit out on her. I can't go into a lot of details with you, Drake, but I need your help in keeping her alive until we find out who's behind it."

For the first time since moving to Stinson Beach, Tori was aware of how dark the two-lane road leading from the beach was at night, especially around two in the morning. So far her Maxima was the only vehicle on the road and a part of her felt good about that. Once she crossed the Golden Gate Bridge into Frisco she planned to avoid less traveled roads like this one. She had no idea where she was going but decided to just head east.

She replayed back in her mind pieces of Hawk's conversation. She had worked with him long enough to know he wasn't one to make rash decisions and relied on his gut instincts about things. She hadn't felt easy since the attempted break-in into her home and even before Hawk's phone call she had planned to sleep with her pistol beside her in bed.

She suddenly felt her body tense when a car pulled out of a side road and began following her. Glancing back in her rearview mirror she saw it was traveling a safe distance behind. She sighed deeply, her gut clenched with anxiety, although she was trying not to let her nerves get the best of her. She wanted to believe that whoever was in the vehicle was someone who enjoyed the nightlife and nothing more. A few minutes later she knew that was not the case when the vehicle picked up speed at the same time the driver suddenly killed the lights.

"Don't worry, little one. Your mother is going to keep

you safe," Tori whispered as she reached across the car seat for her pistol and flicked off the safety at the same time she pushed her feet to the accelerator to speed up. Speed signs were posted for sixty-five miles an hour but she was doing eighty-five with all intention of doing more if she had to. She wasn't sure what she was dealing with and her Beretta may not stand a chance against a high-powered rifle or any type of automatic weapons.

Releasing a curse from her lips when the car behind her increased its speed again, she attempted to concentrate on her driving on the hilly road, trying to make it to the highway that would take her across the Golden Gate.

She blinked when up ahead she saw another vehicle approaching, which looked like a SUV or a truck. She hoped the driver following her wouldn't try anything while another vehicle was around. However, there was no doubt in her mind that once the truck passed her by, the driver would make their move.

Somehow she had to try and lose whoever was following her. She didn't have the option of getting the local police involved. There would be too many questions with too little time to provide answers.

She glanced back in the rearview mirror. The vehicle behind her was gaining speed. It seemed that approaching truck or not, the driver intended to make their move. Holding the steering wheel with one hand, she held her gun in a position ready to take aim if she had to. No matter what, she intended to survive.

"Damn." Drake took stock of the two vehicles coming toward him at full speed. There was certainly a chase going on and first car fit the description of Tori's vehicle.

As soon as he passed the two vehicles he jerked his steer-

ing wheel to the left, made a sharp U-turn and became the
third man in pursuit. He floored it and in no time at all, the
Tahoe he was driving had gained ground and was bearing
down on the dark sedan chasing Tori. The driver had gone
from being the pursuer to being the one pursued.

"You want to act crazy, then let's do crazy," Drake said
through clenched teeth as he increased his speed and
rammed into the back of the vehicle. Gripping the wheel
hard, his gaze stayed glued on the car ahead. Almost in-
stantly, a series of shots sounded and when he heard the
sound of metal shattering, Drake knew the side of his vehicle had been struck.

"Now you've really pissed me off," he snarled, unsnap-
ping his seat belt and taking his pistol and firing back. Suddenly he heard a loud *pop,* then the vehicle swerved to the
right when the driver apparently lost control on the hilly
road and slammed into a tree before bursting into flames.
With an impact such as that Drake knew there weren't any
survivors and at the moment he didn't give a damn.

He glanced up ahead and saw that Tori had slowed down
but had not stopped. She was being cautious and that was
good. He decided to let her know that he was there to help
her by using Morse code with his headlights.

Tori saw the lights on the third vehicle blinking out a Morse
code that she deciphered.

Drake?

What was he doing here? Hawk had been so sure that
Drake hadn't been the person who had decoded the information at CIA headquarters, and if that was true, how had
he found her?

She glanced in her rearview mirror and saw Drake was

sending another message, telling her to pull over. Someone was after her and with all the unanswered questions she had, she found herself wondering whether she could trust him.

She blinked. Evidently adrenaline was making her shaky, crazy. For God's sake, of course she could trust Drake. He was the man she loved . . . but still, was he the same man he had been five years ago?

No.

Tori found she was turning cold as she glanced back into her rearview mirror. Drake Warren had always been arrogant, rough and tough, bullheaded as hell with a kick-butt kind of attitude, but it seemed that over the years he'd also become hard, inflexible, unapproachable and jaded. She had immediately picked on it that day she had faced him down in Casey's office. Because of what had happened in Haiti, he looked at things differently.

He had changed but then so had she. Five years of looking over her shoulders had made her wary, tense, and less trusting of people. She'd found herself questioning people's motives about everything and she no longer took anything or anyone at face value.

And at this moment no matter how much it hurt to do so, she couldn't take Drake at face value either. She had more than herself to worry about and protect. She had her unborn child to think about, even if it meant protecting it from the man who was its father.

A plan came into mind. Pulling off to the side of the road, she quickly crawled out of the passenger door and, using the car as a shield, she got behind it and waited for Drake to come to a stop. When he got out of his SUV she gripped her gun, and raised it into firing position as she stepped from behind her car. "Hold it right there, Drake. Don't move or I'll shoot! What are you doing here?"

. . .

Drake's breathing escalated. He immediately wondered how could a man find a woman so beautiful, so damn desirable while she was crouched into a combat stance with a damn high-powered pistol aimed straight at his heart? All he could see was that gorgeous windblown hair that flowed around her shoulders, how her blouse stretched tight across her chest and how her shorts fit her body—too well. His heart, the same one her gun was aimed at, started a slow pounding. Something else other than adrenaline kicked into his system and his senses were heightened, not at the danger he found himself in, but at the reaction of his body to seeing Tori again, even under the most unusual of circumstances.

"I asked what are you doing here, Drake?"

It was more the terror in Tori's expression that made Drake come to a stop than the gun she held in her hand. She was terrorized but he knew hell would freeze over before she would let it show. She also appeared confused. "Put the gun down, Tori. You saw what I did to the driver in that car," he said, indicating the vehicle that was still burning. "I'm not the enemy. I'm here to help you so put your gun down."

Instead of putting the gun down she gripped the weapon tighter. "No. Answer me. What are you doing here?"

Drake ran a hand down his face, getting madder than hell. He was trying to understand her position. Someone had tried taking her out tonight and that would give her a reason to doubt him or anyone else. But still the idea that she thought that he would harm her hurt like hell. "Hawk."

She raised a dubious brow and the hard line of her mouth relaxed somewhat. "Hawk?"

"Yes."

She raised the gun a little higher and kept it aimed at him. "Now I know you're lying because I talked to Hawk less than a couple of hours ago and he didn't mention anything about you coming here."

Drake's eyes narrowed. "I know that, dammit. He called me after talking to you. He said you might need my help and evidently you did."

She met his gaze. "I didn't need your help. I could have handled things."

"Bullshit."

She shrugged. So maybe it was. But still . . . "How did you know where to find me?"

Drake almost smiled. Almost. He still didn't like the fact that she doubted him. "I hired a private investigator."

Tori frowned. "I tried covering my tracks."

"Well, you did a piss-poor job of doing so." Drake then glanced around. "Look, with that car burning to a crisp, we need to get the hell out of here. I don't want to hang around for the cops to ask questions."

Neither did she.

"You can follow me back to the hotel and call Hawk from there to verify my story, or better yet you get him on your mobile phone. But whatever you do let's get the hell out of here. Now!"

Without saying another word Drake got back inside his SUV, started the ignition and pulled off. Knowing Drake had the right idea, she lowered her gun and quickly got back into her car. She fastened her seat belt and began following behind him as she punched in Hawk's number.

"Tori?"

"Yes, it's me, Hawk. Drake's here."

There was a slight pause. "Yes, I know."

She said nothing for a time, then, "But why?"

She heard Hawk draw a deep breath. "Because he's the only man I trust to help you, so let him."

Tori struggled to ignore the pounding of her heart as she followed Drake. She blinked her eyes several times, almost finding it impossible to believe that he was actually here. After they made it across the Bay Bridge she kept up with him on Interstate 580. A few miles later he exited and she followed as he pulled into a hotel parking lot.

She parked in the space next to his and watched as he got out and came around the truck and stopped. "May I approach or do you still want to put a damn hole in me?"

She flinched. Although he had tried to tease, there was a twist to his lips and she knew that her doubting him had rubbed him the wrong way. "I talked to Hawk. You're safe."

He glanced around. "I may be safe but this place isn't. We need to get the hell out of this area as soon as possible. Come inside while I repack my stuff so we can head out. We'll leave the truck and take your car. While going across the Bay Bridge I called Hawk and gave him the license plate of that car following you. He's contacting the local FBI to fill them in on what happened. I also told him we would leave the truck here and take your car. He'll use his old contacts and have the FBI make sure nothing is traced back to me."

Tori opened the car door and got out. Glancing around as she followed Drake to the hotel's door. She was glad they didn't have to go through the lobby to get to his room but were able to gain entrance through one of the side doors.

"When we leave we'll continue to head east, making sure we aren't followed," Drake said. "We're going to ditch your car in San Jose. Hawk has arranged to have another vehicle waiting for us at a hotel there for us to make the switch."

Tori shook her head. Hawk had retired yet he was placing himself at the head of this investigation and a part of her appreciated that fact. When it came to his agents, present or former, he did anything and everything to protect their backs. Until they figured what was going on, he would be the lone person they trusted. "Do you know who was in that vehicle and why they were after me?"

"No," Drake answered immediately, "I don't have a clue. It was definitely a man, though. When I turned on the high-powered headlights, I saw that much. White male, blond hair, crew cut."

He glanced up the hallway and met Tori's gaze. She knew the routine. From here on out they would not be taking any chances. In unison they both drew their guns as Drake slowly opened his hotel room door and when she made a move to step ahead, he moved swiftly in front of her, searching the room first to the right and then to the left. Tori did the same.

Closing the door behind him and locking it, he quickly checked the bathroom. When he returned Tori was standing in the middle of the room glaring at him. A part of him wanted to cross the room and kiss that damn glare right off her face. "What's your problem?" he asked, putting his gun back into his holster.

"I think we need to get one thing straight, Drake."

"What?"

"I don't need a guard dog."

He leaned against the dresser and stared at her. He knew she was referring to how he had opened the hotel room and entered the room before she did. He had to remember that she didn't like playing the part of a weakling in any situation and liked kicking butt as much as he did. At the moment she was pissed. Too bad. Whether she liked it or not he *was* her guard dog, but now was not the time to tell her that.

"I'll keep that in mind," he finally said, just to appease her. "If Hawk sent you all the way from South Carolina then—"

"Hawk didn't send me."

She lifted a brow. "But you said that—"

"I said that he called me. I was already here in Oakland when he reached me."

She eyed him. "You were here? Why?"

Drake smiled. "I came to see you." As if that one sentence explained everything, he then said, "Make yourself comfortable while I repack."

Tori shook her head. He had come to see her? She then began chewing on her lower lip, not ready to ask him why. She sighed as she watched him pack. He evidently knew where they were going but she didn't have a clue. "Where're we going, Drake?"

"To my home."

Tori blinked at him, not sure she'd heard him correctly. "In the mountains in Tennessee?"

Drake straightened his frame and raised a brow before answering, "Yes." He studied her features for a few moments, then asked. "How did you know my home was in the Tennessee Mountains, Tori?"

CHAPTER 7

Ah hell, Tori thought as she scrambled for an answer to Drake's question while pretending to get something out of her shoulder bag. Anyone who worked for the Agency knew that an agent's permanent place of residence was a top secret, even with someone like Drake, whose family had owned an entire mountain. The government had pretty much established bogus paperwork to protect Drake's anonymity so Cross could never find the exact location of Drake's family home.

"I think Hawk mentioned it a while back. He said he'd been your colonel when you were in the marines. It was right after you pulled that stunt in Russia. Everyone thought you were crazy to climb those mountains the way you did to rescue that other agent, but Hawk said climbing mountains was a piece of cake for you since you'd grown up in the Tennessee Mountains."

Tori sighed. That hadn't actually been the way the conversation between her and Hawk had gone but it was close enough to suit her purposes and hoped it suited Drake's curiosity as well. She peeked up at him, noticing in relief that he seemed to buy it.

A mischievous grin touched his lips. "Oh, yeah, I'd almost forgotten about that time in Russia. My mountain-climbing skills had gotten rusty, but I still managed to do what needed to be done."

She nodded. "Do you need help packing?"

"No, just keep your eyes and ears open."

She glared at him. "You don't have to tell me that."

"Sorry. My mistake." While stuffing everything back into his overnight bag, Drake watched as Tori paced the room. His gaze followed her movement, appreciating the sexy sway of her hips with every step she took. Her thighs seemed curvier since he'd last seen her. She was wearing a blue tank top and a pair of khaki shorts that showed off her long, shapely legs.

And those perfect, round breasts pressed against her tank top; breasts that he knew would fit right beautifully in the palms of his hands. He could barely take his eyes off of her. Her hair was somewhat longer, the curls framing her face and flowing down her shoulders. He liked the new style and thought it enhanced her features even more.

He knew tonight's experience had probably thrown her for a loop. Going out of the country on a mission was one thing; you expected the unexpected. But right in your back-yard where you felt safe and sound, was a different matter. The last thing you would expect was to become someone's target. He knew Hawk was probably working with the local FBI as well as the CIA to determine who was behind what was going on and why.

She stopped pacing, turned to him and caught him staring. He saw the look of wariness in her eyes. "Are you sure you don't need help?"

"Yes, I'm positive." He snapped his overnight bag shut and had a deep feeling that something wasn't right. She was hiding something and he could feel it. He didn't like sur-prises. Crossing the room to her, he closed the distance between them, cocked his head to one side and looked down at her. He could tell his close assessment was making her nervous.

"What are you looking at?" she snapped.

He smiled. He knew she had to feel vulnerable, her stony control shaken somewhat. But this was the Tori he wanted to see: the feisty woman who had been his partner when they had gone into the jungles of Costa Rica; the lady who was full of fire and had one smart-assed mouth on her. A luscious mouth he'd enjoyed kissing.

"I'm looking at you," he finally answered, his tone challenging. "For some reason I think you're holding back, that you're not telling me something. Are you sure you have no idea what's going on, Tori, or why anyone is after you?"

She placed her hand on her hips and glared up at him, holding his gaze boldly. "No, I have no idea what's going on or why anyone is after me." She breathed in deeply. She had her thoughts but she wouldn't share them with him. "All I know," she continued, "is that one evening I received a phone call and the person hung up. A week later, someone tried to break into my home. Then earlier tonight I received a call from Hawk telling me I needed to go into hiding. In the process of following his orders, I encountered that sedan who was dead-set on ending my life and probably would have if you hadn't shown up when you did."

Drake shook his head. "No."

Tori lifted a brow. "No, what?"

"I don't think they wanted you dead."

With an exhausted sigh, Tori tipped her head back and looked at him. "Excuse me?"

"Whoever was after you tonight didn't want you dead."

Tori continued to stare at him, confused. "What makes you think that?"

"Because you're still alive. The person driving that car

had plenty of time to blast you away had they wanted to. I think they intended to run you off the road and take you alive."

Tori swallowed deeply. What he was saying didn't make sense but when she thought about it, he was right. Even before Drake had shown up, there had been plenty of time for the other car to take her out if that had been their intent. Although she had tried staying way ahead, she would have been defenseless against a high-powered rifle.

He watched the lump form in Tori's throat indicating that what he said had her thinking and she was getting more nervous. "And you're sure you've told me everything?"

She sighed deeply and met his gaze. "Yes, I've told you everything."

He stood there, staring down at her. She was so beautiful and all of a sudden he was very much aware that they were in a hotel room with a king-sized bed only a few feet away and his imagination kicked into overdrive.

His mind was suddenly swamped with visions of a naked Tori laid out on that bed, the look in her eyes soft and welcoming as she waited for him to come to her. The thought had his zipper nearly bursting from the force of his arousal. He quickly forced the vision from his mind, deciding that now was not the time to think about anything sexual. His main focus needed to be on keeping them both alive. But damn if he couldn't help but think about the sounds she'd made when he was thrusting into her, over and over again, and how . . .

"Drake? You okay?"

He snapped out of his haze, realizing that he had just been standing there, staring down at her like a hungry lion. He quickly turned away before she could notice the state of his body. He needed to give his body time to cool down so he turned back to his packing. "I'm fine," he said. "Just trying to figure out who could be after you."

Tori studied him, positive that hadn't been what he'd been thinking about at all. But she decided to let it go for now. "You said you had arrived earlier today to see me. Why?" she asked, sitting down on the edge of the bed.

Feeling more in control of himself, Drake turned toward her. "No one at the Agency gave me your information so you don't have to worry about that. And I wasn't the one who retrieved information off the CIA database if that thought crossed your mind. Like I told you earlier, I hired a private investigator. And as to the reason why I'm here, it's because I needed to see you, Tori."

Blood sizzled through her veins just from the way he said her name. It wasn't the first time tonight, but not quite like that; not with the sound rolling off his tongue in a way that made her think of deep, hot kisses and tangled sheets.

"Why did you need to see me?" she asked, a little breathlessly and almost hated herself for it. The thought that he was actually here sent her off balance again. Even now, after all that had happened tonight, his presence exuded an energy that was slowly zapping her strength. He appeared larger than life, his vitality simply awesome. That's the way Drake had always been.

When he continued looking at her without answering her question, she nervously licked her lips. "Please answer my question, Drake."

"Okay."

She sucked in a deep breath when he slowly crossed the room to her. She was aware of every step he took and when he came to a stop in front of her, she had to force herself to breathe.

"The last time we were together, we made love and I didn't use protection. You were going to let me know if you had gotten pregnant."

Tori was completely unprepared for the jolt that shot through her and she stared up at him with wide eyes. She had thought that when he didn't hear from her that he would just believe she wasn't pregnant. Most men would have. But then she had to remember she wasn't dealing with most men. She was dealing with Drake Carswell Warren. He was a man who made his own rules and left nothing to chance. There was a directness about him that let her know he expected an answer of either, "*Yes, I'm pregnant*" or "*No, I'm not pregnant*." There would be no assumptions.

She breathed in deeply, knowing she couldn't tell him the truth. After this episode in her life—the reason someone was after her—was resolved, she would go her way and he would go his. He would never know that she carried a life within her womb; a life he had placed there. That was something he must not find out.

Drake wasn't a man who would walk away from his responsibilities. He was a former marine, a man with honor and conservative views. A man who believed in family although he didn't have one of his own. But at one time he had. He had been raised by grandparents, and a father he had loved and who had loved him. Years ago when she had been Sandy Carroll, they had talked about having children and raising them in the Tennessee Mountains. But that was then and this was now. She was not the same person and neither was he. Danger lurked in their pasts. If Solomon Cross had even an idea that Sandy Carroll was still alive, he wouldn't hesitate to kill her, Drake, and their child.

After deciding what her response would be, she met his gaze for a long moment, then said, "I thought it would have been obvious when I didn't contact you, Drake. But if you need to hear it directly from me then so be it. I'm not pregnant."

She quickly got up and said, "Here, let me take your jacket. You have enough to carry out."

Drake stared at her for a long moment. Then he nodded as he picked up the overnight bag he had placed by her feet. "Okay, come on. I paid by credit card so I don't have to check out at the desk. I'll feel a lot better when we're on our way to Tennessee."

He looked at her, his mouth tightening; his features suddenly became serious, deadly, and his gaze held her captive. "In Tennessee I'll be on my own turf and if anyone wants you, they'll have to come through me."

Tori swallowed. In other words, he wouldn't make it easy for them. In fact, he intended to make it damn impossible. His words made her feel safe, secure, and she knew at that moment there was no other person she would rather trust with her or her baby's life.

"Are you hungry?"

With a quiet intake of breath Tori glanced over at Drake. The sight of him warmed her skin and she felt more feminine than she had in a long time. She had been very much aware of each and every time his gaze had touched her body. She had known when his eyes had lingered on her breasts or when he had glanced down at her thighs. Following every movement, every nervous shift; he had been watching, aware.

Heat rushed her cheeks when she met his gaze. "I am a little hungry," she decided to admit. They had stopped for breakfast hours ago and now it was lunchtime.

"No problem. You have a taste for anything special?"

"No. Anything will do as long as it's filling," she said.

Filling. Drake recalled how wonderful it had felt filling her that night and he couldn't stop the fierce arousal seeping through him as he remembered how it felt going deep inside her body. Frustration suddenly stabbed at him. He needed to concentrate on the business at hand and not on the very sexy woman sitting beside him. But then, he had to admit that she was the business at hand.

They had only heard from Hawk once and that was to let them know the truck had been disposed of and the FBI had pulled the records at the rental agency. The Bureau had also informed the California Highway Patrol as well. There were so many unknowns that they could use every pair of eyes and ears.

The inside of the car had gotten quiet. He wanted to hear Tori talk, liking the sound of her voice. "Tell me about yourself, Tori."

She glanced over at him, wondering just what he wanted to know, and specifically just what she could tell him. "There's not a lot to tell about me, Drake."

"I want to hear what there is. All I know is that you're an agent who once served in the marines in Pendleton, California. I also know you're an ace in martial arts and the use of firearms. And although our paths never crossed, we both were under Hawk's command, which I find interesting."

"What? That we were both under Hawk's command?" she asked, trying to bring a light teasing to their conversation.

Drake didn't return her smile. "No, the fact that our paths never crossed."

Tori nodded. "I don't think anything is really unusual about that, Drake. You mainly worked alone and in different countries than I did. There really was no reason for our paths to cross."

He met her gaze. "Not even at Diamond Bay?"

"Especially not at Diamond Bay. Unlike some agents who made DB their home away from home while in-between assignments, I preferred not to do that and rented a little place in Charleston. The only time I went to Hilton Head was when I got a summons from Hawk or to leave on assignment."

He nodded. "You once mentioned you had lost someone you loved; a marine you were going to marry. What happened to him?"

Tori sighed deeply, knowing the story she and Hawk had fabricated for others. "He was killed in a car accident when he went home on leave one Christmas. I was supposed to join him there later."

"I'm sorry."

"Yeah, me, too." She stopped talking and glanced up at him. "Is there a reason for all of these questions, Drake?"

The eyes that met hers were serious, intense. "The night you mentioned losing your marine was the same night you brought up my relationship with Sandy Carroll. You had heard that she and I were engaged to be married at the time she was killed."

Tori swallowed deeply, wondering why Drake was bringing up anything about Sandy. She cleared her throat, knowing he was waiting on a response from her. "Yes. I think most people had heard the two of you were an item."

Drake smiled. "Sandy and I were a lot alike. A perfect fit and everyone knew it. I respected her deeply and loved her more than life itself."

Tori glanced over at him and looked into his eyes. She immediately saw the pain still lodged there. It was pain that touched her heart. "In some ways, I think you still love her, Drake," she said softly.

"Yes, I do," he said honestly. "What about you, Tori? Do you still love your marine?"

She turned away from Drake and glanced out of the window to look out at the stretch of rolling meadows they were passing. Her gaze then returned to his. "Yes, I still love him. It's been five years, but I still love him with all of my heart," she said quietly.

He accepted her response. Understanding it. For the next few minutes neither of them said anything. Then he spoke, "Do you ever compare other men to him? Look for similarities?"

Tori let out a sigh when she realized what must have happened. That night when they had made love, something had triggered a memory of Sandy. Someone once said that a person would know his or her lover no matter what face he or she had, due to something called a soul connection. Had Drake felt such a thing the night they had made love? The night their child had been conceived?

She knew that she wasn't at liberty to find out. Neither did she have a right. No matter what, she had to keep up with her facade and make sure he never discovered her true identity. "Sure, I think when you've lost a person you love deeply, you have a tendency to always compare and to go so far as to look for similarities in others although you don't intend to. But it was easy for me not to compare or look for similarities since my fiancé was a tough act to follow."

She glanced over at him. "What about you? Do you compare? Look for similarities?"

"Yes," he said, "I do, actually. I think that's the reason I've been drawn to you. There's a lot about you that reminds me of Sandy."

Tori glanced over at him. A part of her was touched. Then another part, the one who had buried Sandy Carroll five years ago, was crushed.

Her life as Sandy had ended in that explosion. She was Tori now and wanted him to accept the new person that she was. Something snapped inside of her, making her feel angry, let down and upset even when she wasn't sure she had a right to feel that way.

For the longest time neither of them spoke again and Tori feigned sleep so he wouldn't ask her any more questions. She needed time to think about everything he had said and to deal with the fact that deep down, he saw her only as Sandy's replacement.

Drake pulled off the Interstate at the next exit when he noticed a variety of restaurants to choose from. They had switched cars in San Jose and were past Fresno. His goal was to reach Phoenix by nightfall. He pulled into the fast-food restaurant and since the drive-through line was long, they decided to eat inside. He had just parked the car when his cell phone rang. He glanced over at Tori who was now awake and hit the talk button. "Yes?" He paused then said, "Hey, Hawk."

For a long moment he didn't say anything, but grimly listened. Then he said, "Yes, that's the best thing to do. And I plan to take every precaution."

Drake ended the call, then sat there staring straight ahead, the seconds stretching out until Tori wanted to scream at him to tell her what was going on.

"Are you going to tell me what Hawk said?" Tori finally asked, barely restraining from clenching her teeth.

He glanced over at her. "With the use of dental records they were able to determine the identification of the person who was driving that car."

When he didn't say anything else she arched a brow. "And?" she asked, wanting to shake him.

"He was Scott Rangel, a DEA agent."

Tori blinked and a knot suddenly caught in her throat. "A

DEA agent was after me?" When Drake nodded, she shook her head, stunned. "Why? I don't get it."

Drake sighed raggedly as he checked his rearview mirror. "Neither do I, and I think that even has Hawk stumped. According to Hawk, you were never assigned to any missions having to do with the drug cartels."

Tori shook her head again, still confused. CIA agents on occasion worked alongside a DEA agent, but Hawk was right. She had never been on any of those assignments and was more than certain that her and Rangel's paths had never crossed.

She glanced over at Drake. Something he'd said caught her attention. "Drug cartel?"

"Yes. The last couple of assignments Rangel worked were related to the drug cartels, specifically ASI." He shook his head gravely. "Whenever I hear anything about that group, it quickly brings one man to my mind. Solomon Cross."

"Solomon Cross?" Tori whispered in a low voice as pain ripped through her body at the mention of the man responsible for all the trauma that had occurred in her life. He had been the first person she had suspected when Hawk had called and told her about the incident with the CIA database . . . and now this. It was too much of a coincidence.

"Solomon Cross is a sick individual, a damn psychopath, and one of the biggest drug lords out there," Drake said, his voice tightening in anger. "He's pretty much kept a low profile for the past five years and it wouldn't surprise me that he's finally decided to crawl out from whatever rock he's been hiding under."

Drake's gaze narrowed as he continued. "Seven years ago he operated a lab in South America to develop this highly potent form of hallucinogens that would make LSD from the sixties seem harmless in comparison. His goal was to have it on every street corner in the United States within a year's time. Fortunately, he had a snitch in his group and the American government got wind of his plans. The marines sent the Recons in to close down his shop and I'm the one who headed that mission. We showed up in the dark of night and caught them unawares. Unfortunately, Cross's wife was killed during the raid and he still holds me responsible. He got away, but not before he promised that he would make me suffer the way he suffered in losing the woman he loved. 'An eye for an eye' is what he said."

Drake inhaled deeply. "Unfortunately, I didn't take him seriously and while on an assignment in Haiti a couple of years later, he made good on his threat. He arranged the kidnapping of a couple of American dignitaries knowing that I would be the one to head the team to go in and rescue them. He'd also found out that I had fallen in love with one of my fellow team members."

"Captain Sandy Carroll?" Tori asked quietly.

Drake nodded. "Yes, Sandy. It was a setup and he intentionally had Sandy killed on that mission and there was nothing I could do to save her."

Tori swallowed deeply; in her mind she suddenly relived that day. Leaning forward, she said, "But you did try to save her, Drake."

She'd said it as a statement, but he took it as a question. He met her gaze and the eyes looking back at her were filled with remembered pain. "Yes, I did try, but there was nothing I could do," he replied with anguish in his voice. "The explosion caused a piece of flying debris to knock me out cold. When I came around, it was too late. There was nothing anyone could do. The building was gone. There was no way she could have survived."

There were a few moments of silence, and then Drake said, "If Rangel was on the take and is connected to Solomon

Cross, then there's a chance that you're in this mess because of me."

"Why would you think that?" Tori asked, startled.

"Like I said, Cross hates my guts and strongly believes in this principle of 'an eye for an eye'. Evidently Cross assumes we're serious about each other," Drake replied.

Tori frowned as she cast him a quizzical look. "Why would he assume that? We've only slept together that one time and we've never dated or anything."

"Yes, but I asked a lot of questions about you when I returned from South America and discovered you had quit the Agency. Due to company policy, no one would tell me anything as to your whereabouts, so I began doing a little digging on my own although it got me nowhere. It's possible my interest in you may have gotten back to Cross and he intends to make good on his threat again." He slammed his fist into the steering wheel. "It never ends!"

Tori shook her head, feeling bad that he was blaming himself when he was probably all wrong in his thinking. "Are you saying that you believe the reason someone is after me is because you asked a couple of questions about me and wanted to find me?"

"Yes."

She studied him for a few moments. "But haven't there been other women in your life since Sandy? Does Cross makes a habit of getting rid of every woman you *seem* interested in?"

There was a guarded look in the gaze that met hers. She watched as he took a deep breath. "You're the only woman that I've shown any interest in beyond that one night I spend with them. This time was different and somehow he found out about it."

Tori's eyes widened and she wanted to ask how the situation with her was different? They had gone on a three-day mission together and had ended up sleeping together. Until he had shown up last night, they'd had no contact with each other, so how in the world was their situation different from any others he'd had? What they'd shared sounded pretty much like a one-night stand to her, although it had meant more than that to her. Could it have meant more to him as well?

He evidently read the questions, the doubt in her gaze. He reached over and took her hand in his. "It *was* different, Tori. That one night that we made love, I connected with you in a way I've never connected with another woman."

Drake's words touched her deeply. Her heart pounded in her chest as all the love she had for him rippled through her. But a part of her knew she had to let go and reject what she was feeling. Being with him was hard enough without adding complications. He thought Cross was after her because Drake was interested in her. She wondered what he would say if he knew that there was a even stronger possibility that Cross was after her because he knew she was Sandy and hadn't died in the explosion. Someone deranged and cold-blooded like Cross would go into an absolute rage at the thought that she had cheated death; especially the one he had meticulously planned for her.

Tori knew that no matter what, there could never be a future for her and Drake. More than ever, they needed to go their separate ways. She slowly pulled her hand from his and said, "Since Sandy."

Unknown to him, he had just given her the perfect excuse to put distance between them and she intended to use it. Being so close to him was bad enough, she didn't need either of them thinking there could or would be a repeat performance of what they had shared. His instincts were good and his perception was excellent. Sooner or later he would figure things out and she couldn't let that happen. When she walked away from him the next time, it would be for good. She needed a clean break and an involvement with him wouldn't give her that. All it would give her was pain and misery and she intended to have a happy life . . . just her and her baby.

"I don't intend to be any woman's substitute, Drake," she said, giving him a measured look.

He looked back at her with darkened eyes. "And you're not."

She narrowed her eyes. "For some reason I don't believe you." Taking the 9mm off the seat beside her, she placed it in the holster underneath her jacket. "Come on, let's get something to eat," she said as she turned to get out of the car.

"Rangel is dead."

The hand not holding the phone clenched at Cross's side. "That's a pity. What about the woman?"

The voice on the other end took a long breath. "She got away. It seems she had help."

Cross frowned. "Help?"

"Yes. Warren may have reached her before we did."

Rage flowed through Solomon Cross's body. Blood pounded in his head. His lips twisted. "You let Warren get to her!"

The man on the other end of the phone heard the demented anger in Cross's voice and it made his insides flinch. "We'll get her," Red Hunter said in a shaken voice. "I'll call in some more men and—"

"Shut up and listen to me! I want both Warren and the woman. It will save me from having to ship her remains to him. I want him to sit and watch everything I do to her. I want him here when I cut her into tiny bite-size pieces." Cross chuckled. Of course it would be after he had his fun with her, and he intended for Drake to watch that too, and not be able to do a damn thing about it.

"Do you hear me, Red Hunter? I want them brought to me alive."

"Trying to take them alive would be suicide; damn near impossible."

"You'd better make it happen. I'll send Miguel and a few of my men to your country to help you."

"I don't need your men. I have my own who are just as capable."

"For your sake, I hope so. How you do it is your problem and you'd better not disappoint me. Keep in touch with periodic reports on your progress."

Cross hung up the phone and then slammed his fist onto the table. When he was finished, Drake Warren would regret the day that he was born . . . and unfortunately, his woman would, too.

CHAPTER 8

Tori glanced around the restaurant as she waited for Drake to return with their food. The place wasn't all that crowded. There were a number of mothers with small children, a couple of men sitting together who appeared to work for some business or another since they were wearing dress pants and ties, and then there were the two women who were about her age who appeared to have just ended a game of tennis.

A twinge of jealousy shot through Tori when she saw how one of the women was trying to get Drake's attention. She frowned. For all the woman knew, she and Drake could have been an item, but that wasn't stopping her from flirting.

Although she didn't appreciate the woman's brazen behavior, she did understand her interest in Drake since everything about him shouted of his masculinity. And the way he looked dressed in his jeans wasn't helping matters. Even with his rough appearance, he would be at the top of the list as a man who belonged in any woman's fantasies.

Not that she was any better. She couldn't keep her eyes off of him either. She loved watching the way his well-defined, incredibly developed biceps flexed when he moved, and his broad shoulders made him seem commanding . . . the dominant alpha male.

"Here you go and I brought plenty to hold us for a while."

The deep timbre of his voice sent a shiver all the way down her spine to settle between her thighs. "Thanks." She watched as he lowered his body into the seat across from her after setting the hamburgers, fries, and milk shakes in the middle of the table.

He glanced at her. "You all right?"

Other than wanting to scratch that woman's eyes out, I'm fine. Instead she answered, "Yes."

He grabbed one of the hamburgers and began unwrapping it.

"Can we say the grace before we eat?"

He lifted a brow and his gaze fixed on her face. "I knew someone else who used to be adamant about saying grace before eating."

Tori nodded, remembering and knowing who he was referring to. Sandy. "Doesn't surprise me," she said softly, trying to sever any connection that may have popped into his mind. "Traditionally, most people thank God before eating their food. I was raised in a foster home by a minister and his wife so saying the grace is second nature to me. Reverend Parker used to say we shouldn't put anything in our mouths until we gave thanks for it." She shrugged. "Old habits are hard to break."

An understanding grin touched his lips. "Hey, I don't have a problem with it."

"Thanks."

After she said grace for the both of them they began eating. Either the food was terribly good or she'd been extremely hungry because the food tasted like ambrosia. Probably both, she thought, taking sips of her milk shake. So far she'd been lucky with her pregnancy. She hadn't suffered morning sickness and her energy level had remained high. She woke up every morning feeling on top of the world and she seemed to have more energy than ever. During her initial visit to the doctor he had given her a prescription for prenatal vitamins that she took each day.

She glanced over at Drake. Like her he seemed to have a healthy appetite, but then he'd always had one. "I feel there's something we should be doing instead of running away and hiding. I packed my laptop. As soon as we get settled into a hotel I plan to use it and see what information I can find out."

Drake nodded. He knew how she felt. He was getting antsy as well. At one time the ASI had become one of the most feared drug cartels in the world and seemed unstoppable until several major countries had joined forces to shut them down. The United States had been their biggest consumer so it stood to reason that to keep being a major drug supplier, the ASI paid off just about anyone to keep their operations moving—including DEA and CIA agents who were willing to become corrupt for the right price.

Drake wanted to believe that most of his fellow operatives were clean, but he wasn't stupid enough not to believe there were some who weren't. He hated to admit it but even honest men could be bought if enough money was thrown their way. And September 11 had shifted a lot of people's attention off drug trafficking and onto terrorism. The shift in focus had helped the cartel's cause, and the illegal organization was more profitable than ever.

Drake had also known that keeping a low profile for the past five years hadn't been Cross's choice. The mess he'd made by putting those United States dignitaries' lives on the line in Haiti, as well as the casualties that had resulted . . . his actions had caused immediate international repercussions. Because of Cross's need for personal revenge, he had put his fellow drug lords' businesses at risk and ASI hadn't been too happy about it. However, instead of taking him out and eliminating him altogether, since Cross's fraction had always been a very profitable one for the cartel, they decided to spare his life but had ordered that he hang low and stay out of trouble. Now it seemed that their bad boy was trying to cause problems again, which meant he either had the ASI's backing or he was operating without ASI knowledge. Drake rubbed his chin. Now that was an interesting theory; one he planned to check out when they got to the hotel and Tori booted up her laptop.

A half hour later they walked back to the car, Drake's eyes scanning the parking lot. "Do you want me to drive?" she asked, feeling a lot better now that she had a full stomach.

"No, I don't mind driving. In fact, I prefer it. You can continue being the lookout."

"All right." He wasn't going to get any argument from her since she detested driving for long periods of time. She glanced around the parking lot and didn't see anything unusual. A part of her hoped that she and Drake had gotten a clean getaway but she knew that probably wasn't the case. If Cross was the person looking for her then he wouldn't stop until he found her. And they could show up at any place, at any time. That alone was enough to drive her crazy.

"What do you think their next move will be?" she asked Drake once they were in the car. She snapped her seat belt on.

Out of habit, Drake scanned the parking lot one more time before turning the key in the ignition, mentally cataloging his surroundings and finding nothing suspicious. "By now they know that Rangel has failed and chances are they're looking for us. If they've done their homework, they know we've left the area by now, but they don't know if it was by plane, train or car. Their first assumption would be

by plane since it would be the quickest mode of transporta-
tion. There's a chance they might have someone posted at
various airports looking for us. I think we should stick to
driving. It's less risky."

He looked around before backing the car out of the slot,
and then continued. "It won't take them long to figure it out,
but all I expected was a head start." His eyes narrowed.
"They still don't know where we're headed. Let's see how
long we can keep it that way."

"Do you think it's wise to stay on the interstate?" she
asked as they pulled out of the restaurant's parking lot and
entered the four-lane highway that would lead them back to
the expressway.

"Let's do so for now. We can always change our plans
later if we have to. Besides," he added, "I want to reach
Phoenix before dark."

At first traffic was pretty congested then the further they
drove the less traffic there was. They had driven less than a
hundred miles when Tori happened to notice a car weaving
out of traffic behind them. "It may be paranoia slipping in,
but I don't like the look of that black sedan a few cars behind
us. It's been passing other cars trying to keep up with us."

Drake glanced into his rearview mirror at the same time
he shifted to reach for the pistol he had placed on the seat
next to him. "Yeah, I noticed that, too. Let's get off at the
next exit to see what it does."

His first thought when he'd noticed the car was that a
professional would have had better tailing skills and
wouldn't have been this obvious, which meant the person
driving was an amateur or someone who wanted them to
know they were being followed.

The next exit was a good ten miles away and sure enough
the black sedan was right behind them. Not knowing who or
what they were dealing with, Tori had already taken the

safety off her gun and was ready, grateful there weren't many cars on the road. No matter what, she wanted to consider the safety of others.

"We don't want to give him the appearance that we're on to him, so let's keep driving for a while," Drake said, turning down a two-lane road that contained even less traffic. "It may not be the actual hitman but someone who's been ordered to tail us. I think a hitman would have made a move by now."

Tori nodded at the same time Drake's mobile phone rang. He snatched it out of his inner jacket pocket and hit the talk button, his hand still steady on the wheel. "Yes?"

"I've called in a few favors with the Bureau," Hawk said. "Don't panic. The black sedan that's following you is on our side."

Drake sighed deeply. "I was beginning to wonder."

"Thought you might be and the driver called suggesting that I let you know that the Bureau will have someone posted every so many miles until you're out of California. They won't interfere with you, but will be there for protection just in case you need it. Once you reach Arizona you'll be on your own for a while."

Drake nodded. After Phoenix he would head for Texas. He had plenty of friends who he trusted in Houston; especially Ashton and Trevor.

"Must have been a hell of a favor you called in," Drake said, knowing it wasn't the usual protocol for the Feds to assist the CIA this way.

Hawk chuckled. "It was."

"Any more information about Rangel?"

"Nothing concrete. I've contacted Casey and of course he's concerned with what's going down. He's going to do a check on a number of things in-house and get back with me. He knows I'm the middleman between the two of you for now."

Drake nodded. He definitely preferred having Hawk at his back than Casey. There was something about the man he just didn't like.

"How's Tori, Drake?"

Drake glanced over at her. She was watching him and evidently had been trying to follow his conversation with Hawk. "Tori is fine. Do you want to speak with her?"

"Yes."

"Hold on." Drake passed the phone to Tori. "It's Hawk and he wants to talk to you. And thanks to Hawk, that car following us is the Feds and they're clean."

Tori nodded and placed the phone to her ear. "Yes, Hawk?"

"I didn't mention this to Drake but we found a definite connection between Rangel and Solomon Cross. You may have to accept the fact that he's discovered your true identity, Tori, and that's the reason he's after you. Time has run out."

Tori released a deep sigh. She had accepted that possibility long ago. She glanced away from Drake to look out the window as he turned the car around to head back for the interstate. "What are you suggesting?"

"That you tell Drake the truth."

"No!"

The word had been quick from her lips. She knew Drake's attention had been drawn to her. "That's not an option right now, Hawk."

"Then make it one. Drake has to be told. He needs to know what's going down and why. He needs all the facts, Tori. That's the only way he can protect himself as well as you."

Tori shook her head. The thought of telling Drake her true identity wasn't something she wanted to think about. "I can't. Not now."

"You don't have a choice, Tori."

She breathed in deeply. "We'll talk again later." She then quickly ended the call.

"What was that about?"

Tori turned to see Drake staring at her. *If only you knew.* "It was nothing," she said, returning her attention to the traffic.

Drake's hand tightened on the steering wheel. "You're holding something back, Tori, and I don't like playing games."

Tori sighed deeply. She didn't like playing games either but there was no way she could level with him right now. But then Hawk was right. If Rangel was connected to Cross, then time had run out and Drake needed to know the truth as to why Cross had reappeared in both of their lives.

"Tori?"

She met Drake's eyes and said, "I don't like playing games either, Drake. But there are some things in my past that I'm not ready to share with you just yet." She nervously licked her lips. "Things only Hawk knows."

Drake nodded. "Does it have any bearing on what's going down here?" he asked, sighing heavily.

She shrugged. "It might, but until I know for sure, I prefer not saying anything."

Drake was silent. Had she been involved in some high-classified secret mission that may have involved Cross at one time, although she'd claimed that she hadn't? He could understand why she might feel duty-bound to keep her lips sealed, but if it would give him the edge in keeping them both alive, he wanted to hear it and told her as much.

Tori heard Drake's words and knew both he and Hawk were right. But how on earth could she tell the man she loved and who had once loved her with a passion that the woman he thought had died, the same one he had mourned for the last five years, was alive and well and had a new identity? She shuddered when she thought of what his reaction might be.

She hiked up her chin and met his gaze. "You're going to have to trust me on this, Drake. I'll tell you everything when I feel I should and not a moment before."

Drake saw the worry lines darken between her brow and around her eyes. Whatever it was that she was holding back was eating at her, so he decided to pull back for now, but he intended to bring it up again later.

"When we get to the hotel in Phoenix, it will be best if we share a room," he said, glancing over at her again.

Tori frowned. She knew that was practical and that she would be safer but the thought of sharing a room with Drake for the night didn't sit well with her. Just being this close to him was wreaking havoc on her nerves.

"You don't have a problem sharing a room with me, do you, Tori?"

She swallowed, thinking, If only he knew. Already her body was tingling at the idea of one bed and two bodies. *One bed and their two naked bodies.* Of course they would request a room with two beds. That was the only way she would survive the night.

"Tori?"

She lifted her chin and met his gaze. She had to remember that she was a professional and she had to think about them together as being on a mission—a mission to save her life. "No, Drake, I don't have a problem with it as long as there are two beds in the room." She wanted to make it clear that they would not be sleeping together.

He nodded. "Of course. That shouldn't be a problem," he said, with more gruffness than he'd intended.

Tori glanced out the window, refusing to meet his eyes. She certainly hoped that it wouldn't be a problem.

. . .

Getting a room with two double beds wasn't a problem. The problem was the coziness of the room. With the two of them together it seemed to shrink in size. Drake, Tori noticed, didn't seem at all bothered by it. On the other hand, the thought of being in such proximity to him had her in knots.

They had shared tight quarters on their mission, but then her concentration had been focused almost exclusively on rescuing Robin Thomas and not on seducing Drake—almost.

They had unpacked and she had set her laptop up on the desk in the room. She had a few contacts of her own—those she felt certain she could trust—and she intended to see what they could find out. One person in particular was a woman—another agent—whom she had befriended a few years ago when they'd teamed up together for a job in Pakistan shortly after the September 11 attack. Jody Barrow was still with the Agency and was a whiz at finding a connection to information on the computer.

"Why don't you go ahead and take a shower? It will probably relax you. After everything that's happened you must be pretty tense right now," Drake said as he double-checked the doors.

His back was to her and Tori thought from behind he looked just as good as he did from the front. There was just something about a good-looking man in a fitting pair of jeans, and boy, did his fit. Her skin suddenly felt warm and the stirrings of hot desire began flowing through her. She needed a shower, all right. A cold shower.

"Yes, I think I will," she said, barely able to get the words out. And when he turned and looked at her, she felt that emotional connection again, that physical attraction, and wondered if he felt it as well. By some miracle she hoped not. Anything other than business would complicate things, especially raging hormones.

Turning, she walked over to the dresser and pulled open a drawer to get out a couple of items. Her hands felt numb as she pulled out an extra large T-shirt, bra, and panties. Closing the drawer she turned around holding the items to her chest like a shield.

"I won't be long and promise to save some hot water for you," she said, her voice sounding odd even to her ears.

He stared at her intently, thoroughly, as if he could see right into her soul and knew all her secrets. There was that look in his eyes, that heated, passionate look, that signaled he was thinking sexual thoughts. The sudden softening of his mouth and the unfolding on that sexy grin of his almost took her breath away.

"That's all right," he said in a voice so sexy and low, the area between her thighs began to ache. "I think I need a cold shower right now anyway."

Swallowing hard, Tori turned and forced one foot in front of the other, determined to cross the room to the bathroom without throwing herself at him and onto the nearest bed. She almost made it to the bathroom door when he called her name. She turned reluctantly as if afraid she would turn to salt. Her nerves were stretched to the limit.

He was standing less than a couple of feet away from her. "Yes?"

"You dropped these."

Her black lacy panties dangled from his fingertips. Her breath hitched and a surge of heat flooded her body. Words caught in her throat. Tori held out her hand silently and waited for him to give them to her, but he seemed in no hurry to return them.

"Nice underwear," he said as she watched him skim his fingers across the satiny material. "Real sexy."

Tori took a deep breath, trying to force his opinion of her panties from her mind. He had seen her in underwear before. He had slowly removed them and then had made the sweetest, hottest love to her. Even now she could remember the feel of his callused fingers grazing her skin before slipping those same fingers inside the edge of her panties, seeking the very heat of her. And when those fingers had found the spot he wanted, they had slipped inside of her and begun stroking her, driving her insane, touching every sensuous passion point in her body and deep-wrenching sounds of pleasure had escaped her lips.

A door slammed next door and Tori blinked and straightened. She had to step back from the hot current passing between them and keep her mind on the situation at hand. Drake insisted on looking at her with unadulterated passion in his eyes. It was a look guaranteed to have her removing her clothes in five seconds flat.

But those times were over and she needed to accept that. She lifted her chin. "Thanks. I'll take those now," she said, ignoring the rush of heated desire consuming her.

"You're more than welcome," was his response, and he held her gaze boldly as he placed her underwear in her hand, allowing himself to touch her. The touch of his fingers on hers was deliberate and she knew it. A hot current tore through her, lighting her up from the inside out.

She took a deep breath and stepped back. She needed distance from this man and fast. She quickly turned and went into the bathroom and closed the door firmly behind her.

Tori stepped into the shower, hoping the hot water soothed her body, calmed her down. How the heck were the two of them supposed to share a hotel room while hot torrid thoughts raced through both their brains?

It wasn't fair that her feelings could still be this intense, her body filled with this much need that only Drake could satisfy. That night two months ago should have been enough to last her a lifetime. He had been pretty damn potent, she thought as she lovingly lathered her stomach, thinking of the life deeply embedded there.

She smiled when she recalled when she was Sandy Carroll, the few times they had talked about a life beyond the Marine Corps; a life that included marriage, children, and a beautiful home in his Tennessee Mountains where they would watch their children grow under the glow of their love. Sometimes they would lie together for hours, appreciating stolen moments even if the cot was barely big enough to hold both of them. Sometimes she would have to lie on top of him for them to fit into the cramped space. But still, those had been special times she had cherished.

A lump rose in her throat and she fought back the tears when she thought of how different dreams were from reality. In reality she was pregnant and on the run for her life. It wasn't her life that concerned her right now but her child's. She had to put it first and take whatever precautions she needed to keep her baby safe. Boy or girl, it didn't matter to her. All that mattered was that it was a part of her and a part of Drake, the way it was meant to be. She couldn't think of any other man she would have wanted to father her child.

Remembering she had promised to leave Drake some hot water, she reached for the fixtures and switched them off, stopping the flow of water. Grabbing the plush towel on the rack over the stall, she began toweling herself dry.

She had fantasized about this moment when she would be with Drake again. Somehow she had to control the feelings he evoked, no matter what it took.

. . .

Drake logged off the computer when he heard the shower stop and inhaled deeply. Tori Green was something else. And it seemed the woman was destined to drive him insane. He got the feeling she was doing all she could to downplay the passionate drama unfolding between them and it wouldn't be difficult if they hadn't been lovers before. He knew firsthand how it felt to be held between the warmth of her thighs, how it felt to have her fingernails digging deep into his back while he thrust into her over and over again, gripping her hips in his hands so he could go deeper and deeper.

He took a deep breath, deciding that he needed another distraction. He had gotten on the laptop to try and find any recent news accounts on ASI but lately, news of terrorism and Iraq dominated the news. He walked across the room and picked up his cell phone to call Trevor. His friend picked up on the third ring. "Trev, this is Drake."

"Drake? Where the hell are you, man?"

"I can't give you a lot of specifics right now, but I wanted you and Ashton to know what's going down. I reached Tori just in time. There was a car chase. Someone was after her and I managed to intercede. The car crashed and the driver was killed, but was later identified as a DEA agent."

Trevor gave a long whistle. "DEA? Damn."

"Yeah, my sentiments exactly. And the kicker is that there's a possibility that he's connected to Solomon Cross." He heard Trevor swear. The words were fiery enough to even burn his ears. "Yes, Cross." Trevor and Ashton had been on that mission with him five years ago in Haiti and knew who Solomon Cross was. They also knew the pain and heartache the man had caused him with Sandy's death.

"Cross is after Tori Green?" Trevor asked, putting two and two together.

"Yeah, it seems that way—and mainly because of her connection to me—but I plan to make sure that neither he nor his men lay a finger on her."

"How is the woman doing?"

Drake smiled. "She's fine, a real damn trouper and it shows. You know what they say, once a marine, always a marine." His face then turned serious. "I need you and Ashton to do me a favor. I'm in Phoenix and will be leaving out first thing in the morning. I know it might be a stretch, but I want to reach Houston by nightfall. I need a place for me and Tori to hole up, at least a day or two, to get our bearings and plan further strategies. Can we borrow that cabin you own not far from Jake Madaris's ranch?"

"Hell, yeah, you can use it and Ash and I will make sure it's stocked when you get here. If you can think of anything else you might need, let me know."

"I could use more ammo," Drake said. He wanted to make sure he had plenty on hand.

"That's no problem. Call us when you reach the place. We want to come see you."

Drake sighed deeply. "You and Ashton may not want to get involved, Trev."

He heard Trevor laugh in the background. "Like hell we won't. If you're involved then we're involved."

"Thanks. I'll talk with you again later."

"Was that Hawk?"

Drake whirled around. He hadn't heard the bathroom door open. A stirring of desire flooded his body and the dark hairs on his arms tingled as his gaze moved over her body. A rush of body heat settled right below his belt. He was glad that he was standing behind the desk, otherwise there was no way Tori would not be able to see the huge erection he had that was pushing against the zipper of his jeans. His breath felt tight in his throat and his mouth suddenly felt dry.

She was wearing a large T-shirt that actually covered a little more of her thighs than the shorts she'd been wearing had. But it was the overall picture of her, looking utterly seductive after a recent shower that had him swallowing hard. She looked fresh, revived, and luscious. He felt the palms of his hands get warm, wet, and remembered how warm and wet she had gotten for him once and how he would love to get her that way again.

"Drake?"

When she said his name he realized that he hadn't answered her. "No, that wasn't Hawk. That was a friend of mine, Trevor Grant. He and another good friend, Ashton Sinclair, live in Houston and are two men I trust explicitly. I wanted them to know what was going down and make arrangements to stay at Trevor's cabin tomorrow night."

Tori nodded as she walked over to her luggage to pull out a small plastic bag and placed the clothes she had taken off in it. Of course, Trevor and Ashton. They had been close friends of hers like they had been friends of Drake and were two men that she had trusted as well. They were known to other marines as the "Fearless Four." They had gone through basic training together and had done a number of missions together before that fateful day in Haiti. She had been surprised as well as glad to see Ashton that night in Drake's hospital room. It had made her feel good to know their friendship was still as tight as it had always been.

Deciding that talking would be a way to ward off the sexual currents in the room, she decided to ask him about their two friends. "Are Trevor and Ashton CIA agents?" she asked, knowing they weren't.

Drake leaned against the desk. "No, they're former Marines, Recons. We use to do a lot of top-secret missions together."

"Are they still in the marines?" she asked as she sat down on the edge of the bed she would be sleeping in. Alone.

"Ashton is. He's made it up the ranks to colonel. Trevor got out of the marines, but is in the reserves, so he still gets to see some action every once in a while."

She nodded. "Are they married?" Back when she knew them, they swore they would remain bachelors forever. She watched as Drake pulled out a chair from behind the desk and sat in it and rebooted the laptop. She also watched as he placed his pistol on the desk in front of him, within close range. She had placed her gun in the nightstand that separated their beds.

A smile touched Drake's features. "Yes, Ashton and Trevor are both married to some pretty feisty women who manage to keep them on their toes. Trevor's wife is Corinthians and Ashton's wife is Netherland, but we call her Nettie."

Tori smiled. "Corinthians and Netherland. Those are unusual names."

"Yes, but then it takes unusual and very strong women to deal with Trevor and Ashton."

"Any children?"

"Yes, and I happen to be the godfather to their four children collectively."

Tori raised a brow. "Four?"

Drake chuckled. "Yes, four. Trevor has a little boy who celebrated his first birthday a week ago and Ashton has triplets, all boys."

"Triplets? I bet they keep her busy."

He chuckled. "They do and they're only four months old."

Tori nodded. She wondered if Nettie was breast-feeding and if so, how on earth she was managing. Tori had decided to go the breast-feeding route and couldn't wait. She was definitely looking forward to motherhood.

Then the room got quiet and she noticed Drake staring at her. "What do their wives do? Does either work outside the home?"

"Yes. Nettie owns a big restaurant called Sisters and although Ashton goes out on assignment, the military allows him to spend the majority of his time at the marines office there. He just so happened to be in Iraq when I got shot a few months back."

Tori could only assume that Drake was talking so freely about what had happened to him in Iraq since practically everyone at the Agency had known about it. So there was no reason to pretend otherwise. "In that case you were blessed."

Drake gazed at her and slowly nodded in agreement. "Yes, I was."

Silence covered the room as they stared at each other and for a moment time seemed to drift away. She tried not to concentrate on the broadness of his shoulders and how his muscular chest tapered to a flat, firm stomach. She recalled the many times that same stomach had been naked and pressed up against hers while he'd made love to her over and over again, and the feel of his chest hair when she ran her fingers through it.

Tori began to feel hot, turned on. She also felt panicky, like she was slowly losing control. She felt her defenses lowering as her world began tilting and for a brief moment, when sanity flowed from her brain, she was Sandy Carroll and the man across the room looking at her like he wanted to eat her alive was Drake Warren, the man she loved and would always love. He was the man who'd wanted to marry her, give her his children and take her to live with him forever on his family homestead in Tennessee—Warren Mountains.

"Drake," she said, her voice sounding hoarse. She wanted to tell him about the elaborate, state-of-the-art plastic surgery that had been performed on her face and other parts of her body that had changed her face but not her heart. She wanted to tell him about the baby, their baby and how much this pregnancy meant to her.

She also wanted him to know how the memories of what they had once shared had sustained her over the past five years, and how she would often go to bed at night with an ache for him so intense she would cry herself to sleep to get rid of it, but the feeling never totally went away.

Tori couldn't recall when he got up and crossed the room. All she knew was that she blinked and he was there, standing in front of her, and when his mouth found hers she was ready. His tongue immediately captured hers, claiming it, declaring it and her as his, sending intense flames tearing through her body.

A sense of urgency ripped through her as his mouth mated with hers as if he were determined to taste every last bit of her and she reciprocated in kind, returning his kiss, stroking whatever heat that was driving him to the bittersweet end. Fervently, he continued ravishing her mouth in a way that almost brought her to her knees. She would have melted into a heap on the floor had his hand not been securely around her waist. Those same searching hands eased up her T-shirt to touch bare skin.

She knew the exact moment his fingers touched her flesh, the feeling so erotically painful yet at the same time so sensuously mind-boggling. She pressed closer to him, dissolving into his arms while he continued to kiss her into a hectic urgency she couldn't break away from. She felt his hard erection against her stomach where their baby was nestled safe inside and cuddled even closer, wanting her child to know the feel of its father and all his strength.

Frenzied emotions tore through her and when she felt Drake's hands skim the waistband of her bikini panties, those same panties he had picked up off the floor and handed to her a while ago, she knew what he wanted and also knew that she couldn't let him have it, no matter how much she desired otherwise.

With all the force of mind she could muster, she pulled her mouth from his, almost finding it impossible to do so when he followed and began kissing her again. She once again became a willing victim, letting him give her more of heaven and wondered if after this kiss, her life would ever be the same.

Moments later it was Drake who broke the kiss and pulled back, needing to regain control of his mind and his senses. Tori Green had broken through his restraints. She had rocked his world, had left him off-balance but oh, so damn satisfied. For now. Kissing her wasn't enough. He knew it and from the dark, sultry, *I want you, too*, look in her eyes he knew that she knew it as well.

He wasn't ready to remove his hand from beneath her T-shirt where he was gently cupping her backside, needing the feel of her bottom in his hand, and the front of her so close to his hard erection. He wanted her to know what she was doing to him, at a time when all his concentration should be on other things, like keeping her safe.

"You know what I think?" he asked as he continued to cup her bottom in both hands. It seemed that touching her this way, in addition to the size of his erection, was limiting his vocabulary. He couldn't seem to think coherently with a raging hard-on.

"No, what do you think?" she asked, her gaze still connected to his.

"I think I could get pretty damn used to kissing you."

She wouldn't have a problem with that if the situation were different. In fact she would welcome his kisses, anytime and anyplace. But she had to remember that the situation was different. They had a past but could never have a future. "And do you know what I think?" she asked, feeling her nipples tighten even more with his hands touching her so intimately.

"No, what do you think?"

She took a step back, giving him no choice but to let her go. She watched as he dropped his hands to his sides and immediately felt a sense of loss. His hands on her had filled her with a rush of desire that wasn't going to ease any time soon. And speaking of ease, there was something he wasn't trying to ease or to hide for that matter, she thought as her gaze lowered. And that was the evident swelling in the front of his jeans. He had an erection nearly the size of Mount Rushmore and she knew from past experience that any time Drake Warren got this big and hard, making love with him was as good as it got. She couldn't think of anything better.

She glanced back up and met his gaze. He wanted her. It was there for her to clearly see in his eyes that were filled with such intensity it nearly took her breath away.

"I think you should go on and take your shower. When you're finished we can see what information we can pull up on the computer about ASI. Maybe there's something that will give us a clue as to whether they're backing Cross or if he's working alone in this vendetta."

Drake nodded. "I'm sure you're probably hungry again right about now," he said, moving over to the dresser and pulling out clean clothes. "If you want, go ahead and order room service. I want the biggest cheeseburger they have, all the way—but have them hold the onions. And I want French fries and lots of ketchup."

"All right." The thought of food eased some of her tension, but not all of it. Without saying anything she watched as Drake went into the bathroom and closed the door behind him.

CHAPTER 9

"Did you have to scare the poor man to death, Drake?"

Drake glanced up at Tori but didn't stop eating. The intimacy of them sitting at a table together in their hotel room was bad enough, not to mention how the glow of light from a nearby lamp accentuated her features. He could barely eat his meal, his nerves endings were tingling so bad.

"Drake?"

When she said his name again, he decided to respond. "What did I do?" he asked innocently.

Tori frowned knowing he knew exactly what he'd done. When the guy had wheeled the dining cart into the room, Drake had drilled him with a stare that would probably have made even the Terminator tremble. He had stood and watched the man's every move as he uncovered their meal, which included a chilled bottle of wine.

"I gave him a tip," Drake decided to add for good measure.

Evidently she didn't think there was anything good about it. She glared at him. "And he was almost too scared to take it."

Very subtly, the corners of Drake's mouth eased into a smile. "Yeah, I noticed that."

Tori leaned back against her chair frowning. "Do you take pride in putting the fear of God into people?"

He shrugged, seemingly not bothered by her question. "I'd rather put the fear of God in them *before* they have a chance to put it in me. Besides, something about him made me suspicious."

Tori lifted a brow. "What?"

"The way he was looking at you."

She raised her eyes to the ceiling before tilting her head to look at Drake. She wondered if jealousy and not suspicion had ruled his brain. The thought that he was actually jealous made her spirits soar although she didn't want them to.

"What's so funny?"

"Oh, nothing." She cleared her throat. After he had returned from taking his shower, it seemed the room had moved from being clouded with sexual tension to sexual frustration. They were beginning to nip at each other's every word and get on each other's nerves, when what they really wanted to do was to get on each other's bodies. The kiss they'd shared earlier hadn't helped matters and sitting across from each other, eating wasn't helping either.

She'd always thought that the way Drake ate his food was a total turn-on. He chewed his food the same way he made love: methodically slow, savoring every taste, enjoying the flavor. Then there was the way he licked his lips and she remembered how those same lips used to lick her. At one time she thought his mouth was lethal and should be ruled illegal. She shifted in her chair to ease the heat that had settled between her legs.

He was watching her and she was getting utterly turned on by the look in his eyes. Again.

"Want some dessert?"

His question gave her pause. It wasn't what he'd asked;

but how he'd asked it. Her breathing suddenly became shallow and she wondered if he could tell. By the darkening of his eyes, she knew that he could.

Tension was building up again and she was helpless to stop it. There was definitely a strong current flowing between them, making her pulse accelerate. "What kind of dessert do you have?" she asked hoarsely, as a delicious pressure continued to rise in her stomach. She wondered if this was way too much excitement for her baby.

He leaned over the table. "Something hot, chocolate with whipped cream on top."

Heat rose in Tori's face when she had visions of that very thing and knew that what she was thinking about was probably totally different from what he was thinking about. Or was it? she wondered, after seeing the devilish gleam in those dark eyes of his.

"So, could I possibly convince you to try it?"

In a heartbeat, she thought, thinking of one of her darkest fantasies that always involved him. And over the past five years she had piled up quite a few.

Tori was about to answer when her cell phone ring. She quickly crossed the room, checked to identify the number before taking the call. It was Jody.

Drake listened to the conversation between the two women. He knew Jody Barrow and although he had never worked with her, Tori had and felt she was an agent who could be trusted. And for that reason, he would trust Tori's judgment.

He listened and noted she was careful not to mention where they were. In fact she wasn't telling Jody much at all, but stating that she needed to know how to retrieve the Agency's most recent records on the ASI. Evidently the two women had an understanding. Their conversation was short and after jotting down the information, Tori ended the call.

Tori crossed the room back to him, fanning herself with the hotel's notepad before tearing off the top sheet of paper. She held it up. "We should be able to tap into the Agency's file on the ASI using this code."

Drake smiled. All his attempts at getting into the records had failed. "Then let's do it."

A few hours later, Tori was fanning herself again. She and Drake had been sitting close together while checking out information on the ASI on her laptop. At one point she had leaned over him, to look over his shoulder at the screen, and his scent, manly and robust, had infiltrated her mind, started her hormones raging and made her feel intoxicated with need. She let out a breath of air as she gently brushed back the hair that had fallen in her face. "It feels hot in here," she said taking a step back and crossing the room for a drink of cold ice water.

Drake pushed back from the desk and stood. "Well, at least we now know just about everything there is to know about ASI."

Tori nodded after taking a big sip of water. Her body started feeling cooler. However, when she glanced over at Drake, it began getting hot again. She took another sip of water before saying, "It would be great if we had the names of all the CIA agents assigned to them."

Drake shook his head. "That sort of list would be suicidal in the hands of the wrong people."

"Yeah, but it would help us tremendously. Someone knew you were asking questions about me and didn't waste time tipping Cross off. That meant that person was aware of the grudge Cross is holding against you. That only leads me to believe that same person was also in cahoots with Rangel who has a connection to Cross." She met Drake's gaze. "Do you remember the names of anyone you asked about me directly?"

Drake frowned. "It's not like I posted an 'I'm trying to find Tori Green' message on my forehead. I merely asked a couple of people, but word evidently got out since I've never sought out a woman before. The only persons I asked directly were Lucille, Casey, Daniel Horton, and Tom Crowley. The only reason I asked the last two was because I'd heard you had dated them at one time or another and thought perhaps they were still in contact with you."

She frowned. "They weren't."

He nodded. "Yeah, that's what they were quick to tell me." After a few moments he said, "And I also called Hawk."

Tori nodded as she sat down on one of the beds. Of all those he'd named, the only one who'd known her whereabouts was Hawk.

Drake picked the notepad up off the desk and scanned the list they'd made. It was a list of places Cross had last been seen and the men he'd been seen with. It would be easier if they could recognize the enemy. Chances were that now that Rangel had been eliminated, Cross would use other corrupt agents to do his dirty work. There were only a few places on the list, which meant Cross had followed the cartel's orders and kept a low profile.

Drake was about to make a comment about one of the places and glanced over at Tori. She had stretched out across the bed closest to the door and fallen off to sleep. She had put on a robe when the waiter had arrived with their food but had removed it after the man had left. The overlarge T-shirt had been sufficient enough in covering most of her . . . until now. With the way she was lying in bed, too much of her thighs were showing, which equated to way too much temptation.

Crossing the room, he pulled down the covers on the

other bed and then picked her up in his arms. She came awake immediately and looked up at him with tired, drowsy eyes. "What are you doing, Drake?"

He smiled as he gazed down at her. "Putting you in bed."

She glared. "I was already in bed."

"Yeah, but the wrong one. I'm the one who's taking the bed closest to the door."

Tori sighed. She knew it would be pointless to argue with him. Besides, she was too tired and sleepy to do so. She hadn't slept in well over twenty hours; more than that if you didn't count the catnaps she'd managed to squeeze in during the time they'd been on the road.

The bed felt wonderful and she curled into her usual sleep position as soon as Drake placed the covers over her. She was too tired to care that he continued to stand next to the bed, staring down at her. The last thing she remembered when she closed her eyes to go to sleep was the feel of his hand as he gently caressed her cheek.

Drake sat at the computer and forced his mind back to what he was doing. He had a map on the screen that showed all the routes they could take to reach Houston, especially back roads. He needed that information in case they needed to get off the interstate at a moment's notice.

He glanced back over to the bed where Tori was sleeping. This was the first time he'd ever seen her sleep. She had taken catnaps while he'd been driving and on their last mission together they had taken turns keeping watch. But this was the first time he could actually study her for a long period of time while she was at rest. She had let her guard down and put her trust in him to keep her safe . . . and he would. He'd lost one woman to the cruelty and craziness of Solomon Cross, but didn't intend to lose another.

He tried to refocus his attention back on the computer map and found it straying back to Tori time and time again. He couldn't help but wonder what deep, dark secret she had that only Hawk knew about, and how was it connected to what was going on? He was trying to be patient but patience wouldn't keep them alive.

He glanced at his watch. It was just past midnight and he needed to get some rest himself. Standing, he rechecked the door and, deciding he wouldn't undress but would sleep on top of the covers, he kicked off his shoes and stretched out on the bed closest to the door, with his pistol within close reach.

"Just what kind of animal you plan to bring down with this?"

The Red Hunter ignored the old man's question as he continued to count out the money he was paying for the tranquilizer gun. It was a high-powered cartridge-fired rifle; a special type of weapon that had a unique side lever where darts could be loaded and unloaded from the chamber with ease. By adjusting the power on the control valve, close shots could be taken without injury to the animal . . . or in this case, the humans.

Cross wanted Drake and the woman alive and he intended to give the man what he asked for. Like he'd told Cross, overtaking two seasoned, highly skilled agents without fuss wouldn't easy, and he would have to find them first. But he hadn't earned the name the Red Hunter for nothing. And he preferred working alone although he had reinforcements in the way of contacts if he needed them. He enjoyed tracking people down. Before joining the CIA he had worked for over ten years as a bail enforcement agent.

He glanced up into the rugged face of the old man who

was waiting for an answer. It was dark and the meeting was in a rural area of town on a deserted back road. The sale of this rifle was regulated by federal law, and shipment was restricted to military institutions, sheriff's and police departments or holders of federal firearm licenses. Just the mere fact that the gun was being sold to him warranted a lot of questions, so in his book the geezer had best tend to his own business while he tended to his.

"That about does it," the Red Hunter finally said after counting out every single dollar the old man had charged him. "Are you sure I have enough darts?"

The old man licked his lips when he stuffed the money into his back pocket. "Yeah, I gave you plenty. Just remember that the serum in the darts is more potent than most. With just a single shot, in a range of up to one hundred and fifty yards, it has the ability to immobilize an animal as large as a bear rather quickly and lasts a little longer."

The Red Hunter nodded. "But it won't cause injury?"

"No, just renders them unconscious just long enough for you to do whatever you want to do with them."

The Red Hunter nodded again. He knew what Cross's plans were once he notified him that Warren and the woman had been captured. But what Cross didn't know was that he had plans of his own, and if Warren and the woman were such a valued prize, then Cross would do things his way. With Rangel dead things might start unfolding and he needed enough for a fresh start someplace.

After he was sure the old man had gotten into his car and driven off, the Red Hunter got into his truck and, using a flashlight, he pulled out the map he had studied earlier. From the information he'd been able to gather, Warren and the woman were traveling by car, headed east. After checking with the airlines it seemed that Warren had flown to Oakland from Houston so chances were he was returning there.

Red Hunter also found out that Warren had friends in Houston, old military buddies who would probably assist in keeping him well-hidden for a while.

Red Hunter smiled. He had friends in Houston, too, and he would call on those friends for information, and assistance if he needed it.

Houston, Texas

Ashton Sinclair woke up abruptly. He'd had another vision. Thanks to his African-American heritage, which included ancestors who had been fierce tribal medicine men with mystical powers, and his Cherokee Indian heritage, which included a great-great-grandfather who'd been a shaman, he had been born with the gift of visions. He looked down at his wife, Nettie, who was sleeping peacefully next to him. He'd had a vision that she would one day be his wife. Of course, she hadn't thought so. And on top of that, he'd also had a vision that she would give him three sons, triplets. Again, she hadn't believed that either, mainly because doctors had told her she could never have children. Now with his sons sound asleep in the other room, it was a testament to the power of his visions. He sat up. That's why he was concerned about the one he'd just had. It hadn't made much sense.

Trying not to disturb Nettie, he slipped out of bed and walked over to the window. It was a beautiful night, he thought, as he stared up at the full moon. He didn't have visions often, but usually when they occurred there was also a full moon. The last one he'd had over eight months ago had involved Sir Drake. This one had involved Drake, too.

When he heard a stirring behind him, he turned and watched as Nettie reached for him and when she found the spot beside her empty, she sat up and drowsily searched the room. When she saw him she pushed her hair back from her face and smiled.

He returned her smile thinking that he was definitely a blessed man. Nettie and his sons meant everything to him and he loved them dearly. Friendships meant a lot to him as well and he immediately thought of his two closest friends, Trevor and Sir Drake. He was 100 percent certain that Trevor was home in bed with his own wife Corinthians. Drake, however, was a different story. Usually, there was no telling where he was or what he was doing at any given moment. Trevor had talked to Sir Drake earlier tonight and had passed on the message that Drake wanted him to know. He was on the run with the woman he'd been looking for, Victoria Green. Knowing Drake, Ashton felt his friend had things pretty much under control, but still, there was something that hadn't set well with Ashton since hearing the news about Drake; and his vision tonight had proved him right.

"Something wrong, Ashton?"

He saw that the smile on Nettie's face had turned into a concerned frown. He quickly walked back over to the bed, sat on the edge and pulled her into his arms. "I had a vision about Drake tonight, Netherland."

She pulled back and looked at him. He knew how much his rough and gruff friend had come to mean to his wife as well as to Corinthians. Sir Drake had managed to wiggle his way into both women's hearts.

"Do you think he's hurt again?" Nettie asked with deep concern in her voice.

He gently caressed her cheek. "No, not physically, but something is going on that I can't figure out and the vision wasn't exactly clear. All it revealed was turmoil in Drake's life and for some reason I'm seeing flashes of that woman."

Nettie raised a brow. "What woman?"

"That woman who lied to me about being a doctor, so she could be left alone in Drake's hospital room."

Nettie nodded. "But you said her visit probably saved Drake's life. Whatever she said to him made him want to fight to live, right?"

"Yes, but I still would like to know who she was. I refuse to accept Drake's theory that she was an angel. I saw the woman. She was not a figment of my imagination."

He sighed deeply. "I'm also curious about who's this other woman, this female agent. She's the same woman who accompanied him on his last assignment and I've never seen him react so strongly to a woman since Sandy was alive. It's seems so coincidental that he arrives in California just in time to save her life; the same woman he'd been trying to find for the past few weeks. All of a sudden, Sir Drake, who'd avoided women is now suddenly obsessed with one."

Nettie cuddled deeper into her husband's arms. "Maybe after five years he's finally let go of Sandy's memory and moved on with his life, Ashton. Even you and Trevor have said numerous times that he should put that mission in Haiti behind him."

"Yeah, but I'm not sure he's doing that. I think one of the main reasons he's attracted to this woman is because there's a lot about her that reminds him of Sandy. He even admitted that."

Nettie sighed as she stared into her husband's eyes. "If that's true then he's not being fair to her. No woman wants to think she's another woman's replacement." An intense look appeared in her face. "Tell me about the vision you had tonight."

"All right," he said, placing her in bed then stretching out beside her, holding her in his arms. "It was kind of sketchy and involves Drake and two women, Sandy and the woman

I saw at the hospital that was masquerading as a doctor. The three of them were together in a deeply wooded area and the two women were surrounding him, trying to protect him."

Nettie raised a brow. "Protect him from what?"

Ashton shook his head. "I don't know."

"What about the woman he's with now? The one *he's* protecting?"

Ashton shrugged. "She wasn't in my vision. Perhaps because I don't have a face to go along with Victoria Green." For a few minutes he didn't say anything, then he added, "Or another reason is that perhaps she is what Sandy and the mystery woman are protecting him from."

Ashton felt the sudden tension in Nettie's body. "Are you saying that this woman Sir Drake is protecting is someone he can't trust? That she might be a double agent or something?"

Ashton took another deep breath. Nettie had put his very thoughts into words. "I don't know. I plan to talk to Trevor in the morning and run everything by him to see what he thinks."

"Good. Drake is a part of our family and I don't want anything to happen to him, Ashton."

Ashton was touched by the love and devotion she felt for his friend and was suddenly filled with a need to kiss his wife. He felt her quiver the moment their lips met and within seconds he was lost in the welcome and warmth of her arms and her body.

Albuquerque, New Mexico
Abram Hawk paced the confines of his living room, waiting on an important call. He needed information from the Agency, information he no longer had access to, but hoped to obtain. No one worked as many years within the CIA as

he had without building trust and confidence in certain people. He still had one person he could depend on: the woman who had been his assistant for over eight years, Lucille Mitchell. Although he'd never seen reason to divulge any information to her regarding Victoria Green's history, Lucille was someone he trusted implicitly. She'd always been his accomplice in making sure the agents in his operations were well cared for and that their personal well-being came first. She had always been his eyes and ears when he'd not been around and had kept him in the loop on what was going on in the lower ranks.

As a favor to him, Lucille had agreed to check out a few things. Until he was certain of his theory involving Solomon Cross, he wouldn't go to Casey. He'd known from first meeting Ronald Casey that the man intended to do things his way, which wasn't always the best way, and that was the main reason he hadn't told him Tori's history. A part of him knew he couldn't trust the man to look after Tori's welfare if she had stayed on as an agent. It was obvious that Casey had his mind set on a higher goal and his present position was just a step in that direction. The agents who worked under him were supposed to make him look good by doing what they were told and not give him any trouble.

Hawk smiled. He wondered if Casey had been ready for the likes of Drake Warren. Since he had once been Drake's commander when Drake had been a marine, he'd understood Drake. Casey wouldn't take the time to do so, which was a big mistake.

So lost in his thoughts, Hawk jerked when he heard the phone ring. Crossing the room he quickly picked it up. "Yes?"

"Hawk, this is Lucille. Sorry it took so long to get back

with you, but Casey called an unscheduled meeting with Robert Chisholm."

Hawk raised a brow. Chisholm was the man at the Agency in charge of the entire South American investigation; a man determined to bring Cross to justice after that Haiti incident. His son had been one of the marines who had been killed in the explosion. "What was the meeting about?" he asked, definitely interested.

"The informant the Agency has on Solomon Cross reported in. It seems that Cross found out that Drake has a love interest and has ordered that the two of them be found. According to the informant, Cross has been bragging to his men that they are about to have special houseguests and just what he intends to do with them when they arrive."

Hawk frowned. "Arrive?"

"Yes. Whomever he's sent to hunt them down will deliver them to him alive at a drop-off point, somewhere in South America in the hills near some rebel camp. Cross is supposed to be waiting there for them. The Agency plans to have their men in place when that happens and hopes to finally apprehend Cross."

Lucille sighed deeply before she continued. "Chisholm is excited at the thought of finally capturing Cross and it seems that he and Casey are willing to use Tori and Drake to do it."

Anger gripped Hawk's entire body. He didn't want to believe that Chisholm and Casey would go as far as to willingly place two agents' lives in danger. But then, a part of him knew they would. In their minds Drake and Tori were nothing more than sacrificial lambs for the cause of justice, as well as their own individual personal causes. After all those years of working hard to forge a bond of trust between the agents and the men they worked for, men like

Casey and Chisholm were willing to destroy that trust for their own personal gains and he refused to let that happen.

Hawk breathed in deeply. "Thanks for the information, Lucille. You've been most helpful."

After hanging up the phone, Hawk glanced at his watch. It was late and he needed to thoroughly think things over before calling Drake and Tori. He also needed to consider what actions he needed to take to make sure Casey and Chisholm's powers were stripped from them. Men who put their own selfish needs before their men didn't need to be in control.

But one thing was for certain, for Drake and Tori, time had definitely run out.

CHAPTER 10

"You certainly have a hearty appetite this morning."

Drake made the observation as he sat across from her at an IHOP restaurant. They hadn't done much talking while getting their gear together that morning before they left the hotel. But she had asked that they get something to eat before getting on the interstate. Deciding a good breakfast would hold them a while, they decided to get buffet and Tori's plate was loaded.

He remembered how much she had consumed at dinner the night before and wondered where the woman was putting it all. Although he had to admit that her hips appeared a little fuller since the last time he'd seen her, he actually liked the way she looked, especially in her shorts and jeans. He knew he would like her even better wearing nothing at all.

"I was hungry," she said.

"Evidently." He actually liked seeing her eat. A lot of women he had dated over the years ate like birds, for fear of putting on weight. Personally, he much preferred a woman with meat on her bones and the first thing he had noticed about Tori when he had first seen her was that she was well-built, with everything in the right place. In addition to that, she was in good physical shape. That became evident when they had gone on that mission together.

He glanced around the restaurant. It had been crowded when they walked in and was getting even more crowded by the second. He took a sip of his coffee and decided from the remaining food on Tori's plate that it would take her a little longer to finish it all.

They hadn't heard from Hawk and already it was eight in the morning. "I noticed you don't drink coffee anymore," he said when the waitress came to refill her glass of milk and she had taken several huge gulps. When they'd been on that mission together, she had consumed the stuff like it was going out of style.

Tori glanced up at Drake, startled by his question. She hadn't thought he would notice her preference for milk over coffee but it appeared that he had. "Once I left the Agency, I decided to try to live without it."

He took another sip of his coffee and decided it was just the opposite for him, he couldn't try and live without it. In fact he damn needed it this morning. He hadn't gotten a good night's sleep due to fantasizing about her. He hadn't been able to close his eyes just knowing she was in a bed just a few feet from his own.

He hadn't been able to stop his mind from remembering the one time their bodies had joined. Her legs had parted so eagerly for him and the womanly essence of her had been drenched with desire. That night he had found heaven and he hadn't been the same since. Her flesh had been tight as if she hadn't mated with a man for a long time and he had gloried in the feel of that tightness holding him, squeezing him, clutching him, and making him lose every ounce of control he'd had, all the way up to the point where he hadn't given thought to using a condom. The only thing he could think about that night was getting his engorged flesh inside of her.

Drake inhaled deeply, trying to get his mind and body

under control, something he'd been doing a lot lately. He glanced around the restaurant again. They were sitting at a table near the entrance and his position at the table faced the door. He wanted to be aware of everything, who came in and who went out. He also had a good view of the parking lot through the huge window.

"How long will it take us to reach Houston?" Tori asked, setting down her now-empty glass. Drake smiled and leaned forward in his chair. He surprised her by taking his napkin and wiping the milk ring from around her mouth.

Their eyes met. Drake felt that same awareness of her; the one that would strike him full force in the chest whenever he gazed into the darkness of her eyes. He struggled for breath and for control. From the one time that they'd made love he still knew the signs. It was there in her gaze. The uncertainty. The caution. The desire. Heated desire.

"Drake?"

He blinked, immediately becoming aware of their surroundings again, as well as the fact that he hadn't answered her question. "I want to make it there before nightfall," he said, his voice deep and unruffled. "Trevor and Ashton are setting up this cabin for us to stay in for a day or so until we can decide our next move. I think we should stop hiding and go after the bastards and let them become the hunted for a while. But first we have to identify just who they are. Although everything is pointing his way, we still don't know for certain that Solomon Cross is behind this and we can't assume anything."

Tori forced her gaze from his. There was no assumption about it, Cross was behind it and she knew that she would have to tell Drake just as Hawk had said. Only then could he fully prepare for the fight they had on their hands. For all she knew, Cross had targeted them for death and had dispersed a hit squad to take care of things.

Panicking at the thought of the danger she had placed Drake in, she sighed deeply. There was also the thought that once he saw her, Ashton Sinclair would immediately remember her as the woman who had pretended to be a doctor that night. Her hands suddenly felt cold thinking about the mess she was in.

And it didn't help matters whenever she looked at Drake and saw the raw, naked look of sexual hunger in his eyes. When she had awakened this morning and had glanced across the room, he was up already, sitting at the computer and staring at her.

"Then I guess we should get going if we want to make that deadline," she said. Rubbing her hands together, she stood.

Drake also stood and reached out and captured her hands in his. "Your hands are cold," he whispered softly, coming around the table and stepping closer to her. "Are you okay?"

She tipped her head back, met his gaze and nodded. "Yes, I'm fine."

She had lied. She wouldn't be fine until this nightmare was over.

Tori's phone vibrated and while Drake paid for their meal, she told him she needed to go to the ladies' room. Once inside a stall she returned Hawk's call.

"Hawk, this is Tori."

"Time has run out, Tori. I just talked to Lucille last night and she shared information as to what's going on. Casey heard from an informant that Cross has sent someone else to take care of Rangel's screwup and the person has a reputation for getting the job done. Cross wants you and Drake brought to him alive."

Tori arched an eyebrow. "Alive?"

"Yes, alive, so knowing how he feels about Drake, you can imagine what that means."

Tori nodded. She didn't have to imagine.

"And it's my understanding that Chisholm's department has been called in. He and Casey are willing to let you and Drake be used as bait to lead them to Cross."

"What!"

"Yes," he said. He hated to be the one to tell her, but she needed to know that the same agency she had dedicated her life to for the past five years was willing to use her and Drake to bring a wanted man to justice. "So you can't trust Casey to help you."

Hawk sighed deeply, angrily. "Drake has to be told, Tori. There's no longer a reason to keep him in the dark. It's too dangerous for the both of you. Either you tell him everything or I will."

Tori didn't say anything for a long moment as she tried to come to grips with everything Hawk had told her. "All right, but I want to be the one to tell Drake the truth about who I am, Hawk. He deserves to hear it from me. We're on our way to a place near Houston; a cabin owned by Trevor where we'll be hiding out for a couple of days. We should be there by the end of the day. I'll tell him when we get there."

"And will you call me after you do?"

"Yes, either Drake or I will call you."

She heard Hawk's long, hard sigh. "I know this can't be easy for you, Tori."

"No, it's not, and what scares me the most is not knowing how Drake will react when I tell him."

"Once you explain everything to him, he'll understand. He loves you and—"

Tori shook her head. "No, Hawk. Drake loved Sandy. He still does. Drake is a different person than he was five years

ago and so am I. Five years ago we were young, in love, full
of fire and ready to take on the world."

"And now?"

She didn't say anything for a long moment, and then she
said, "And now I'm a woman who beat death only to become a totally different person than I was before. I've lived
each day looking over my shoulder, knowing there was a
possibility that Cross would find out my secret."

"And I'm still not certain that Cross has found out your
secret," Hawk said. "I think if he had, he would have taken
more drastic measures by now. He would have come to this
country himself to deal with you and Drake, and not send
someone to do it. I agree with Drake that the only reason
you're involved is because of your association with him."

Tori nodded. "That might be true, but either way, Cross
wants me. Just give us time to reach the cabin and then I'll
tell Drake everything, including how the Agency is willing
to throw us to the wolves." She ended the call and placed
the mobile phone back in her purse.

Her hands, the ones Drake had recently warmed, had
turned cold again.

"You're shivering."

Tori blinked, surprised at Drake's comment. He must
have been watching her pretty hard to have noticed the
trembling of her body just now. He needed to keep his eyes
on the road and not on her—but the thought that he had
been watching her sent an unwanted spark through her; especially when his voice was filled with concern. But would
he still be filled with concern once she told him the truth?

"No, I'm fine although I have noticed the change in the
weather since leaving California."

Drake nodded his head. "Yes, the days are cooler, aren't they?" he said gazing over at her.

They had been driving for quite some time and had stopped for lunch. Drake suggested that instead of them stopping someplace for dinner that they should continue driving until they reached the cabin. Trevor had indicated that he would make sure it was well-stocked, which meant there would be food for them to eat.

For the past couple of hours she had racked her brain trying to decide how she would tell him the truth and decided that once they reached the cabin and after unloading their stuff she would just do it and get it over with. Then the two of them would have to deal with it. But how they dealt with it was what had her worried. She was more worried about the knowledge that Cross wanted them brought to him alive.

Needing something to take her mind off of what lay ahead, she decided to get Drake talking about something else; something she knew meant a lot to him, his home in the Tennessee Mountains.

"I bet your home in Tennessee is beautiful," she said, knowing that it was. He had taken her there one year for Christmas. That had been the last holiday they had spent together and memories of that time had sustained her through all the cosmetic surgeries, skin grafting, and implants that she'd endured.

"It is beautiful."

She heard the love and pride in his voice. It had been there the first time he had told her about Warren's Mountain. He was proud of his family's history and his great-great-grandfather's ability to hold on to the huge parcel of land he had been given as compensation for dedicated service as a Buffalo Soldier. Warren's Mountain had been passed through the Warren family for generations and now with Drake being the only Warren left, all land rights had been passed down to him. Because of the beauty of the land, he had been besieged with offers from various land developers ready to make him the deal of a lifetime. But he had turned all of them down, deciding to keep the land his family had worked so hard to hold. It was his haven, a place he could go after returning from missions abroad when he needed to feel in tune with the great country in which he lived. He had shared all those things with her as Sandy Carroll and it was there in his home on Warren's Mountain on Christmas Eve night when he had asked her to marry him.

She listened for the next hour while he told her about his home and just listening to him made her fall in love with it all over again . . . as well as with him. She would always love him, but the big question was whether or not he could still love her. She was different. She looked different. Could he handle the changes? Would he want to? But more importantly, did she even want him to? Would it be best when this was over for them to go their separate ways?

Something he said about being a loner caught her attention and as she reclined her seat back she knew that was true. Drake Warren was used to doing things alone. She remembered the exact point in time when Sandy had convinced him that he would never be alone again, and that she would always be there to share his life with him. They had been words freely spoken with all the sincerity of her heart. But less than a year after she had spoken them, both of their worlds had come tumbling down and in the end they had been forced to go their separate ways. Alone.

Solomon Cross's hand tightened on the phone. "You have good news for me, Red Hunter?"

"No, not yet, but I wanted to let you know that I'm getting close. I have everything set in place and have an idea just where they're headed. I just wanted to keep you posted. As soon as I have them I will let you know so we can make the exchange. I'm excited about getting that bonus."

Cross's eyes narrowed. "I never said anything about a bonus."

"But I'm sure you'd agree that they would be worth me getting one when I bring them to you."

Cross tried to hold back his temper. This man was a fool if he thought he could use Warren and the woman with him like dangling carrots. He was already getting paid well enough and Cross didn't intend to give him another cent. But now was not the time to let him know that. He would let him deliver Warren and the woman at the agreed drop-off point and then he would make sure Red Hunter got what was coming to him.

"Yes, maybe you're right. If you pull this off then you'd be most deserving of a little extra. Just keep in touch."

After hanging up the phone, Cross knew he would teach the Red Hunter a lesson in trying to pull one over on him.

Tori noticed when Drake pulled off the interstate and glanced over at him. He deciphered the question in her gaze and said, "We made better time than I thought we would. This road will take us to the cabin, but first I want to circle around a bit just to make sure we weren't followed."

She nodded, knowing they needed to take every precaution. A little more than a couple of hours later Drake turned off the highway and onto a dirt road where a sign was posted indicating *Private Property*.

It took them almost thirty minutes before they came to a small clearing where a huge cabin sat on a lake. Her breath caught when she saw a black truck parked out front, and standing beside it were two men whom she immediately recognized, Trevor Grant and Ashton Sinclair. When Drake brought the car to a stop she caught Ashton's astute gaze and knew he had recognized her—not as Sandy Carroll but as the woman who had pretended to be a doctor and entered Drake's hospital room that night.

She swallowed deeply. Hawk was right. Time had run out.

Ashton narrowed his eyes as he watched Drake and the woman get out of the car. He glanced at Drake and then back at Tori Green, and at that moment he knew Drake didn't have a clue that the woman he was putting his life on the line to protect was the same woman who had visited him in his hospital room.

Drake's angel. The same woman who had miraculously given Drake the will to live.

Ashton leaned against the door of his truck. His trained gaze was focused on the woman. He picked up on her nervousness when she met his gaze. His inner intuition, that same sixth sense that had kept him alive over the past thirty plus years, alerted him that she was definitely hiding something, and he intended to find out what.

"Tori, I'd like you to meet my two closest friends, Trevor Grant and Ashton Sinclair. I've mentioned them to you before," Drake said.

Tori knew that now was not the time to tell Drake the truth, not with an audience. She decided she would stick to her plan and tell him later when they were alone, which meant she would pretend just a little while longer. After making that decision she extended her hand first to Trevor and then to Ashton, who was drilling her with a piercing look. There was no doubt in her mind that he remembered her from when she'd visited Drake at the hospital.

"It's nice meeting the both of you."

"Same here," Trevor said, smiling.

Ashton, however, continued to stare at her. "Have we met before, Tori?" he asked, knowing damn well that they had.

With a shake of her head, she pulled her hand from his. His features were hard, unreadable. "I don't think so."

"Umm, that's funny. For some reason I thought that perhaps we had."

Drake, who hadn't picked up on the tension between Tori and Ashton, said, "Tori used to be in the marines before going to work for the Agency. Perhaps you ran into her somewhere." He smiled as he glanced over at Tori. "She's not a woman a man can see one time and easily forget."

Ashton nodded as both his hands slipped into the pockets of his jeans. "Yeah, I can definitely agree with that."

Drake turned to Trevor. "Thanks for letting me use this place."

Trevor smiled. "Don't mention it. Come on and let me show you a few things before we leave. And we stopped by a restaurant and got take-out dinners so you two won't have to do any cooking tonight."

"Thanks," Tori said, appreciating his thoughtfulness.

"I'll stay here and help Ms. Green unload the car," Ashton volunteered.

Drake nodded. "Thanks, Ash."

Tori swallowed. She knew no matter what Ashton had told Drake, the main reason he was hanging back was because he had questions and intended to get answers.

Tori pulled her luggage behind her while following Ashton as he carried the rest of their things into the cabin. It was a spacious one-story dwelling that had two bedrooms with their own private baths, a huge living room with a pool table and an eat-in kitchen.

"Who the hell are you? What were you doing in Drake's hospital room that night? And what the hell are you doing with him now?"

Tori had just completed a quick tour of the cabin and had retuned to the living room the exact moment that Ashton had walked into the cabin with the last of their stuff. She shook her head and inwardly smiled. Ashton wasn't wasting any time. This was the Ashton she knew and loved as a friend. When it came to finding out something he wanted to know, he didn't believe in beating around the bush and he was worse than a dog with a bone.

"The answers you want are complicated, Ashton."

"Who gives a damn? I want them anyway."

She could feel his anger and knew that because of the unknowns, he didn't trust her. "Be careful what you ask for, you just might get it," she said softly. Inhaling deeply, she crossed the room and sat down on the sofa. "You always were a pain in the ass when you wanted to know something."

He lifted a brow and stared at her. "What the hell are you talking about?"

"I'm talking about that time in the Philippines when you were determined to find out the reason behind our mission instead of just following orders and doing what we'd been sent to do."

Ashton's gaze hardened, his nostrils flared and his jaw tightened. He slowly crossed the room and stood over her, staring, looking at Tori for a long moment, studying every feature on her face, giving her his full attention, his total concentration.

He opened his mouth, shut it, then opened it again. "Who

the hell are you?" he asked incredulously, with tightly-held restraint.

Tori sat very still. Then she looked up at him. After five years she was about to share her secret with someone she knew was a friend. Someone she trusted.

She leaned back against the sofa. "It's me, Ash. Sandy." Her mouth curved into a tight smile. "And before you ask the answer is no. Super no. Hell no. Damn no. I still don't like okra."

CHAPTER 11

"Sandy?"

Ashton's voice trembled and Tori knew it wasn't from fear but emotion. He wasn't afraid of anything or anyone, however, when it came to those he cared about, he felt deep.

"Yes, Ash, it's me with a new face, nice dental work, and better skin in some places—all compliments of my country. I asked for a boob job, but they turned me down claiming it wasn't medically necessary."

She watched as his features, which had been full of tension, slowly relax. He continued to stare at her, speechless. Then he smiled, a huge rich grin, and reached out and pulled her into his arms. He held her tight and all the emotions he felt poured straight through to her. He finally let go and gazed down at her. "But—but how? Why?"

She took his hand and together they sat down on the sofa. For the next fifteen minutes she told him what had happened after the explosion in Haiti. He listened attentively, not saying anything but she could tell by the intense look on his face that he was taking everything in. Deep understanding lined his eyes.

"Now I know why you were at the hospital that night to see Drake."

Tori inhaled deeply. "When I heard that he was . . . dying, I had to do something, Ash, even if it was against Hawk's orders. What I did may be the reason I'm in this mess now, but I'd do it again in a heartbeat to help Drake."

"And you think Cross has discovered your real identity?"

"I'm not sure. Hawk doesn't think so. He thinks if Cross knew that I was Sandy, he would be furious enough to come after me himself."

Ashton nodded. "Knowing how much he hates Drake and blames him for his wife's death, I have to agree with Hawk. Cross has gloated at the thought that he's been the cause of Drake's pain and suffering for the past five years. And if he found out that he'd been duped, I don't want to think about what method of revenge he would use on the both of you."

Ashton then looked at her and asked, "I take it that Drake doesn't know you're Sandy?"

Shutting her eyes, Tori felt the weight of the world on her shoulders. She slowly opened them. "No, but I plan on telling him tonight. According to Hawk, the agency intends to use me and Drake as bait to get Cross." She then told him what Hawk had told her about Cross wanting them taken alive and how her abductors were supposed to deliver them to some drop-off point. It was the CIA's intention to monitor the exchange and be there to apprehend the elusive Cross.

"I can't believe they're willing to take a chance like that on your and Drake's lives. Anything can go wrong and I don't trust Cross to do things according to plan."

Tori nodded. "Neither do I, and knowing Drake, he'll have those same thoughts as well."

When they heard the sound of Trevor and Drake returning, Ashton stood and pulled her up. "Is it all right for me to tell Trevor you're Sandy?"

"Yes. I plan to tell Drake later anyway."

Ashton nodded. "Trevor and I will leave so you can talk to Drake. As soon as you tell him the truth the better."

Tori nodded. She knew that was true but she definitely wasn't looking forward to it.

Tori could barely drink her water with Drake standing across the room, leaning against the kitchen counter and watching her every move. They had eaten the food that Trevor and Ashton had left and now Drake stood waiting. She had told him during dinner that she wanted to talk to him after they'd finished eating.

He had asked to take a shower first and he had come back into the kitchen afterwards. He stood tall, powerfully built and wearing nothing but a pair of jeans. He possessed a commanding presence.

Over the rim of her glass her gaze roamed his body, centering in on his wide shoulders and muscular arms. Then there was the hair on his naked chest and how it tapered down his flat stomach going past the waistband of his jeans. Although her vision stopped there, she was well aware of how things looked beyond that point, specifically how well endowed he was. Some men were blessed in that area but others like Drake had been more than just blessed. He had been awarded more than generously. The very first time she had seen him completely nude she had quickly reached the conclusion that he definitely broadened the definition of the word *big*, had redefined the word *sexy*, and had clearly escalated the term *powerfully masculine* to a whole other level.

When she placed the empty glass on the tiled counter, she felt a tingling sensation in her stomach. Although it was way too early in her pregnancy to feel her baby move, she believed in her heart that her child was letting her know that it felt its father's presence and felt safe.

"Ready, Tori?"

She nodded, although she doubted if she would ever be fully ready for Drake Warren. Even as Sandy, she had thought he was overwhelming. There had always been something about him that preyed on her sensual side and always sparked her with potent desire whenever she was around him. The only time she'd been able to tone it down was when they were on a mission together. Then she would put business first. But then alone, with whatever privacy they could manage, they would tumble into each other's arms like mating was the most natural thing for them to do.

"Yes, I'm ready," she replied, unable to calm the rapid and intense thump of her heartbeat when he crossed the room to her.

"Then let's sit at the table and talk."

She swallowed deeply. "All right."

Before she could recover from his closeness, he took her hand in his. His touch immediately sent a sexual current radiating through her that she felt all the way to her toes. She glanced up at him and knew he had felt it, too. But he didn't say anything as he led her over to the table where they had eaten earlier.

He took the chair facing her. "Okay, what's going on, Tori? What do you have to tell me?"

Tori swallowed as she gazed at him. "It's about Sandy." She watched his reaction at the mention of his fiancée's name.

He raised his brow. "Sandy?" he asked in surprise. "What about her?"

She hesitated, swallowed again. Then said, or tried to say, "She didn't . . ."

Drake sat forward in the chair, attentive, waiting for her to finish what she was saying. When it appeared that she wouldn't, he leaned closer. "She didn't what?"

Tori glanced away from him, feeling the tension radiating in him. He was picking up on her nervousness and she could tell that it was making him uneasy, agitated, and edgy. When moments passed and she didn't say anything, he reached across the table, cupped her chin, turning her face back to his. "Answer me."

Tori met his gaze. The tension she had seen in his features had extended to his voice. It was shaky, strained. "Sandy, sh—she didn't die in that explosion, Drake. She survived."

Drake stared at her like she had gone stone crazy, absolutely foolish, seriously deranged. Then she added quietly, "She *did* survive, Drake. Sandy didn't die in Haiti."

Something in Tori's eyes told Drake that she believed what she was saying, no matter how far-fetched her words seemed. He continued looking at her and suddenly felt as if he'd gotten punched in the stomach and his breath was cut off, making breathing difficult. "You want me to believe that Sandy survived that explosion and I, of all people, didn't know about it?" he asked, his words forced, and his voice barely recognizable even to his own ears.

"Yes." She inhaled deeply and gazed intensely into his eyes. "The reason you didn't know is because she couldn't tell you, and—"

"No!" Drake jumped out of his chair, turning it over in the process. The crash sounded loud when it hit the floor. He put up his hand to stop any further words Tori was about to say. "I don't know where the hell you got your information, lady, but I don't believe any of it. I was there. After I came back around, I saw that warehouse. I read the reports. I saw—"

"What you didn't see," she said, standing and cutting off his words, "was Sandy's body because there wasn't one, Drake. She didn't die. She survived and under tight security she was rushed to a hospital and provided top-priority medical treatment."

Drake shook his head, still refusing to believe any of what she was saying. "No, that's not true. Don't you think that I would have known if Sandy would have survived? She was my fiancée! We were to be married in six months. There's no way in hell she would have lived and not contacted me to let me know she was alive, so you can shut the hell up about it," he said, anger consuming him, clawing at his insides. He was again reliving the anguish he'd suffered knowing he had lost the one woman who had meant everything to him. Just thinking about that time and what he'd gone through made his hands suddenly feel numb. His entire body felt paralyzed as he remembered the grief that had forced him into their grips.

He glared at Tori. "And what makes you think that you know so damn much about it anyway? How dare you stand here and tell me Sandy didn't die like you're an expert on what happened? What kind of sick game are you trying to play?"

Tori didn't say anything for a few moments, and then she lifted her chin and met his stony glare, the hostility she saw in his eyes. "Who I am makes me an expert, Drake. I can stand here and tell you that Sandy didn't die because I know that she didn't. And the reason I know is because," she took a deep breath, then said, "Because I *am* Sandy."

Moving beyond the shock that immediately covered his face, she continued. "I am the woman you made love to the night before the explosion; the one you sneaked off with into the woods to lie with next to that stream. I'm the woman who you convinced that night not to wait another year to marry but to move the date up and marry in six months."

Tori blinked back tears. "I'm also the woman you told that night that you wanted our first son to be named Deke, after your father, and for our daughter to be named Savannah, after your grandmother. I'm the one, Drake."

She watched him suck air into his lungs as if he needed to relieve some of the pressure overtaking him by breathing. He was remembering that night, every detail, and knew everything she had just said was true. "No," he said, barely getting the word out, taking a step back, as if her claim was too much to bear and he needed distance between them. "You aren't Sandy. You can't be. There's no way."

She shook her head sadly. "Although I don't look like her, I am. There's a lot that's happened and there was a good reason I couldn't tell you the truth. But more than anything, Drake, you have to know that I am Sandy. That's why you felt so many similarities between us. Because of the extent of my injuries, I had to have plastic surgery over more than eighty percent of my body, which is the reason I don't look the same. And Hawk decided that I needed a new identity. When I got better he insisted that I go into the Witness Protection Program since Solomon Cross was still on the loose, but I refused. After begging and pleading, he finally gave in and agreed to let me work for the Agency. You hadn't begun working there at the time so there was no chance our paths would cross."

The force of Drake's glare nailed her to the spot where she was standing, and she knew what she was saying was finally sinking in as he was trying to make sense of everything she was telling him.

"You survived that explosion and didn't tell me? Didn't want me to know?" he snarled, like a wounded animal. "You let me go through those five years believing that I had lost you? How could you do that to me?" he asked, in a voice so incredulous with pain, Tori had to blink back more tears. "The Sandy that I loved would not have done that to me," he added.

"Oh, yes, she would have if it meant keeping you safe," Tori said through clenched teeth. "Don't you see that I *had* to do it, Drake? Solomon Cross was a psychopath. Had he known he'd failed to carry out what he thought was the ultimate revenge against you, and that I was still alive, he would have tried again and his second attempt may have cost you your life. I couldn't let that happen."

Fury ignited Drake's features. "Who the hell made you God?" he shouted, staring at her. Nothing about her looked like Sandy, but he knew about the similarities she'd mentioned. He'd felt them. Experienced them. He'd thought at one time he'd been about to lose his mind, especially when he had made love to her. And all this time . . .

Rage consumed him; tore into him and his mind seemed to snap when he remembered the hurt, the pain, and the anguish. "Damn you, how could you do that to me!"

Tori flinched like she had been struck and anger consumed her as well. It overtook her mind and ripped through her senses. "Damn you back, you selfish bastard!" she shouted, tightly wound and springing into action with his words—words that had been like a knife cutting into her. "Do you think you're the only one who suffered those five years, Drake Warren? I went through several painful surgeries, at times just barely holding on to my life. I awoke from a coma only to be told I had a new identity and the man I loved more than life itself, could never know that I was still alive. Do you know how hard it's been for me these past five years? You're not the only one who was hurting. But for me things didn't end there. I had to live looking over my shoulder and stay in constant fear that one day Cross would find out the truth and retaliate. Then there were those reports I would hear about you acting like a jackass and playing Russian roulette with your life. Don't you know the risk I took defying Hawk's orders and going to that hospital to see you eight months ago? Do you know what—"

"You?" he asked, cutting into her words, clearly stunned. "You were the woman who came into my hospital room? The woman Ashton actually saw?" The question was asked in an unbelieving quiet tone.

"Yes," she snapped. "And I'd do it again if it means keeping you alive, but I won't let you stand here and make it seem like you were the only victim in this. Damn you, I was hurting, too."

Drake sucked oxygen into his lungs, refusing to believe that any of this was happening. He was in some type of a dream, worse yet, some friggin' nightmare. When he woke up everything around him, including his life, would be back to normal—at least as normal as he'd known it for the last five years. But all he had to do was stare at the woman glaring at him to know that was not the case.

He couldn't think rationally. Hell, he couldn't think at all. He was a man who was forever galvanized for action, and his body was radiating with anger of the worst kind. The room suddenly felt like it was closing in on him. He needed to think. He needed to come to terms with what Tori had just told him. He needed to beat the hell of out something, kick somebody's ass, break someone's bones, or better yet, bury a body alive.

He needed to get the hell out of there.

He inhaled sharply, turned abruptly, crossed the room and walked out the kitchen door, slamming it behind him.

Tori watched him leave and, unsure of the strength of her legs, she made it to the chair and sat down. She knew that in time she would feel calm again but for now, her body was wired, coiled tight, filled with anger. For five years she had been her own tower of strength, her own voice of reason, her own source of sanity. But now, tonight, at that very moment, she felt alone, weak, forsaken.

As tears fell from her eyes, she dropped her head onto her arms and cried.

Trevor Grant and Ashton Sinclair.

The two names were on the Red Hunter's list as friends of Warren. Friends who would eventually lead him to Warren and Green. He sat in a rental car, parked at the curve on a residential street of beautiful, stately homes. A couple of times a few joggers had come by, given him a curious glance, but had kept moving.

Damn. People were so leery these days but he could understand why with the way sickies were snatching up kids and all. He didn't like sitting and waiting for Sinclair to come home but had no choice. He breathed a sigh of relief minutes later as he watched Ashton Sinclair pull into his driveway. Since he hadn't driven into the garage to park, it stood to reason that the man planned to go back out again later, so he needed to act quickly.

As soon as Sinclair went into the house, the Red Hunter eased his car forward, glad it had turned night and that the illumination from the streetlights wasn't directly on him. Moving quickly, he got out of the car and attached a small transmitter underneath the side of Sinclair's truck. Getting back into his car he quickly drove off, satisfied with what he had accomplished and totally convinced that in due time, Sinclair would lead him straight to his prey.

CHAPTER 12

Sandy was alive.

Drake was sure he had walked the circumference of Trevor's property and he was still consumed with anger and filled with disbelief, although deep down he knew Tori's claim was true. There had been something about her that had pulled him in to her from the first. That day he had sat in the coffee shop and watched her walk in, he had felt some sort of an affinity to her, a connection.

Tori Green was Sandy.

He shook his head. In some ways she was Sandy and in other ways she was not. He frowned, knowing that it didn't make sense, but it was something he needed to accept and somehow get beyond the anger and betrayal that he felt. He knew all that should matter was that she was alive and hadn't died in that explosion but for some reason he couldn't accept that Tori was Sandy. The only two people who knew about their secret rendezvous the night before were him and Sandy. No other person had known they had made love by the stream, the conversations they'd shared and the promises they'd made.

For five years she had been alive and hadn't told him.

She claimed she had done it to protect him. He hadn't

needed her to protect him, dammit! Drake Warren could take care of himself. He could have protected them both. And even if they'd had to go into the Witness Protection Program for a while, he would have made do as long as the two of them were together. How dare she decide his future for him.

And she'd insinuated that it had been Hawk's decision, one she had meekly followed. Drake inhaled deeply. Of course it had been Hawk's decision, and Drake could very well see him almost single-handedly pulling things off. The man was well respected for being fair, honest, and aboveboard. The top brass, the upper honchos in the executive office—all the way up to the president—respected him, admired his integrity and had basically let him run his own show. No one had been surprised last year when he'd been offered the job of deputy director of the CIA, which would have placed him in a position to exercise the powers of the director when the director's position was vacant or in the director's absence or disability. And those who also knew him hadn't been surprised when he had turned the position down, deciding to retire after serving his country for over thirty years, first as a marine then as operations chief in the CIA, in charge of international organized crime as well as arms-control intelligence.

Drake sighed deeply, wondering who else had known about Tori being Sandy. Had Trevor and Ashton known? He shook his head, knowing that wasn't the case. There was a chance Ashton knew now, after seeing Tori today and putting two and two together; but Drake believed that like him, neither man had had a clue. Sandy had been their friend and they had also mourned her death.

Her death.

Now that was a laugh since Sandy hadn't actually died.

He continued walking, too mad to think straight. Then there was the reality that a seriously crazy bastard was after them. Had all Hawk and Tori's carefully laid plans been for nothing since it seemed that Cross had found out she was alive anyway? There were questions he needed to ask, answers he had to have straight in his mind; but at the moment he needed to be alone.

He *had* to be alone.

Tori lay in bed. When she head the sound of Drake returning she glanced over at the clock. He'd been gone for two solid hours. The agent in her had to be sure it was Drake returning and not an intruder. Grabbing her pistol off the nightstand, she flicked off the safety and eased out of bed. Making her way to the door, she slowly opened it.

From the light shining in the hallway from the kitchen, she could see that it was Drake. She lowered her gun the exact moment he turned and saw her. Their gazes met for the longest time and then he turned back around to gaze out the window. "It's me, so you can go back to bed."

Outwardly, Tori tried not to react to Drake's harsh tone but she did. He was still pissed. But then, so was she.

She drew in a deep breath and smelled his scent from across the room. He was sweaty, hot, musky. He had been engaged in some sort of physical activity. What? Sparring with the devil, she thought as a smile eased on her lips. He was an ace at martial arts. Had he been outside working out, doing a lot of his maneuvers, trying to rid the anger within him? Drake was a unique human being whenever his anger combined with high adrenaline. And if you threw in a dose of sexual frustration, that particular part of him between his legs would swell to gigantic proportion and deliver the best lovemaking possible—as good as it could get.

That thought took over her mind as she stood there, her breasts rising and falling with every breath she took; the area between her legs suddenly feeling hot, wet.

Without saying anything to him, she slipped back into her room and closed the door. Now was not the time for her hormones to start acting crazy. She had gone five years without sex before that night they had spent together on the ship. She placed the pistol back on the nightstand and eased back into bed. She would just love to beat the crap out of Drake, literally pound some sense into that arrogant head of his.

She had called Hawk earlier, after taking her shower and had told him that Drake now knew the truth, and how badly he had taken the news. Hawk felt that eventually Drake would come around and see that every decision that had been made had been for the both of their protection, and that she had not betrayed him as he wanted to believe.

She knew Hawk was right and that Drake was battling shock and denial and she needed to give him time to come to grips with everything.

What had she expected?

As she curled under the covers, she knew exactly what she had expected. It had been a forbidden dream that would creep into her sleep-induced unconsciousness every once in a while. In this dream she would tell Drake the truth, that she was alive, and then he would sweep her off her feet, tell her how much he still loved her and then carry her to the nearest bed and make passionate love to her, wiping out five years of need, separation, and turmoil.

But that was not the way it happened. It hadn't even come close to that.

She heard the sound of water running and knew he was preparing to take a shower. She tried to remove both him and his anger from her mind and discovered that she could not. A part of her resented that he felt that he was the only one who had suffered, and that she had outright betrayed him when she had made the ultimate sacrifices to make sure he was kept safe.

Tori was glad the cabin had two bedrooms and was grateful she'd had the foresight to be ready for bed when he returned. She couldn't deal with him and his anger any more tonight, but she knew that tomorrow they had to talk. She needed to let him know about the CIA's plan to use them as pawns.

Her breath caught when she heard footsteps outside of her door. Moments later Drake moved on. She turned in bed. She would deal with him soon enough in the morning. She knew his anger and he knew hers. But tomorrow, they needed to put their anger aside to deal with the issue of keeping them both alive.

Tori couldn't sleep. She spent her time tossing and turning in the most comfortable bed she had ever slept in. But still she was restless, angry, and even worse, agitated and frustrated.

She eased out of bed, making sure all the buttons on her nightshirt were securely fastened. She wanted to go outside for some fresh air but knew that would not be a good idea.

Deciding it was safer to go into the kitchen for a drink of water, she opened her bedroom door. A light that shone under Drake's bedroom's door indicated that he was still awake. The lights in the other parts of the cabin were off but the silhouette of the moon shining through one of the windows provided just enough illumination for her to see.

She had started down the darkened hall to the kitchen when she suddenly bumped into a hard, broad chest. Immediately, she went into a defense mode, ready to put her skill as a karate expert into action.

"It's me, Tori."

Drake's voice almost knocked the breath out of her. She had been more than prepared to take him down. She took a deep breath to calm her racing heart. "Drake, I thought you were in your room."

"I was but I couldn't sleep so I got up to check on things."

"Oh." She tried not to let the fresh scent of his recent shower get to her, but a jolt of desire rammed through her body anyway. And the bad thing about it was that she was still mad at him and knew for sure that he was still angry with her. But her mind stopped dealing with anger when Drake stepped out of the shadows and into the flow of the moonlight. He wasn't wearing a shirt, and a pair of sweatpants rode low on his hips. She was suddenly bombarded with a heated sensation.

"Where were you going?" he asked, leaning back against a wall, crossing his arms over his broad chest. There was a "climb into bed with me" look about him. She was all too familiar with that look.

She wondered if he could hear the pounding of her heart. "To the kitchen. I was thirsty and wanted something to drink."

"Milk?"

Tori lifted a brow, wondering if he was getting suspicious about anything.

"What makes you think I'd want milk?"

"Because you seem to drink a lot of the stuff. I'm sure you're keeping some dairy farmer happy."

She shrugged. From his tone of voice she could tell he was trying to downplay his anger for the same reason that she was. Emotions were suddenly taking over their senses. They were together for the first time in five years, not as strangers or two people who barely knew each other and who had met less than six months ago. But they were two individuals with a deep history; two people who had once loved each other . . . and had lost each other.

"Tori."

"Drake."

They said each other's names at the same time that he pulled her to him and captured her mouth. His lips were firm, his mouth eager, and his tongue hungry. And that hungry tongue took control of her mouth, making her senses swim. She became entrenched by feelings she hadn't felt in a long time. His tongue was leaving no area in her mouth untouched and untasted.

Moments later when he slowly broke off the kiss, she felt consumed with a need so great, she wanted to forget Cross and mainly concentrate on their awareness of each other, their reaffirmation of life and the realization that they were together again.

Right now, at this very moment, she only wanted to dwell on the man who was building an incredible ache all through her body; an ache she had to have filled.

"Knowing who you are is making me crazy," Drake whispered against her lips, taking the tip of his tongue and outlining her mouth from corner to corner. "Just to think you're here and with me again is driving me insane."

That makes two of us, she thought, her panties completely drenched. The air was chilly but they were building up a lot of heat and the scent of aroused bodies permeated their surroundings, adding an extra zing to their lust.

They were desperate. Hungry. Out of control.

It seemed that all the anger of that afternoon was gone, but she knew it was still there. It had only been put on hold. It would resurface in the morning and they would have to deal with it. Something within them crashed at the same time their control snapped. Emotions they had tried holding at bay toppled over in a heated frenzy as their tongues continued to mate desperately, urgently, relentlessly.

Moments later Tori pulled back, drew in a sharp breath, taken aback by the intensity of the kiss they'd just shared and the need that was ramming through them. She was suddenly feeling delirious with desire, hot with a need that only Drake had the ability to quench.

She wanted him to take her, hard and fast. Now.

He must have seen the deep hunger in her gaze, heard it in her breathing, felt it in the shiver that raced through her. In one smooth feat he reached out and gripped her nightshirt, sending buttons flying across the room with the strength of his pull on the silk material. With no buttons to hold the garment together it fell open, exposing her body. Before she could say anything, utter a single word, he pushed the nightshirt from her shoulders, leaving her standing before him stark naked.

The look in his eyes, fervent and aroused, caused the longing in her to rise to another feverish pitch. Mindlessly delirious, she reached out and tugged at the waistband of his sweats. "I want you, Drake. Now!"

As if that was all he needed to hear, she watched as he took a step back, quickly discarded his sweats and swung them away. He wasn't in the mood to take things slow. Neither was she.

When he stood totally naked in front of her, she was unable to think about anything and anyone except him. *Get ready to meet your daddy*, she silently communicated to the child she carried within her womb. *He's coming for a visit and Mommy intends to make him feel very welcome.*

She met Drake's gaze and all the love she could ever have for one man was there, shining in her eyes, although she doubted that he could see it. She was opening herself in the only way she knew how for the second time in five years. The turbulent storm that had been raging inside of her had finally come to a head and it was almost next to impossible not to get caught up in it. She was too far gone.

He quickly covered the distance separating them and pulled her to him, kissing her with a hunger that matched her own. He released her mouth to let his tongue trail a path downward to her breasts. Catching a nipple between his teeth, his tongue went on the attack, tugging, licking, sucking, as she moaned out his name. And when she felt his hand dip lower to stroke her intimately, she inched closer, wanting everything.

"Drake!"

"Do you have any idea what it means having you back with me? What losing you did to me? Do you know how much I missed you?" he growled in her ear.

"The bedroom is too far away," he said, swinging her up into his arms. And then he was gently laying her back on the pool table, opening her legs in the process, and drinking in the sight of her positioned that way before him, seeing everything. Tori felt no shame, just need, and her eyes fluttered close just thinking about how much she wanted him.

"For the last five years I have been a man living on the edge, not caring if I lived or died," Drake said huskily, his voice the one of a man whose life had been torn. "Living a life without you was more than I could bear. Believing you were gone nearly destroyed me. My life virtually ended the day I thought you died."

He saw the tears sliding slowly from her eyes. "Look at me. I want you to see how much I missed having you with me. How much I missed loving you."

Tori met his gaze. She swallowed with the intensity in his dark depths. And then he smoothly eased to stand between her opened legs and before she could catch her next breath he thrust into her, pushing past her ultra-damp flesh while going further, moving deeper, making the flame within him scorch her already hot body.

He threw his head back and she saw the tightening of the muscles in his neck. He groaned and the sound echoed in the room and came across like a male animal that was about to mate.

He pushed deeper and when he had gone as far into her as he could go, he leaned over and skimmed a fingertip down her breast, while looking down at their connected bodies. He inhaled deeply and she knew he was taking their aroused scent into his nostrils and somehow she could tell it made his own need flare to greater heights.

She felt wild, wanton, out of control being spread atop the pool table, yet at the same time she felt a sense of feminine satisfaction that she was the one who had put that deep look of heated lust in his eyes.

Suddenly he began moving, holding her hips tight in his hands while thrusting in and out of her, mating with her in a way that had her emitting breathless cries to mingle with his rough groans.

She dug her nails into his back with the feel and sound of bare flesh slapping against bare flesh. Their mating was intense with no sexual restraints; passionate in the most overpowering way. And when he spread her legs wider for deeper penetration, she knew that for as long as she lived she would always have special memories of this night with him.

Tori couldn't stop the convulsions that began shuddering through her, racking her body, sending her over the edge. And when she felt him stiffen before pushing into her for one hard final thrust, she knew what was coming.

They were.

A crescendo of sexual sensations that she felt all the way to her toes ignited into an explosion that tore through her. That same explosion tore through him as well and she felt him come, in a torrential release deep inside of her. She cried out his name at the same time he cried out hers. Her inner muscle tightened, clutched him, loving the feel of him buried deep inside of her, coming in her that triggered her own climax.

He leaned down and captured her mouth in a kiss while doing all sorts of things to her with his hands, as the two of them climaxed and shuddered uncontrollably. Together.

And Tori knew as sensations after sensations continued to explode inside of her that Drake Warren had done more than come for a visit. He had come home and she had a feeling that no matter what problems they had to face, he intended to stay.

CHAPTER 13

It was twelve A.M., the midnight hour.

Drake came fully awake as memories of the past hours flooded his mind. He glanced down at the woman sleeping beside him as emotions, stronger than any he'd ever encountered before knotted his stomach.

First he had taken Tori on the pool table, not once but twice, with an urgency and desperation that had nearly driven him insane. Their mating had been wild, uncontrollable, and intense. Then he had placed her in bed and made love to her again, several times, before the both of them, mindless with exhaustion, sated with passion, had succumbed to sleep.

And now he was wide awake and dealing with the fact that Sandy and Tori were one and the same. He leaned up, rested on his elbows and studied her. In his mind, Sandy was dead. She had died five years ago in that explosion. The woman he held in his arms looked nothing like her, and a part of him was having problems accepting that she was, although he knew it to be true.

But then there was something his mind wasn't finding it hard to accept. What she had said was true. He had acted like a selfish bastard when she had told him the truth. Now that he had come to grips with a lot of things, he was glad, thankful that she was alive. And he had a slew of questions to ask her . . . as well as wanting to ask for her forgiveness.

He thought of some of the things she had said, about all the surgeries she'd had to go through, and the type of life she had lived over the past five years. She had known he was alive, which had to be just as bad as him thinking that she was dead. And she had done it to protect him.

It would probably take a lifetime to make up for the way he'd acted earlier, but Lord knows that he would try. It didn't matter to him whether she was Sandy or Tori. What mattered was that he still loved her, and would always love her.

The sound of curtain blinds being raised, as well as the smell of fresh-brewed coffee, made Tori open her eyes. She stared up into Drake's face as he stood beside her bed with a cold glass of milk in his hand. "Good morning," he said, placing the glass on the small table next to her.

Tori felt slightly sore as she slowly raised up in bed and studied Drake's features. For some reason there was a guarded look on his face, and not a single hint in his gaze of what they'd shared the night before. A thought suddenly came to her mind. "Did you hear from Hawk?" She watched Drake study her and wondered why he was staring at her so intently.

"No, I haven't heard from Hawk," he said in a quiet yet husky voice. "I think we should talk before I contact him, but first you need to eat something. I've cooked and left breakfast for you warming in the oven. There are a few places I need to check out around here and I'll be back in about an hour."

She nodded. "All right."

She then watched as he turned and left.

. . .

An hour or so later Drake returned to the cabin. Tori had eaten breakfast and changed into a pair of denim shorts and a top. He walked into the living room where she sat curled on the sofa reading a magazine that she had found somewhere in the cabin.

He came and sat beside her. "Okay, what do you want to talk about first? Cross or us?"

Tori closed the magazine, not sure there was an "us" even after last night. The question that still plagued her mind and stoked her uncertainty was whether or not Drake could accept the woman she was now? Five years ago her life had been filled with being a soldier, a marine, one of those few good men—or women. It had also been about becoming his wife. But she was not the woman he had fallen in love with and he needed to understand that. She didn't look like the same woman, not even remotely. And although he basically looked the same, she knew deep down that he wasn't the same. Over the years they had changed on the outside as well as the inside; their values, their ideals and the very things that had made them fall in love. For the past five years she had lived alone, without a man in her life, without sharing a relationship with one. She looked forward to loving and caring for her baby but she wasn't sure she wanted to deal with an overbearing male, even one that she loved as much as she loved Drake. They would drive each other crazy in no time.

"Let's talk about Hawk," she said, deciding it was safer to go there. Besides, the sooner Drake knew what they were up against, the better. She had kept things from him long enough.

"Hawk is pretty positive that Cross is behind what's going on," she said, uncurling from her position on the sofa and turning toward him. "But he doesn't think the reason Cross is after me is because he's found out that Sandy is alive. Hawk thinks your earlier assumption is correct and that Cross is after me because of your interest in me."

Tori inhaled deeply before continuing. "It seems you were also right about something else."

Drake raised a brow. "What?"

"Rangel didn't waste me because he'd been ordered to bring me to Cross alive. According to an informant, Cross planned to torture me and send you my leftover body parts to make you think twice about involving yourself seriously with another woman again."

She watched Drake flinch at the candid picture she had painted. She also saw the look of hard, cold anger that appeared in his eyes but he needed to know what they were dealing with. Cross may have kept a low profile over the past five years, but his mind had gotten even more demented.

"There's more," she said, after giving Drake what she'd felt was enough time to digest what she'd said.

"What?" His voice was as hard and cold as the look in his eyes.

An icy chill crept up Tori's spine and she was glad his anger wasn't directed at her. What she saw in Drake was deadly anger; the kind of anger she had never seen in him before. During their days in the marines, she had seen him get angry, but never to this degree.

"You threw a monkey wrench into Cross's plans when you grabbed me before Rangel. According to Hawk, Cross got furious and has hired someone to hunt us both down and bring us to him alive."

To Tori's surprise, Drake smiled. "Alive?"

"Yes."

"How is this person supposed to accomplish that, dealing with the likes of the two of us? We're not just ordinary people."

Tori shrugged and she couldn't help returning Drake's smile. He was one cocky, arrogant, son of a—

Suddenly they heard the sound of a vehicle pulling up and, like a flash, they were off the sofa with pistols raised. Ashton and Trevor had said they would be returning some time today, but neither Tori nor Drake intended to take any chances by assuming anything.

Drake quickly eased to one window while Tori covered another. "It's Trev and Ashton," Drake said, lowering his gun and shielding his eyes against the brilliance of the rising sun that was flooding through the window.

"Yeah, but who're the other two men with them?" Tori asked, deciding not to lower her gun just yet.

Drake glanced over at her and grinned. "The younger one is Alexander Maxwell, private investigator extraordinaire, and a friend. The older gentleman is Jacob Madaris."

Tori snapped her head around and looked back out the window. She then glanced back at Drake with disbelief on her face. "Jacob Madaris? *The* Jacob Madaris? Wealthy rancher, investment genius, husband to movie star Diamond Swain-Madaris?" she asked, lowering her gun.

Drake chuckled. "Oh, I guess you've heard of him?"

Tori rolled her eyes. "Who hasn't? The man is a good friend of the president, although they belong to different political parties."

Drake shrugged. "So what of it? They're both Texans."

Tori shook her head grinning, knowing that Drake might pretend the relationship between Jacob Madaris and the president wasn't such a big deal, but she knew that it was. Over the past five years, she might not have had much of a social life, but she had kept pretty well informed by reading newspapers and magazines. Even before Jacob Madaris's marriage to movie actress Diamond Swain became news, he'd been a man who had influence in high places.

She couldn't help but check out the two men. Both were extremely good-looking. Jacob Madaris was tall, every bit of six-feet-seven or taller. He had dark eyes, chestnut colored skin, hair—a succulent blend of black and gray, and a hard-muscled body. He looked mature and sexy as hell. Everything about him said Texan, from the jeans and western shirt he wore, to the Stetson he had taken off his head.

Alexander Maxwell, she noticed, was also tall, handsome, and sexy, and where Jacob Madaris displayed an innate roughness, Alex appeared more debonair, definitely a business type. He was impeccably dressed in a chambray shirt, blazer, and starched blue jeans.

"Why do you think Trev and Ash brought them here?" she asked, her curiosity piqued.

"Probably as additional security. Alex has former FBI connections and Jake owns the land that surrounds this place, and the men who work for him are good. They would alert him if they noticed anything suspicious and we need all the help we can get; especially if Cross has sent his top gun to bring us in."

Drake put his gun back in the holster. "Also Jake Madaris's contacts are out of this world and those just might come in handy."

Tori put her gun back in her holster as well. "So in other words, we can trust them."

Drake nodded as he crossed the room to the door. "Yes, implicitly."

Trevor Grant was the first to enter the cabin and his gaze immediately went to Tori. Barely giving Drake a nod, he quickly crossed the room and pulled her into his arms.

"Ash told me," he whispered softly, hugging her tight. "I can't believe you're alive. God, how on earth did you manage?"

Tori felt herself getting emotional, but with Trevor she had no choice. He'd had a sister, just a few years younger than her, and had always treated Sandy like a big brother.

"It's okay, Trev, and I did manage," she said in a choked voice. "I learned to survive without you guys, although it wasn't easy."

He released her and smiled down at her and she knew that, as Ashton had done yesterday, he was looking for something that had remained the same, but was finding everything had changed. "Well, we're damn glad to have you back," he said. "So what will it be? Sandy or Tori?"

She glanced across the room at Drake before meeting Trevor's gaze. "Tori. I'm Tori now."

A huge smile touched Trevor's lips. "Good enough, Tori. Now let me introduce you to two men who want to help."

Taking her hand, he led her across the room to the two men Drake had indicated were Jacob Madaris and Alexander Maxwell.

Introductions were made and immediately Tori appreciated Drake, Ashton, Trevor, and their two friends.

"All right, Sir Drake, what do you think Cross's plans are?" Trevor asked as he leaned back in the chair. The kitchen had become a mini-office. Both Alex Maxwell and Jake Madaris had their laptops open. Jake's laptop monitor was displaying a computer map of all the land surrounding the cabin and was advising Drake and Tori as to what areas a vehicle could gain access without them knowing about it. He was also pointing out where, if there became a need, they could hide out and take refuge.

"If Cross wants you and Tori brought to him alive," Ashton was saying, "his guys might try using tranquilizer guns, so there are no mistakes, plus it's less messy."

Drake stopped his pacing. "Makes sense. Can't do much about a bullet wound . . . but is there any way to fight off the effects of a tranquilizer?"

"There's more than one kind of tranquilizer and the tough job is figuring out what type the men coming after you will be using," Alex said, leaning back in his chair. "If they are using the most sought-after brand on the black market today, then that's the one that's used mostly with animals, specifically livestock. However, I recall reading somewhere that there was a special antidote being tested that is supposed to counteract the serum that's used in most tranquilizer guns." He sat up straight in the chair. "Jake can explain that better than I can since he works with livestock."

Drake quickly crossed the room to Jacob Madaris. "Is that true, Jake? Is there an antidote that works against most tranquilizers?"

Jake slowly nodded. "Yes, but like Alex said, it's in the testing stages. It works more like a vaccine than an antidote in that it's injected into the body at least twelve hours before a hit might take place and stays in the system for only a limited amount of time, usually seventy-two hours. The good thing is that it's supposed to counteract most kinds of tranquilizers, but I haven't heard anything about it being tried on humans. I'd hate for you to be the first since it might be risky, Drake."

Drake shrugged. "Hey, what do I have to lose?"

"No!" The word was torn from Tori's lips before she could stop it. Everyone in the room turned to stare at her. "You heard what Jake said, Drake. It hasn't been tried on humans. You'll be placing yourself at risk."

He frowned. "And I'll be placing myself at risk if I don't try it. Someone is hunting us down and at least we have an advantage in knowing how he plans to do it. If there's a way that one of us can retain control of our capabilities and take him on, then I'm willing to give it a try."

"But what if it doesn't work? What if the antidote does more harm than good?"

He met her gaze. "Those are risks I'm willing to take."

Tori inhaled deeply. Over the past five years Drake had become a man without illusions; a man who thrived on taking risks. He didn't avoid danger, he embraced it. When he'd been a marine, he had a job to do, but he hadn't taken unnecessary risks. He hadn't been as hard, as unyielding; but not anymore. The years had changed him.

And she knew at that moment that the two of them could never have a future together. She would always love him, but when this incident with Cross was over, she would go her way and he would go his. That thought made a pain settle around her heart, but she knew there was no other way. She owed their child a normal life, not one filled with chaos and danger lurking around every corner.

"Then do what you think you must," she said, before turning to walk out the cabin.

Drake stared after her. He knew she was upset with his decision, but there was no other way. He would not sit and wait around for someone to hunt him down like some animal. And he'd be damned if he would continue to run. But more importantly, he would die before letting Cross or his men put a hand on Tori. He had nearly lost her before and didn't intend to lose her again.

"Are you sure about that antidote, Drake? Like I said, it's pretty damn risky."

Drake slowly turned around and met Jake Madaris's intense stare. "If someone had placed Diamond's life in danger and there was a way, even a small chance, that you could protect her, even if it meant putting your own life at risk, would you do it?"

"Yes," Jake said, without hesitation. "I would do anything to protect the woman that I love."

Satisfied with Jake's answer, he glanced at the other three men in the room. He knew he could ask Trevor and Ashton the same question about Corinthians and Nettie and he would get the same response. And although Alex might not realize it yet, Drake was pretty sure the man was in love with Christy Madaris, so he felt certain he would get the same response from him as well.

Drake nodded. "And so would I. I would do anything to protect the woman that I love."

The Red Hunter smiled as he tracked Sinclair on his computer. Unknowingly, Sinclair had led them straight to Warren and Green's location. This job had been a piece of cake and he couldn't wait to tell Cross.

He pulled out his mobile phone and hit the power button and immediately punched in Cross's number. "Let me talk to Cross," he said to the person who had come on the line.

It seemed like a full ten minutes passed before Cross came to the phone. "I hope you have good news for me, Red Hunter."

"I do. I'll be making the hit tonight."

"Remember, I want them alive! I have my own brand of punishment for them."

Red Hunter couldn't help the icy chill that shivered down his spine. Solomon Cross was one of the most heartless, ruthless, and cunning men that he knew. His reputation had been well-earned. The man was a sadistic killer. The sooner he was through doing business with Cross the better.

"You'll get them alive. Go ahead and make the necessary flight arrangements. I can transport them so far in my car, then I'll need a plane to get them out of the country."

"And you'll have one."

"And my money?"

Cross smiled. "One of my men will be at the airport. He will pay you off then."

Red Hunter frowned. "That was not our original plan. I was supposed to accompany Warren and Green to South America. I was to be there for the exchange."

There was a moment of silence on the other end of the line. "Very well, then. I was trying to save you an unnecessary trip."

The frown slowly eased from Red Hunter's face. "I don't mind the inconvenience," he said, relaxing again. He had worked too hard for anyone to discover he was a double agent. Casey and Chisholm had promised him a lot of money if he led them straight to Cross and he intended to do just that. Cross, on the other hand, was paying him a lot of cash to deliver Warren and Green to him alive, and he intended to collect on that as well.

"Call me when you have them," Cross said. "I'll give you further instructions at that time."

"Good," Red Hunter said, then hung up the phone.

Cross handed the phone back to Miguel. A smile touched his lips. "Tell Dominic he is to kill Red Hunter as soon as he turns my houseguests over to him. I much prefer him loosing his life in his own country rather than in mine."

CHAPTER 14

"Would you like another piece of pie?"

Shaking her head, Tori took another sip of her milk. "No, but thank you for asking." She knew her response sounded stilted, way too formal for two people who'd spent the better part of the night mating like rabbits. But here they sat, she and Drake, trying to ease the tension between them. She was still upset about his decision to take the antidote.

"I'm surprised we haven't heard from Hawk any more today," she said, putting down her glass. Earlier Hawk had been advised of Drake's decision. In fact, Drake had already been injected. Once Jake Madaris had been certain Drake knew what he was doing, he'd had one of his ranch hands bring over the medication, and once it had been delivered, everyone had waited while Drake had gone into the bathroom to inject himself.

According to Jake, the drug needed to be in the system for at least twelve hours, which meant Drake had a couple of hours to go. The only drawback to that was the uncertainty that this was the night Cross's men would make their move. Jake Madaris had posted a couple of his men in strategic locations to serve as watchmen and they had a remote alarm to send him a signal if they spotted anything unusual. For some reason, Drake thought the strike would come tonight and wanted to be prepared. Tori didn't want to think what would happen if nothing happened within the next three days. Did that mean he would give himself another injection?

"I did hear from Hawk again," Drake said after taking a sip of his coffee.

She met his gaze, surprised. "You did? When?"

"While you were taking a bath."

Tori's eyes narrowed. "And why didn't you tell me?" she asked coolly, upset that he hadn't mentioned the call to her.

Drake leaned back in her chair and looked at her. "There was nothing to tell. He's still checking out a few leads. However, he did mention that an agent is missing."

Tori lifted a brow.

"He found out from Lucille that Tom Crowley didn't report for his assignment a week ago."

"Tom? Umm, that's interesting," Tori said, leaning back in her own chair. And from the way Drake was looking at her she knew he was remembering that she and Tom had dated once.

"Yes, I think it's interesting, too," Drake finally said, getting up and breaking into her thoughts. "Hawk also said the Agency is looking into his disappearance." He looked at her empty plate. "Are you sure you don't want any more pie?"

"Yes, I'm positive and I'll help with the dishes. It's the least I can do since you did all the cooking."

He glanced back over his shoulder at her on his way to the sink. "That's not necessary. Besides, I want to stay busy."

Tori studied him. "How are you feeling?"

He turned around and smiled. "You've asked me that five times already and my answer is still the same, Tori. I feel fine. If I didn't know that I injected myself with that drug, I'd believe I imagined the whole thing."

"No side effects then?"

"No." He crossed the room to her and took her hand in his. "Hey, don't worry, I'll be fine."

A corner of Tori's lips flexed upward, annoyed, and she eased her hand from his. "This is nothing but a game to you, isn't it, Drake?"

He lifted a brow. "I don't think that being hunted down like an animal is a game for either of us, Tori."

She stood and crossed her arms over her chest. "But you enjoy the danger."

It was a statement more than a question so Drake decided to treat it as such. He shrugged. "I would enjoy it better if you weren't involved."

She glared at him. "It's okay for you to be at risk, but not for me. Is that it?"

"If I had my way, yes."

"Well, I don't like it. In fact the main reason I left the Agency is because I didn't want to take risks any longer. I decided I preferred living a safer life."

He narrowed his eyes at her. "Yeah, it's been real safe, hasn't it?"

When she just glared at him, he rubbed his chin as he studied her. "Is that why you didn't want me to know where you were after you left the Agency? You wanted a safer life and saw me as a threat to your tranquil existence?"

She met his gaze. No, actually she had seen him as a threat to her and her baby's tranquil existences. "Yes, that's the reason."

She watched his frown slowly form into a smile. She was surprised when he laughed. It was a deliciously rich sound that filled the room. She placed her hands on her hips. "What's so damn funny?"

"I found you anyway, Tori, and you were lucky that I did."

She took her hands off her hips, knowing he had a

point. "Yes, well, just because you found me doesn't mean anything."

His dark face lit with a grin. "Oh, it means a lot. After last night I thought I made things pretty clear. You're mine now."

Her hands went back on her hips. "What do you mean, I'm yours?"

Drake shrugged. "Just what I said. Last night I claimed you in the best way a man can claim a woman he wants. Heart, body, and soul."

Tori glared at him again. "Oh, but weren't you a tad confused as to just who you were claiming?"

He crossed his arms over his chest. "No. Whether you're Sandy or Tori, no big deal."

Her anger reached boiling point. "What if I think it's a big deal?"

"Why?"

She lifted a brow. Confused. "Why what?"

"Why would you think it's a big deal when I don't?"

She frowned, wondering if he was as dense as he was handsome. "Because Sandy, the woman you fell in love with, doesn't exist anymore," she snapped, wondering if he was deliberately getting her pissed off. "I'm Tori, and I feel differently about things now. In fact, when all this is over, I think we should go our separate ways and continue to live our lives the way we have for the past five years. No matter what, in everyone's mind Sandy will still be dead, you'll still be with the Agency and I plan to move someplace quiet and try to live a normal and peaceful life."

Drake resisted the urge to pull her into his arms to show her how mistaken she was about things. Instead, he said, "I hate to disappoint you, but that's not the way things are going to happen. Like I said, you're mine, and whatever problems there are between us we'll work through them."

Tori shook her head. "How can we work through the fact

that no matter what we felt about each other five years ago, we are totally different people now? We don't think or act the same way. And like I said, I feel differently about things now than I did then."

He lifted his hand to gently caress her cheek and although she wished otherwise, she felt her insides melting and that funny sensation that settled deep in her stomach. Her baby was taking sides. Drake's.

You're nothing but a softy for your daddy, she wanted to rub her stomach and say. Instead she met Drake's gaze as her breathing started coming out slow with his touch.

"Then we will get to know each other all over again, Tori. Whatever it takes, we will do it."

When moments passed and she didn't say anything, he said, "So you think you feel differently about things? About me? Then tell me if you feel differently about this." Deciding he no longer wanted to resist the urge, he leaned down and captured her mouth and when his tongue flicked over her sultry, pouty lips, she released a sigh that matched his own. He entered her mouth, reclaiming, restating. She needed to understand that whether she was Sandy or Tori, she was his. Undoubtedly. Unquestionably.

She didn't resist when, without breaking their kiss, he picked her up and carried her into the bedroom and placed her on the bed. Leaning over he began removing her clothes. Off came the little skimpy terry jumper she'd changed into after her shower. He easily peeled it off her body, seeing she wasn't wearing a bra or panties underneath. She'd definitely made things easy for him.

Once he had her completely naked, he stepped back to remove his own clothes. Their gazes held and he felt a connection and he knew at that moment what he'd said was true. She was his. He also knew that she was fighting that fact.

He returned to the bed and took her into his arms and kissed her again, needing the taste of her. Driven by a sexual need that seemed more overpowering than the night before, he wrapped her legs around him at the same moment he reached and touched her, verifying her readiness. She was hot, wet, and he spread her legs wider and the moan that was released from her throat touched him all the way to his bones.

"How differently do you feel about this, Tori?" he asked, placing kisses all over her body. "And this," he murmured silkily as he captured a nipple between his teeth and lavished it with the tip of his tongue.

"Drake . . ."

He loved the sound of his name from her lips; the voice was different, possibly even parts of the throat, but deep inside, whatever she possessed that had made him fall in love with her from the very beginning, was the same and was still there. He had fallen in love with her as Sandy and then again as Tori. He doubted there were many men who could boast of falling in love with different women who were actually one and the same.

"Love me, Drake," she whispered from her lips.

"I do," he said as he kissed her again, letting his tongue stroke every part of her mouth. And then moments later, he pulled back, gripped her hips firmly in his hand and gave her what they both wanted as he entered her, thrusting as deep as he could go and wishing there were a way to go deeper. His voice was rough, guttural as he began moving inside of her, intending to let her know she was his.

"You're mine, Tori," he whispered as his body continued to surge repeatedly into hers. He threw his head back when he felt her body shuddering and he let out a hard growl when he followed her lead with an orgasm that pulled everything out of him. And just as he knew she would do once she felt him coming, she clenched him and milked him for all he had, holding his shaft hostage inside her womb until she got her fill.

"Tori!"

It was her name that was wrenched from deep within his throat and he knew that no matter how differently she felt about some things now, this soul-deep connection they'd always shared would constantly remain the same.

Drake slipped out of the bed when he heard the alarm go off. Careful not to wake Tori, he grabbed the transmitter from the pocket of his jeans and eased out of the room to go into the kitchen. Everything was dark and he intended for it to stay that way.

"This is Drake."

"There are six men. Get ready."

Drake frowned, recognizing the voice. "Alex? What the hell are you doing here? I thought Jake had two of his men on watch."

"I sent them home. They have families and I don't. Which is also the reason I'm not calling Jake, Ashton, and Trevor like I told them I would. I did a lot of research on Solomon Cross and he's a sick bastard with a long memory. He also likes holding grudges. I wouldn't want anyone I know on his payback list."

Drake nodded. He fully understood. "Thanks. I appreciate the help. Just let me handle things and keep an eye on Tori. She means everything to me."

Alex chuckled. "Yeah, I couldn't help but notice that fact."

Then the line went dead.

Drake quickly returned to the bedroom to wake up Tori. "We have company."

She was scrambling out of the bed like a flash. "How many?"

"Six," he said as he grabbed both of their pistols off the nightstand. He then told her of his conversation with Alex. He gazed down at her. "How about if you stay inside and let me and Alex handle things, Tori?"

She glared at him. "How about if you don't piss me off, Drake Warren? This is my fight, too."

He sighed deeply. He'd known she wouldn't cooperate. Needing to kiss her this one last time, he captured her mouth in his. "That's to keep you for a while," he said after releasing her. "Come on and be careful."

Tori crawled on the ground, slowly, cautiously, firmly holding a rifle in her hand. Her pistol was in the holster for backup. She and Drake had split up. He was circling around the cabin to find a nice spot to lie and wait. According to him, Alex had counted six men but there was a chance there were more. He'd also told her that Alex had contacted Hawk who knew just who to call for their backup. They still wanted things kept quiet until he could work with the powers that be to remove Casey and Chisholm from their positions with the CIA. Until that was done, they were literally on their own.

When she felt she had found a good position she looked back at the cabin. It was dark and if she didn't know better, she would assume the occupants inside were asleep. But she did know better. Cross's men did not.

She didn't have to wait long before she spotted the first man. He was crouched low on the ground and making his way just a few feet from where she was hiding. Making sure he was alone and no one else was in sight, she emerged from the shadows, knocked his legs out from under him.

When he tried to recover, she gave him a quick, effective hard chop to the neck, deciding not to break it. The blow would render him unconscious for quite a while.

She rolled his body to the underbrush and took the gun he had dropped. He didn't have a tranquilizer gun, but had the real thing. She glanced around as she got back down to the ground. One down, five to go.

Unknown to Tori, there were only two more to go. Alex had taken down one and Drake had taken care of two. Drake scanned the darkened area, hoping that Tori was okay. They were unable to use their remotes for fear of alerting Cross's men of their location. He'd overheard the conversations between the two men just moments before they had crumbled to the ground with his blows. They had bragged about their leader, the Red Hunter's expertise in finding any prey he went after.

When Drake had heard the code name, he'd searched his memory and could not make a connection. It wasn't until he got a glimpse of the man sneaking around the side of the house that he'd known who the traitor was. He was none other than the man who had teamed up with Tori on a couple of missions, Daniel Horton. Drake had even approached Horton upon his return from South America about Tori's whereabouts. Drake knew that Horton was good at what he did and that had Drake worried. Not for himself but for Tori.

Drake decided he needed to take Horton out before he found Tori. Knowing he was taking a chance, he eased up from his position to move around to the other side of the cabin when he felt it, a sudden, piercing pain in his shoulder. He looked down and immediately knew he had been hit with a tranquilizer dart. He pulled it out, and then the world began to tilt. He staggered and the last thing he remembered before his body crumpled to the ground was Daniel Horton's smiling face, floating above him.

Tori was getting worried when she saw no signs of Alex or Drake. She started to crawl toward the cabin when suddenly, a heavy weight dropped on her, almost knocking the breath out of her and knocking the rifle from her hand. She tried to recover and pull the pistol from her holster but she suddenly found herself flipped to her back, and a huge male body straddling her, pinning her down.

He leaned in and whispered into her ears. "Just where I've always wanted you," a deep male voice said close to her ear. "On your back beneath me."

Tori flinched, recognizing the voice of Daniel Horton. She didn't want to believe that a man she once liked well enough to let her guard down and date, could deceive her this way. "Get off me, you bastard!" she screamed.

He laughed. "Not until I'm good and ready. And I might as well tell you that I had to put a bullet in your friend's head."

She went still. "Drake . . ."

He chuckled. "No, not Warren. I'm talking about Tom Crowley. He found out about my extracurricular activities and was about to turn me in, and I couldn't let him do that."

Anger consumed Tori. With lightning speed she rolled over, taking Horton with her. The surprise move momentarily gave her an advantage but before she could jump to her feet and give him a good roundhouse kick to the groin like she wanted, he grabbed her ankle and yanked her back down. She landed in a bed of grass and leaves instead of the hard, solid earth.

Horton pinned her with his body again. "Hey, don't fight it, enjoy it," he said, running his hand along her thigh, trying

to work his way toward the zipper of her jeans. "I promise it
will be a hell of a lot better than what Cross has planned for
you. And don't worry about your lover interrupting us. He's
out cold. There was enough serum in that dart to bring down
an elephant so he'll be out for a while."

He grabbed the front of her blouse and was about to rip it
off of her when a loud animalistic growl rent the air, seconds before Horton was abruptly snatched off Tori.

It was Drake.

And he was mad. Fighting mad. She scrambled to her
feet as the two men squared off. Horton had drawn a bowie
blade knife from his boot but it didn't faze Drake. The fury
in his eyes was so potent Tori knew that the knife in Horton's hand wouldn't do the man any good.

"Cross told me to bring you alive but I'm sure he'll understand if I have no choice but to kill you," Horton said
smiling, as the two men continued to circle each other.

"You touched my woman, and you shouldn't have done
that, Horton."

Horton shrugged as if Drake's words meant nothing.
"Hey, she's a looker, you should expect that kind of attention. Besides, I tried like hell for a whole month to get her
in my bed and she outright refused me, so how did you get
so damn lucky, Warren?"

"She has good taste," Drake snapped, just seconds before
he whirled and kicked the knife out of Horton's hand.

Tori blinked. In a series of lightning-quick moves Horton soon discovered he was no match for Drake, but he
seemed determined to come back for more. Horton staggered back and Drake backed away, quickly glanced over to
Tori and smiled.

"You want to finish him off?"

She smiled back, surprised but appreciative that he had
offered. "My pleasure," she said, striding forward.

Horton recovered with a cocky grin when he saw her. "Oh, you made it easy for me, Warren. And you may as well know that I have two other men and they know what to do if something happens to me."

"Shut up, Horton," Tori said, then released a side kick to his throat. He fell to the ground but was back up quickly, with the knife in his hand again.

He sprung forward but she ducked aside. It was time to end this. "You wanted me, Horton, well now I'm going to give you something to remember me by."

She knocked the knife from his hand once again. Faster than the speed of lightning, she made a series of karate kicks, then let loose one hell of a roundhouse kick to his groin. Ignoring his howl of pain, she gave him another kick to the groin, hoping she had pretty much damaged him for life.

And like the typical man, with his precious jewels damaged, he went down.

Drake walked over to her and placed an arm around her. "You okay?"

She breathed in deeply as she tried to smile. "Yeah, he's a good hunter but he can't fight worth a damn."

Drake chuckled.

She shook her head, remembering what Horton had said. "He killed Tom Crowley."

Drake sighed deeply. "Yeah, I heard him bragging and I hope he ends up rotting in jail."

Tori nodded. She hoped so, too. She then met Drake's gaze. "Why?"

He lifted a brow. "Why what?"

"Why did you let me finish him off?"

Drake held her gaze for the longest time before saying, "After what he intended to do to you, you deserved to be the one to kick his ass . . . or in this case knock his balls out of the socket."

A slow smile touched Tori's lips. "I'm glad you thought that way." She then glanced around. "Do you think there're other men around here like he claimed?"

"Probably. But I have a feeling Alex has taken care of them. Come on, let's check to make sure."

Alex had taken care of them.

Tori couldn't help but admire his handiwork as she gazed at the four unconscious bodies spread out on the ground. She jerked her head around when she heard the sound of vehicles approaching. In the first truck she recognized Jake, Ashton, and Trevor. She didn't recognize the four very handsome men who got out of the second truck.

Introductions were quickly made. Three men from the second truck were introduced as Jake's nephews, the Madaris brothers—Justin, Dex, and Clayton. The fourth man was introduced as Trask Maxwell, Alex's brother. She blinked, remembering Trask as a former professional football player, one who was still considered the greatest running back in the NFL history.

"Justin's a doctor," Jake was saying. "He lives near Dallas, but is in town visiting the family, and agreed to take a look at Drake to make sure he's doing okay after that injection."

Tori nodded, appreciating Jake's thoughtfulness. She soon discovered that Clayton Madaris was an attorney and from what she could see, he was a very smooth and efficient one. Dex Madaris was in the oil business, but according to Trevor he had come along because he enjoyed kicking butt every once in a while.

"Why the hell didn't you call us, Alex?" Ashton asked angrily, as he and Trevor approached the younger man. "You said that you would let me, Trevor, and Jake know if anything went down."

Alex grinned. "I changed my mind. I decided all of you had families to take care of and this was no place for you. I figured I could help out if Tori and Drake needed it, but I think they did just fine on their own."

He thought of the damage he'd witnessed Tori giving Horton's precious body parts. He winced and shifted uncomfortably, just thinking about it. "I'd hate to run into Tori in a dark alley. She's one hell of a fighter," he said, nodding over to Horton who was on the ground, his body curved in a fetal position as he moaned and groaned piteously.

Trevor grinned. "Oh, you got to see her in action, did you?"

"Hell yeah, and I don't envy Drake one bit."

"Damn, what a mess," Alex Maxwell said twelve hours later, after everyone was briefed on what had happened. Abram Hawk had arrived after being pulled out of retirement by the Director of Central Intelligence. Also present were the directors of the DEA and the FBI. Alex wondered if there was ever a time when the heads of the three most powerful law enforcement agencies in the country had met in one location other than D.C. There was the murder of agent Tom Crowley to deal with and as a result, a number of their agents who'd been taken into custody were either suspected of murder, on the take or had totally abused their power. Casey and Chisholm had been relieved of their duties pending a thorough investigation by the Justice Department.

Needless to say all three organizations were reeling with embarrassment and trying to find a quick, easy, and quiet way to handle things.

"Cross is still out there somewhere," Drake said as he angrily paced the room.

Hawk nodded his head. "Yes, and he'll go deeper into

hiding once word gets out about his involvement in tonight's activities. He defied the cartel's orders to keep a low
profile and they'll handle him as they see fit. It won't surprise me if they got rid of him."

"That's not a possibility I'm going to wait for, Hawk.
I've lost too much because of him," Drake said, glancing
across the room at Tori, who was being checked over by
Justin Madaris.

"Well, the only way you'll get a crack at him is if he
comes out of hiding," Hawk said, understanding how
Drake felt.

Drake stopped pacing as an idea came to mind. He met
Hawk's curious gaze. "I think I have good reason for him to
want to come out of hiding."

Hawk lifted a brow. "And what reason is that?"

"Me and Tori. You saw how desperate he was to get us,
and according to Horton, the only reason he wanted Tori
brought to him was because he thought I was interested in
her. What if he knew the truth? What if he knew that Sandy
never died in that explosion, that she cheated death and the
last laugh is on him?"

Hawk shook his head as a cold shiver slid down his spine
and spread throughout his body. "The man is demented,
Drake, a bona fide psychopath. If he even suspected she was
still alive, you and Tori's life would become a living nightmare. All hell would break loose. He'd finish the job."

"Yes, and he'd be so damn pissed he would want to do it
himself this time. He wouldn't depend on anyone else failing him."

Hawk nodded his head. "Yes, that would definitely draw
him out, but are you willing to take that chance with Tori's
life?"

"He has no choice," Tori said, from behind them. She
walked forward and stood next to Drake. "I can't continue

to run and hide and look over my shoulder, Hawk. It's time that Drake and I confront Cross face-to-face. He wants us, so it's time that he come and get us."

Hawk sighed deeply and thought about what they were saying. Casey and Chisholm had been willing to use them as bait without their knowledge. Now they were volunteering to be used to draw out Cross in order to finally end this madness. "That means we'll have to leak the information that Sandy Carroll is still alive."

"No," Drake said as a dark frown covered his face. "I have a better way. I'll call Cross myself."

Hawk raised a dark, surprised brow. "And you just happen to have his personal phone number?" he asked dryly.

Drake smiled. He then pulled out a slip of paper from the pack pocket of his jeans. "Exactly. I don't know where Cross is hiding out but thanks to Horton, I do know his private number."

"You have a call, sir."

Cross quickly took the phone from Miguel. He had been waiting for the call from Red Hunter. He had a plane standing by and was anxious to give them the word to take off to bring back his houseguests.

"I assume you're calling to let me know my houseguests will be arriving shortly," he said.

Drake laughed. "Fat chance, bastard. I was calling to let you know that Tori and I won't be visiting after all. We figured we wouldn't like the company."

Cross's hand tightened on the phone and his face filled with rage. "Warren!"

"Umm, I see that you remember me. And don't waste time asking about the Red Hunter. Let's just say he's a little indisposed at the moment."

The vein in Cross's neck almost strained in anger. "You'll pay for what you've done."

"Your ass will be too busy hiding out from the cartel to worry about me. It won't be long before they find out that you defied them. They won't like you being a bad little boy. But I thought I'd give you something to think about while you're on the run for your life. You screwed up, Cross. You screwed up tonight but most importantly you screwed up five years ago. You didn't kill Sandy. The CIA outsmarted you. They let you think you killed Sandy but she still lives, Cross. The woman I love is still living and you were too stupid to put two and two together to figure out who she was."

"You lie, Warren!"

Drake would swear he could feel the heat of Cross's fury all the way through the phone line. "If you don't believe me, find out the truth for yourself. I have my woman back and I plan on spending the rest of my life making up for lost time."

"I will find you and kill you both."

"No, you won't. You'll be too busy hiding out to save your own ass. Face it, Cross, your eye-for-an-eye bullshit has become an 'everybody plays the fool sometime.' You've been played."

The line then went dead.

Cross's knuckles turned almost white as he stood there and continued to hold the phone. Moments later, letting out a loud animalistic howl, he threw it against the wall.

"Miguel!"

The man came immediately. "Yes, sir."

"I need you to make calls to my contacts in the United States. I need information quickly."

"Yes, sir!" He watched as Miguel quickly left. He didn't have time to worry about the cartel's displeasure with him at the moment. He could hold them off for a while, especially when they discovered they no longer had the power they thought they had. One call to a number of rebel groups he had under his thumb would scare off the cartel. Right now he had more important issues to deal with.

Nobody played him for a fool.

Excitement suddenly replaced the anger that was ramming through him. Warren's days were numbered. Sandy Carroll may not have died five years ago but he would make sure she was enjoying her last days of life now. He would take pride in having her blood on his hands; and he would take pride in having Warren's blood on his hands as well.

An eye for an eye.

Cross inhaled deeply. He intended to personally see that Maria's death was avenged.

Drake inhaled deeply and forced himself to breathe out slowly as he hung up the phone. The gauntlet had been thrown down and the battle lines were officially drawn. No, it wouldn't be a battle, it would be a damn massacre, at least that would be Cross's way of thinking.

Drake's gaze slowly moved across the room to the two people who were watching him, Hawk and Tori; but mainly Tori. It was their battle and they were determined to see it to the finish. "Cross will come," he said quietly with absolute certainty. "He's desperate, obsessed, determined, and he strongly believes he'll get his 'eye-for-an-eye' bull."

Drake inhaled deeply again. He didn't want to admit it, but he knew the feeling. He'd felt that way after Sandy had died—or when he'd thought she had died. Especially when Cross had come forward and claimed responsibility. He had wanted to become a one-man hit squad, go after the SOB and blow his brains out; and for a time he had contemplated doing just that.

But Ashton and Trevor wouldn't let him wallow in self-pity or hatred. They had refused to let him sink to Cross's level by becoming a cold-blooded killer, dead set on revenge. But he had thought about it. He had planned and plotted to waste everyone he thought had been responsible for Sandy's death; the entire damn cartel. Dying had not been something he'd worried about. In fact, he'd figured when it happened it would be a blessing. He had gone through those months feeling that he'd rather be dead than alive without Sandy.

His chest went tight as he remembered those times. That was the past and this was the present, and he wished he could consider it as water under the bridge but Cross was still around muddying those waters.

"So what do you think will be his next move, Drake?"

He looked Tori directly in the eye when he answered her question. "First he'll verify my claim that you're alive. Once he's satisfied it's true and it's not a setup, he'll plan our downfall and use every arsenal at his disposal to do so. And because of his position within the cartel, he won't wait to make a hit."

He stepped from behind the pool table and glanced out the window. Trevor, Ashton, Jake, and the others had gone outside to give them privacy. He slowly turned back to Hawk and Tori.

"Horton was a wealth of information and one of the things he told us was that Cross's position with the cartel is better than we think. In fact, it's better than the cartel thinks. While keeping a low profile Cross has been busy gaining support from several leftist rebel forces; rebels who have agreed to protect him. He in turn agreed to provide them the financing they need to fight their bloody wars. They see it as a 'you scratch my back and I'll scratch yours' situation because Cross is willing to aid their fight against the government; something the present cartel has refused to do."

Hawk grimaced. "Heaven help us all if Cross becomes head of the ASI."

"He won't live long enough to take the throne. I'm going to see to it."

Hawk went rigid when he saw the intent in Drake's eyes. "You can't do this alone, Drake. You can't become a one-man hit squad."

Drake smiled slowly. "Believe it or not, that's exactly what I'd thought of doing five years ago, but, no, that's not what I plan to do now. I sort of like to compare myself to the Terminator better."

Hawk's gaze narrowed. "This isn't funny, Drake."

"And you don't see me laughing, Hawk. Cross is coming after me and I plan to use whatever means I can to keep me and Tori alive."

"And you will get help," Hawk said, coming to his feet. "I'll guarantee it."

Drake shook his head, chuckling. "Forgive me for not wanting to fully trust the CIA, FBI or DEA about now. What went on here with Horton has somewhat sullied my opinion of the agencies. The only good thing I have to say about the CIA is that you're back, and I know you'll clean house. But you're only one man, Hawk. You have to take your orders like everyone else and at the moment I refuse to believe that the Agency is going to support everything you want to do."

Hawk sighed deeply, knowing Drake was right. Because of Casey and Chisholm, the Justice Department would be initiating a full-fledged investigation; and in the meantime every department within the agency would have to be on their P's and Q's and play strictly by the rules. "So what do you plan to do?" he asked Drake.

The smile that had appeared on Drake's face moments earlier faded. Now there was intensity in the depths of his eyes, the firmness of his jaw and the flaring of his nostrils that made Hawk glad that he wasn't the enemy. "I plan to do nothing, but sit and wait. I'm sure with all his contacts, Cross will eventually find me."

Hawk took a deep breath. "And when he does?"

"I'll deal with him."

"Then *we'll* deal with him," Tori spoke up and said, glancing from Drake to Hawk.

Hawk studied them both for long moments. They were more than operatives who had worked for him, marines who'd served under him. They were two people he genuinely cared about, and he knew he had to make them see reason. "The two of you are making a mistake. Besides, what you want to do is out of the question. You will be breaking the law and—"

"The only law on Warren Mountain is *my* law."

Hawk stiffened. His heart skipped a beat. "What the hell do you mean?"

Drake smiled. "Just what I said. Pull the documentation that goes all the way back to when the land was deeded to my ancestors. Warren Mountain is as protected as any Indian reservation is. It has its own law and until that changes no federal, state or local governmental agency can trespass its boundaries unless I give permission, and I'm not giving it."

Hawk stared at him. Cold chills crept up his spine. "You're not saying what I think you're saying, are you?"

"Yes. I'm going home, Hawk, and when Cross finds me, that's where I'll be."

Hawk blew out a long breath, raked his fingers through his hair, thinking he needed a haircut, but more important, he needed another thirty years to deal with the likes of Drake Warren. And just to think he had agreed to come out of retirement. Had he taken leave of his senses or what? "Think about what you'd be doing, son," Hawk said, altering their positions from business to personal. "Without backup forces from the government, your mountain will become a war zone—a slaughter territory. Do you honestly think Cross will come by himself? He'll bring men with him, trained killers of the most ruthless and cunning kind. He'll intend for it to be a showdown, one he doesn't plan losing."

"Then it should be interesting because I don't plan on losing either," Drake said quietly. He shifted his eyes and caught Tori's gaze. He drew in a deep breath and tried to rid himself of the anger he was feeling. "But I would like to ask that you do me a favor, Hawk."

Hawk lifted a brow. During the years he'd known Drake, he had only asked for one favor and that had been a few months ago when he was trying to find Tori. It was the first favor Drake had ever asked of him and it had hurt like hell to turn him down. He wondered if he would also have to turn down this second request. "What's this favor?"

"No matter what you have to do, keep Tori safe. She's not a part of this. I'll be operating alone."

Tori whirled on him. "The hell you will. This isn't your fight alone, Drake! I thought we agreed on that. This is also my fight and I'm definitely in." She was so mad, her voice was shaking.

Drake stared at her. He had expected her anger and was prepared to deal with it. He would never forget how he'd felt when he'd gone down from that tranquilizer dart. Luckily, the injection he had taken had kicked in. But what would have happened to Tori if it hadn't? "No, you're not in," he said. "The only reason Cross tried killing you in the first place was because of me. This is not your battle, it's mine, and I'll come and get you when it's over."

Tori's lips tightened as she tried to bring her anger under control. What had she expected? Drake Warren thrived on taking risks, but he was too bullheaded to see that what he was contemplating wasn't taking a risk but setting himself up on a suicide mission. There was no way one man could stand against Cross's ruthlessness.

"You might as well let me go with you, Drake, because there's no way I'll stay behind. Even if I'm locked up somewhere, I'll escape and then what? What do you think Cross will do when he finds out that I'm not on that mountain with you? He'll either finish you off and come after me or vice versa. There'll be no place for me to hide, not that I intend to hide anyway."

Her spine went ramrod straight as she continued to glare at him. "We either deal with Cross together or we deal with him separately, Drake. What's it going to be?"

Drake gazed at her thoughtfully for a long moment and she stared back at him defiantly, haughtily, full of anger and fire. And she was so deep-in-the-gut beautiful. He wished there was some way he could lock her up and throw away the key, but damn her hide, she would probably find a way to escape, and then he'd be too busy worrying about her safety to take care of Cross. At least if she was with him then he could keep an eye on her. And if things got too heavy, he had that room in the basement that had a steel door and no windows. If he had to, he would use it. He'd like to see her get out of that.

"Fine," he snapped. "Just be ready to move out at midnight." He then turned to leave.

Tori didn't stop holding her breath until the door had slammed shut behind Drake.

CHAPTER 15

"This place is just as I remembered, beautiful," Tori said as she glanced at the vast land and the high, rough mountains surrounding her. Although this wasn't her first time to Warren Mountains, the view still left her utterly breathless. As far as her eyes could see the blue sky dipped rhythmically around mountains, plains, and valleys that seemed to have no end.

"Thanks," Drake said, pulling her one piece of luggage out of the car. "I want to get you settled then I'll put the security system in place."

Tori turned and looked at him. "You have a security system here?" she asked in surprise. That was one thing she didn't recall him having before.

"Yes. It became necessary when I discovered people were trespassing on my property. They were camping out and hunting down the animals that consider this home," he said, anger lacing his voice. "I set up security cameras in strategic locations to put a stop to it and to make sure violators are dealt with to the full extent of the law," he continued. "I have no control over what happens while I'm gone, but whenever I'm here I make sure it's kept under control."

Tori nodded. Drake's love of nature hadn't changed. He

would spend hours telling her about all the wild animals that roamed Warren Mountains and found refuge in the five thousand acres that he owned. He had also once told her that since he was the last of the Warrens, he would deed Warren Mountains to the Tennessee Wildlife Preservation Society to assure that his land remained in its natural state after his death.

She glanced around again, as she climbed the steps to the huge shady porch that wrapped around the ranch-style structure, a mixture of stone and wood that provided an overwhelming view of Warren Mountains in all directions. She remembered standing on the porch one night and seeing a deer and before dusk had claimed the evening, she had seen a fox, rabbits, and what looked like a huge wolf as well.

Drake had told her what she'd seen was not a full-blooded wolf, but a half-wolf he called Tender Two. The dog's mother had been a full-blood wolf and the father had been the Warren's family dog, Tender. After the pup's mother had been killed by a trespasser's bullet, Tender had roamed the mountains to claim his son and had returned with him to the ranch. However, Tender Two never fully appreciated the tight reins of domestic life and after Tender's death, he spent more time out in the wilds than he did in Drake's home. But Drake said they understood each other since they both were loners. Before she'd left, she and Tender Two had become good friends.

She looked up at Drake. "Tender Two? Is he still alive?"

Drake smiled, surprised she had remembered his dog. "Yes. The last few times I was home he stayed here, close by my side, as if he knew I needed the company. He might show up while you're here, but don't be shocked when you see him. Now he looks more like a wolf than a dog."

Tori nodded as she followed Drake into the house. The

inside of his home was just as she remembered. As soon as she stepped through the doors she entered a huge foyer made of beautiful tile and whose wall was lined with portraits of deceased Warrens.

Once you stepped out of the foyer into the massive living room the rest of the house connected to halls that went in three directions, each containing bedrooms and baths. There were six bedrooms and four bathrooms in all. Instead of going upward the house had been built spread out to encompass the land. The large eat-in kitchen was on the left and connected to a spacious family room. The house was a huge, rambling single-story structure with a basement.

Drake had once told her that the house had been built to hold a lot of Warrens, but due to health reasons Drake's grandmother had had only one child, Drake's father, Deke. Deke Warren had given his heart to the wrong woman and after a short marriage that produced only one son, she ran off with another man, never to be heard from again. Deke Warren, bitter over his wife's betrayal, never remarried and died years later in a hunting accident, which made Drake the lone surviving Warren after his grandparents' death. Tori knew how much Drake loved his home and was so entranced by everything she was seeing again that she jumped when his hand touched her arm.

"It will be best if we stay on the same side of the house," he said.

"That's fine," she responded, grateful that he hadn't assumed they would be sharing a bed. She followed him down a huge hall to a beautifully decorated guest room with shiny hardwood floors and an intriguing design of wallpaper that enhanced the solid blue curtains and bedspread. Although it appeared to have the tone of a masculine room, a huge vase of dried flowers sat on the nightstand next to the bed. And just like she knew from memory, a stone fireplace was in every bedroom.

"Everything looks neat and comfortable," she said, turning around in appreciation, trying to keep her gaze off the bed. It was too big for one person and just the right size for two.

"Although I'm not here most of the time, I have a woman from town who was a friend of my grandmother, Mrs. Gillette, drop by every so often to keep the place up. I contacted her before leaving Houston and asked that she pick up a few things from the grocery store so I wouldn't have to go out," Drake said, placing her luggage on the bed.

Tori forced her attention away from the size of the bed to what Drake was saying. "That was a good idea."

He turned to face her again. "I'll leave you to rest up while I switch the security system. The one on now is the one I use to alert the local police of anything when I'm away for long periods of time."

She raised a brow. "But I thought you said the law enforcement authorities have no jurisdiction on your land."

"They don't, except for when I give it to them. The local cops and I have an understanding. Besides, Roy and I grew up together."

She raised her brow again. "Who's Roy?"

"The sheriff. You didn't meet him the last time you were here because he moved back to these parts from Wyoming a few years ago." He glanced at his watch. "I'll also start something for dinner." He met her gaze and grinned. "I also asked Mrs. Gillette to make sure she bought a gallon of milk since you seem to enjoy drinking it."

Her pulse accelerated with the look of amusement on his face. He had such a sexy grin. "Thanks."

He nodded. She then watched as he turned and walked out of the bedroom, closing the door behind him.

. . .

Tori wasn't sure how long she had slept but she awoke from her nap to the smell of chicken frying. She slowly pulled herself up in bed, still feeling somewhat tired.

After Drake had left her alone she had quickly unpacked. Then gathering some clean clothes in her arms, and being careful not to drop anything this time, she had walked across the hall to the bathroom where she had indulged herself in a long leisurely bath in the oversized tub. Then she had returned to the bedroom, stretched across the bed, and wearing nothing but an oversized T-shirt and panties, had dozed off.

Standing, she slipped out of the T-shirt and went into the closet to get the skirt and blouse she had hung up earlier. Within minutes she was dressed and walking down the hall to where she knew the kitchen was located.

Drake glanced up from stirring something at the stove when she walked in. "I see you remembered your way," he said, smiling.

"Yes, but it would not have mattered if I hadn't. I would have simply followed the smell of food."

He chuckled. "Hungry?"

She nodded. "Starving."

"Good. Everything is ready and I can bring you up to date on a call I received from Hawk an hour or so ago while we eat."

Tori nodded again. "While you're finishing with that, I'll set the table," she said.

"Thanks."

Drake watched as she walked over to the cabinets and began taking down plates. He stopped stirring the pot of vegetables to watch her. Just like before when he had brought her here as Sandy, she was making herself right at home and he liked that. What he didn't like was the way she was trying to put distance between them, but he was willing to give her the space she seemed to need.

He wasn't stupid. He knew that no matter what they'd shared before, and no matter how many times they managed to occasionally fall into the same bed now, in a way they were virtual strangers. So much had happened for both of them over the past five years; now with the Cross situation, they hadn't had the opportunity to really get to know each other again. He knew he still loved her but he wasn't absolutely sure just how she felt about him. He wasn't the same man she had fallen in love with years ago. Now he saw more bad in people than good, and he no longer trusted easily. He no longer took things at face value. Yes, he wasn't the same man and the big question was whether or not she could accept that.

He inhaled deeply. Once this situation with Cross was behind them, he intended to find out.

Tori turned to find Drake watching her intently. She cleared her throat. "What do you want to drink? I can fix up some tea or something," she said, after seeing the jar of tea bags on the counter.

"Thanks, tea will be fine."

Moments later when they sat down at the table together, she couldn't help but remember what had happened after the last time they had eaten together. He had been driven to prove that although she felt differently about some things now, there were other things she still felt the same about. He'd also wanted to prove to her that he considered her "his" woman.

After saying the grace for the both of them she asked, "What did Hawk have to say?"

Drake glanced up after pouring gravy on his chicken.

"He wanted to let me know that Cross is trying desperately to find us. Like with most operatives, where I live is a closely guarded secret. However, Hawk feels it won't take long for him to find out about this place."

Tori nodded. "Anything else?"

He gazed at her for a moment then said, "Yes. It seems that Cross has checked out my story and although Hawk didn't make it easy for him, Cross got confirmation from whatever resources he's using that Sandy Carroll is still alive and the two of you are one and the same."

Tori went rigid. She knew it was bound to happen, that it was part of the plan, but still it felt eerie that a secret she had worked five years to protect was now out in the open. "So how much time does Hawk think we have?"

"No more than three days, possibly four at the max. There are no signs that Cross has entered the country yet. Hawk also said that getting men together to help him do his dirty work isn't as easy as Cross thought it would be. After what went down with Horton, a lot of the corrupt agents are keeping a low profile, hoping that no one finds out about their extracurricular activities; and those slimeballs connected to the drug scene aren't absolutely sure of Cross's claim that he'll eventually be the head of the ASI and are cautious about doing anything to piss off the present leaders of the organization."

Tori was silent for a moment, then she asked, "So what's our game plan?"

Drake met her gaze. "Get prepared and be ready. As soon as we finish up here, I want to take you downstairs and show you the security system I have in place and how it works."

She nodded. He had told her earlier that he'd converted his basement into a state-of-the-art security room.

"I have hidden video cameras located in various areas on my land," he added. "One of the features of my security system is a huge monitoring screen where I can just sit back and watch all the creatures that are roaming around. How would you like to do that with me later?"

Tori lifted a brow. "Don't you ever feel like you're spying on them?" she asked, forcing a smile. She thought about sitting in a closed room with Drake and watching anything and knew it wouldn't be a good idea.

He chuckled. "They're on my property so that gives me the right. So what about it? After showing you the security system, how would you like to see an authentic wildlife film in the making?"

Tori licked her bottom lip nervously then said, "Okay, I'll spy on your wildlife with you," knowing as she said the words that she was probably making a big mistake. "So you're into modern technology these days?" she asked, curiously. She didn't recall him having such an interest before.

He smiled over at her. "Sort of. I got interested when I had a lot of free time on my hands after that Haiti mission. Because of what happened, the top brass in the Marine Corps felt I needed at least six months off to get myself back together. During that time I distracted myself by doing things with my hands. Roy is a whiz with technology and on his days off he came around and helped me set things up."

A short while later they finished eating and cleaned up the kitchen together. Tori was surprised at how quickly he had gotten over being upset that she had forced her way into coming here. In fact it seemed that her presence was not bothering him at all.

"Ready?"

Tori looked up at him and nodded, but she doubted if she would ever be fully ready for Drake Warren. "Yes, I'm ready," she replied, unable to calm the rapid and intense thump of her heartbeat.

"Watch your step on your way down."

"All right."

Before she could recover from his closeness, he took her hand in his. His touch immediately sent a sexual current radiating through her that she felt all the way to her toes. She glanced up at him and knew he had felt it, too. But he didn't say anything as he led her out of the kitchen toward the hall that went to the basement.

He stood back and let her go down the stairs before him.

The moment her foot touched the last step she gazed around, impressed at what she saw. It looked like a miniature security control room that contained a computer, several television screens and some sort of state-of-the-art control panel. All of the screens were turned on and were showing different areas of his land. Although it was nighttime, the moon's glow provided more than sufficient light to see certain areas.

She took a deep breath. This particular room must have been where he spent most of his time whenever he came home. It was set up like a mini-apartment with a small refrigerator and microwave on one side of the spacious room, a table with chairs and a love seat as well as a double bed on the other side. She tried not to concentrate too long on the bed. Like the one she had been sleeping in, it looked just the right size for two people.

"This is quite a setup," she managed to say when she heard him come to stand directly behind her.

"Yes, and using it to deal with Cross will give us an advantage. Nothing and no one can penetrate Warren Mountains without me knowing about it."

His use of the word *penetrate* caused another image to fill Tori's mind. She would never forget their first time together and how after kissing her senseless, not to mention the way he had nibbled and licked her to sweet oblivion, getting her unbelievably wet, he had slid his hips between her spread thighs, teasing her with a rubbing motion of his body over hers, making her moan and groan till she thought her throat would go raw, before he had finally given her what she'd wanted and entered her, penetrating deep into her virginal core and introducing her to the most wild and erotic lovemaking of her life. All of their mating sessions after that only got better.

Tori fought to steady her pulse, forcing that memory away as well as the others that wanted to follow. Stepping back she watched as he took a step forward and moved toward the first screen.

"This shows the north section of my property. This camera is well-hidden high in the trees with a scanner." He chuckled. "It frustrated the hell out of the squirrels when they discovered it wasn't a huge nut they could carry off somewhere to save for winter."

Tori smiled. "I'm sure it must have been frustrating to find that out," she said, trying not to look directly into Drake's eyes. She glanced at another screen and her smile widened. "Look!" she said, pointing at another screen. "There's a fox out tonight. Isn't he beautiful?"

Drake laughed. "It's a she, Tori."

"Oh." She decided not to ask him how he could tell so clearly in the dark but evidently he knew his animals.

For the next few minutes he went over the security system with her, going into details of how it worked, showing her the other screens and what he often viewed on them. He also told her about the motion sensors he had installed around the house as well as the ones he had positioned at any location where someone could gain access to his land by use of a vehicle or plane.

She listened attentively, for the moment putting her attraction to him out of her mind. She had to remember a killer intended to hunt them down and was coming here to do it.

"So what do you think of this setup?"

Tori smiled over at him. "Like you said, it will be an advantage in dealing with Cross," she said, leaning back in her chair. "When will you show me around the property?"

"Tomorrow; and there are a number of other things we need to do to get prepared."

Tori nodded. She knew the waiting would be the hardest part; the waiting as well as not knowing exactly what to expect. Hawk still wasn't happy that Drake would not use the CIA as backup. He didn't want any restrictions and was determined to work on his own.

"I guess you're tired and ready to go back to bed," he said in a soft voice that was laden with huskiness. He extended his hand out to her to help her out of her chair. The moment their hands touched a sizzling current flowed through her. When she stood, their eyes met and she knew he had felt it, too.

"Drake?"

"Yes?"

"We need to keep our minds focused on other things . . . like staying alive." She watched as he drew in a deep breath.

"All right, but when this business with Cross is over . . ."

She glanced away, not able to look into his eyes any longer because she knew when the business with Cross was over, she still intended to get on with her life without him. There was no way she could share her and her baby's life with a man who continued to take risks. She refused to sit around waiting for him to get himself killed.

"I think I'll go on to bed now," she said, deciding not to comment on what he'd just said.

He lifted a brow. "It's still early."

"I know, but I have a book Corinthians gave me that I'd like to finish reading."

He nodded. "I'm glad that you got to meet Corinthians and Nettie."

She smiled as she remembered the two women and the warmth that had flowed from them. She was happy for Trevor and Ashton. They had married women who were truly as special as Drake had said they were. "I'm glad I got to meet them, too. Now, I'd better go."

"All right. After breakfast I'll show you around."

"Okay." Without looking back, she quickly climbed the stairs to go to her bedroom.

Drake sat in front of the huge monitor screen with his legs stretched out in front of him, as he watched a family of raccoons sprint about, looking for food. He smiled when he thought of Tender Two. A few minutes earlier, he had zoomed in on him and it seemed his old friend had a mate; it also appeared from the looks of his companion that he would be a father soon.

He smiled as he stood up and checked his watch. It was late, almost midnight, but he wasn't sleepy. He was restless. He remembered one night when Tori had been restless and how they had handled the problem, but he knew there would be no relief for him. She was right, they needed to keep their mind focused on one thing and one thing only.

He wished his body understood that.

He sighed deeply. For his own sanity he needed to concentrate on something. He moved over to the bookcase and decided he might try reading a good book when he saw the photo album. He automatically reached for it and slowly opened it up.

His heart caught. They were pictures he and Sandy had taken together and as he looked at them, the woman in the photos looked nothing like the woman sleeping upstairs in one of his bedrooms. Both women were beautiful. Yet there were differences that couldn't be seen in a photograph, but qualities that he loved.

With Sandy, it had been the little things, like the way she could make him laugh no matter how bad his day had gone, the way she would look at him and give him that 'come-and-get-it' smile, the way she was so positive about life in general, even when they were on a dangerous mission. With Tori . . . there was everything about her that drew her to him. She was a grown-up, more matured version of Sandy, who had seen and experienced things that no longer were positive, yet it hadn't made her cynical; more cautious, yes, but not cynical. She had gotten rough around the edges in a way that literally turned him on, and her mouth had gotten sassier. Sandy had been his kind of woman then, but Tori was definitely his kind of woman now.

Closing the album he leaned against the bookcase. There was no way he could risk losing the woman he loved again. He would do anything to keep her safe, even if at some point it meant walking away.

The thought nearly pierced his heart and cut into his soul. He sighed, bowed his head and prayed that it never came to that.

Houston, Texas
Ashton Sinclair suddenly awakened, drenched in sweat. He'd had another dream about Sir Drake. An uneasy feeling settled in his gut.

Easing out of bed, being careful not to wake Nettie, he left his bedroom and went into the kitchen to use the phone.

It was late, but he needed to call Trevor and hoped he didn't wake up the entire Grant household in the process.

He sighed when Trevor picked up on the second ring, and amazingly he sounded wide-awake. "Trev, this is Ashton. What are you doing up?"

He nodded when Trevor told him he was watching a basketball game on television. "Look, man, I just had a vision. Sir Drake needs us."

CHAPTER 16

"Hello, Mrs. Gillette," Drake greeted the older woman who was putting away the additional groceries he had called and asked her to pick up.

He and Tori had gotten up early and walked his property. Then later they had installed additional sensors as well as checked on a few others to make sure they were angled the way he'd wanted. After returning to the cabin he had taken a bath and when he'd gotten out of the shower, he had run into Tori in the hallway. At first she hadn't seen him but when she'd turned, she had caught his gaze and held it steady while heat had thrummed all through him.

Even from the distance separating them, he could feel her temperature rise and the only thing that had stopped him from crossing the room and taking her into his arms was the alarm that had gone off, alerting them that someone had gained access to his property. It didn't take him long to discover it was Mrs. Gillette delivering more groceries. He had introduced her to Tori before Tori had excused herself to go take her own shower.

"I see you and your houseguest are putting down a lot of milk," Mrs. Gillette said, reclaiming Drake's attention.

He chuckled as he grabbed an apple off the counter.

"Hey, don't blame me, it's all Tori's doing. She seems to just love the stuff."

Mrs. Gillette smiled as she watched him take a big plug out of the fruit. "Well, that's understandable."

Drake lifted a brow. "What is?"

"Her drinking milk."

He gave the older woman a reluctant grin and wondered why she would think that such a thing was understandable. So he decided to ask. "Why is it understandable for her to drink milk?"

Mrs. Gillette walked past him to put a couple of canned goods in his pantry. He was right on her heels. "Because of her condition," she said, placing the items on the shelf.

Drake stilled; momentarily stopped breathing. When he was able to breathe again, he grabbed Mrs. Gillette's hand. She glanced up at him, startled. "Drake? What's wrong?"

Instead of answering her question, he had one of his own. "What condition are you talking about?"

Mrs. Gillette studied him for a few moments. Then she looked behind her to make sure Tori wasn't around. "If you don't know, then I'm not sure it's my place to tell you," she whispered. She then moved across the room to get her purse off the table. She looked at him and a tiny smile touched her lips. "All I have to say, Drake Warren, is that after giving birth to eight kids, I know the signs and consuming a lot of milk is just one of them." She lifted a brow. "Being a man I'm surprised you haven't noticed any of the others."

Without saying anything else, Mrs. Gillette went to the door, opened it and walked out, closing it behind her.

Drake leaned back against the counter as his heart started racing. He took deep breaths to calm himself down but it wasn't working. Why did Mrs. Gillette think Tori was pregnant? What signs was she talking about?

He slowly walked into the living room, pulled the drapes back and watched Mrs. Gillette leave. She was no longer there for him to ask. The only person who could answer that question was Tori.

All I have to say, Drake Warren, is that after giving birth to eight kids, I know the signs. . .

The older woman's words rang in his ears. Could she be right? He continued to stand at the window, staring out. Had Tori deliberately lied to him about not being pregnant? God help her if she had, he thought as anger consumed him. He thought of what had happened in Houston—the danger she'd been in, her fight with Horton, and his anger escalated. If she was pregnant, she had placed herself and their baby at risk . . . and with Cross planning to show up any day, they were still at risk.

He balled his hands into fists at his side. He hoped for Tori's sake that Mrs. Gillette had read the signs wrong.

When Tori walked into the bedroom after taking her shower, she stopped short. Drake was sitting in the chair next to the bed holding a cold glass of milk in his hand.

She gently brushed the damp hair back from her face as she studied him. "Drake, what are you doing in here?"

He met her gaze; held it. "I thought you might like a glass of milk," he said, placing the glass on the small table next to the bed.

Tori studied his features and could tell he was upset about something. "Did you hear from Hawk?"

He continued to watch her, silently, intently. "No, I didn't hear from Hawk," he replied quietly, almost in a deadly tone.

Tori pulled her robe together, beginning to feel nervous. What was wrong with him? She clenched her jaw to stop from screaming the question at him. When time ticked on and he didn't say anything, just continued to stare at her, she couldn't take it any longer. "Drake, why are you upset?"

He slowly stood. "Is there any particular reason why I should be upset, Tori?"

She swallowed as she saw the anger that lined his face. "I don't know. Is there?"

He met her gaze and more anger deepened the grooves around his eyes. "Oh, yes, there certainly is." He tossed her bottle of prenatal vitamins on the bed. "Would you like to explain these?"

Tori quickly crossed the room and picked up the bottle. Fire blazed in her eyes when she looked up at him. "You went through my things! My personal belongings!"

Drake lost his composure—the little bit he'd been holding onto. "Damn right! I wouldn't have had to resort to such tactics if you'd been honest with me from the beginning. Are you pregnant?"

She met his gaze, felt his anger. He was going to give her hell. Double hell. She tilted her chin upward. "Yes, I'm pregnant."

"And the child is mine."

It was a statement and not a question but Tori answered anyway. "Yes, it's yours."

Hearing her say it, hearing her admit she carried his child, took some of the punch out of Drake's anger; but not all of it. "Why didn't you tell me the truth when I asked you about it, Tori?" he asked in a somewhat gentler voice. "You'd even told me that you would contact me if you were pregnant. Why didn't you?"

Tori met his gaze and immediately she saw the hurt in his eyes. "Because I knew that we could never have a future together, Drake. You didn't know my true identity and I couldn't tell you who I was. Besides that, you were a CIA operative and I was getting out of the business. I couldn't live my life putting my child in constant danger."

Her quiet answer did little to quell the anger he felt. "What gave you the right to make a decision on my behalf, Tori? For all you knew, I could have been willing to walk away from the Agency."

Tori raised a doubtful brow. "I didn't think there was one thing that could get you to leave the CIA. You live for the risks. It's part of who you are."

Drake's shoulders were ramrod straight, his jaw set and his eyes were dark with emotion. "There isn't one thing that could have pulled me away, but there are two. To keep you and my child from danger, I would have walked away in a heartbeat without looking back."

Tori was stunned. "Are you sure I would have been included in the mix? Even when you had no idea I was Sandy?"

He raised a brow as if surprised at her question. "Of course."

Tori sighed. She had hoped he would be a little bit more forthcoming than that, but she was satisfied. "But I didn't know that, Drake, and maybe you're right that I should have told you, but I didn't. I made a decision based on what I thought was best for our child under the circumstances."

"Your pregnancy was my fault. I didn't use a condom."

Tori shook her head. "It wasn't anyone's fault. We got carried away that night and lost our heads. I knew who you were although you didn't know who I was. More than anything I wanted to be with you that night. I didn't deliberately get pregnant, but when I discovered that I was, more than anything, I wanted our child."

He studied her for a long moment, glad to hear her say those words. Then he asked, "And how have you been feeling?"

She saw concern in his eyes. "I've been fine," she assured him. "So far this pregnancy has been a breeze. I haven't had any morning sickness and feel relatively fit."

He nodded. "How far along are you, actually?"

"Three months as of yesterday."

"You aren't showing," he said, his gaze focusing on her stomach. "Nettie was already showing at three months."

Tori smiled. "Nettie was carrying triplets. I'm having just one baby, Drake."

He lifted a brow. "Boy or girl?"

Tori shook her head and grinned. "I have no idea. It's too early to tell."

Drake shrugged. "Doesn't matter. Either one will be a future marine."

Tori nodded. She could agree on that.

Drake took a step closer to her, closed the distance separating them and, after opening her bathrobe, his hand moved in a shaky path across her flat stomach. "And you're sure there's a baby in here?"

Tori was so mesmerized by the tenderness she heard in Drake's voice that she almost couldn't talk over the lump that formed in her throat. Nor could she hold back the tears that threatened to fall from her eyes. "Yes, I'm sure there's a baby in there. We communicate all the time and it knows you're its father. It has officially met you already."

Drake lifted a confused brow. "It has?"

"Yes. The first time we made love in the cabin," she said, her eyes sparkling with amusement.

Drake looked deeply into her eyes and then he pulled her into his arms, capturing her mouth before sweeping her into his arms and placing her on the bed. She reached up and wound her arms around his neck as he lowered his mouth to hers for another kiss. And as their tongues tangled and mated, Tori knew Drake intended to send her into heaven yet once again.

Slowly, coming back down to earth, Tori became aware of everything around her as she opened her eyes.

Amazing, she thought. Drake Warren was simply amazing. He had used his hands and mouth to drive her so insane that when he had finally entered her with one quick thrust, she had come immediately, screaming out so loud that she thought it was a good thing he didn't have neighbors for miles.

Then he had kissed her stomach over and over while whispering to their child promises that he intended to keep the both of them safe and that he couldn't wait to meet him or her.

Tori had witnessed aside of Drake she had never seen before. The powerfully-built man who possessed such a commanding presence and was known to be tough as nails, as temperamental as they came, had made love to her with such profound tenderness, she'd cried in his arms. And he had held her, kissing away her tears and soothing her fears by telling her that everything would be all right. He would get them through this no matter what.

She turned on her side and watched him sleep. For once, his features were relaxed, peaceful. She glanced over at the clock. It was late afternoon and the perfect time to contact Hawk. Easing out of bed she slipped back into her bathrobe and after getting her mobile phone off the dresser, she tiptoed out of the room, closing the door behind her. Going into the living room she sat on the sofa and placed a call to Hawk.

He picked up on the second ring. "Yes?"

"Hawk, it's Tori."

"Tori, is everything all right?"

She heard the concern in his voice. "Yes. Any word on Cross?"

"We got confirmation that he's still in South America, but he's making plans to come stateside. We think he's waiting for final word as to your and Drake's location. We're not going to leak that to him. We're letting him find it out on his own. As long as no one knows you're on Warren Mountains, you're safe for a while."

Tori sighed deeply. "Drake found out about the baby, Hawk."

She could hear Hawk's lengthy sigh. She had confided to Hawk about her pregnancy when she had seen him in Houston. "And how did he handle it?"

She was silent for a moment, and then she answered. "He's fine with it now, but we had some pretty rough moments earlier. He was pretty pissed to know that I had no intention of ever telling him."

"Well, I hope you realize that now that he knows, he has no intentions of letting you stay on that mountain."

Tori frowned. She knew Hawk was right. Now that Drake knew she was pregnant, he would not let her stay. "I won't leave him here alone," she said and meaning every word. "Please let us know if you hear anything else about Cross."

"You know I will. I want the two of you to take care and stay safe."

She smiled. "We will."

After she hung up the phone, she drew a shaky breath as she rubbed her stomach tenderly. She had to believe that in the end, things would all work out.

She had to believe that.

. . .

Solomon Cross smiled as he read the report. Excitement began to course through his veins. "It took your contacts long enough, Miguel, but this information pleases me. Now we're ready to embark on our adventure to North America. Let the pilot know that I'll be ready to leave in less than an hour."

"Yes, sir."

Cross stood and walked across the room and gazed lovingly at the portrait of Maria. "The time has come, my darling. They will pay for taking you away from me. This time I will not fail."

Drake picked up his mobile phone on the first ring. "Yes?"

"I just got word that Cross is headed to this country. He left from somewhere in South America two hours ago. We're using all our resources to try and intercept his flight, Drake, but in case we aren't successful, you and Tori need to be prepared."

Drake nodded. He thought of the decision he'd made concerning Tori and said, "We will be."

After a long moment, Hawk said, "I wish you would reconsider letting us help, Drake."

"I can't, Hawk. If word leaks out that the CIA is assisting, Cross will think it's a setup and I can't take the chance of him not coming. I'll call you when you can pick up his remains."

Hawk shook his head, laughing. "Dammit, Drake, you're one cocky son of a bitch."

Drake smiled. "Yeah, and the only thing I got to say to that is that I was trained by the best. Good-bye, Hawk."

"Good-bye, Drake, and take care."

He disconnected the call and turned when the alarm on his security system went off. He quickly moved over to one of the monitors. Someone had opened the gate to the north entrance of his property. He knew it wasn't Mrs. Gillette since he had called her earlier and told her not to come back for a while. Moving to the control panel he punched in a few buttons before one of the screens in front of him flitted to life.

Drake's gaze narrowed when he saw the two lone figures step out of a truck. They were mean-looking bastards who appeared ready for action, and he let out a deep, appreciative sigh.

Ashton and Trevor.

Before leaving Houston he had told them not to come. They had families to think about and he didn't want them getting involved. But they had come anyway. In a way he'd known they would.

He chuckled. Solomon Cross and his men were about to get their asses kicked.

CHAPTER 17

"Ashton had another vision," Trevor said, as a way of explaining their unannounced arrival. He stepped onto the porch to stand in front of Drake who was casually leaning against a post. "And since he thought I had nothing better to do with my time than to travel over six hundred miles to reenact my role as a Recon, I'm here."

Drake crossed his arms over his chest. "And I suppose back in Houston you were doing something better with your time?"

Trevor smiled. "Yeah. Corinthians has decided she wants another baby, and of course I'm more than happy to oblige her."

"Of course." Drake shook his head. His gaze shifted from Trevor to the other man who was approaching the porch.

Ashton glanced around. "I didn't come here just to twiddle my thumbs, Sir Drake. Where are they?"

Drake chuckled, not surprised Ashton knew what was going on. Ashton and his visions. "They're on their way."

Ashton said, "Good."

Trevor said, "Damn."

And Drake felt sincere gratitude all the way through his bones for the two men he called friends. It was like old times. The three of them were lethal when they worked together against an enemy. As Recons they had gone on a number of missions together. They had the ability to read off each other, know the others' thoughts even without a single word being spoken.

Ashton glanced around. "And where's the woman who's causing so much damn trouble?"

The smile that eased into the harsh lines of Drake's face had both Trevor and Ashton grinning. "Tori's taking a shower." His smile widened. "The two of you might as well hear my news."

Trevor rubbed his stubbly chin, thinking that he needed a shave but that could wait until after this mission. He stared at Drake. "What news?" he asked.

"Tori is pregnant."

"Damn, how did that happen?"

The question from Ashton had Drake laughing. "The usual way, Ash. I would think a man who produced triplets would have this down pat."

"Don't be a smart-ass, Drake. You know what I'm asking," Ashton snorted. "Being careless isn't your style, so what happened?"

Drake grinned. "I got caught up in the moment."

Trevor quirked one eyebrow as he stared at Drake. "Must have been one hell of a moment."

Drake's eyes sparkled with pleasure as he recalled every sensual second. "Trust me, it was."

Moments later, the three men glanced around when Tori stepped out on the porch. She gasped in surprise when she saw Trevor and Ashton and quickly flew into their arms.

Trevor looked at Drake as he held Tori in a hug. "One hell of a moment. One hell of a woman. I'd say you're one lucky bastard, Sir Drake."

Drake laughed. "Yeah, I'd say the same thing myself."

. . .

Tori glanced around when Trevor, Drake, and Ashton walked into the kitchen after returning from checking different areas of the property. Drake immediately walked over to her and kissed her on the lips. "How's my baby?" he asked, gently rubbing her stomach.

"Fine."

"And my baby's mom?"

Tori smiled. "She's doing fine, too." Her features then took on a serious expression. "Did you notice anything unusual?"

Drake shook his head as he pulled her closer into his arms. "No. It's my guess they'll do what they think will be a sneak attack."

She inhaled deeply. "So what do we do in the meantime?"

"We wait. Trevor has volunteered to take the first watch to man the security room. We've put out enough sensors to let us know way ahead of time when someone arrives, even by air."

Tori nodded. She knew that Drake had covered all bases. "In that case, I'll start dinner."

Drake caught her wrist before she had a chance to move away from him. "Dinner can wait. We need to talk."

Tori raised a dark brow. "About what?"

He took her hand and tugged her out of the kitchen. "You'll find out soon enough."

Drake watched Tori angrily pace the confines of his bedroom. She was mad. Furious. Boiling over with rage. But that couldn't be helped. He had made his decision and intended for his order to be followed. After all, Warren Mountains was his land, Solomon Cross was his personal enemy, and Tori was having his baby.

He would ignore the fact that she had told him to go to hell, after saying a couple of other not-so-nice words. He would even ignore the fact that she had kneed him—in the groin. According to what Trevor and Ashton had told him while they had been covering his land earlier, expectant women had a tendency to have emotional moments. He would chalk this up as Tori having hers.

And from the look of things, she wasn't through.

He leaned against the door and braced himself when she stopped pacing and turned to him. Fire was still in her eyes. But he thought she was beautiful when she was mad.

"You cannot tell me what to do, Drake. I am not a soldier under your command. I am a grown woman and if I want to fight, then I will."

"No, you won't, Tori. You have more than yourself to think about. Think of the baby."

She tossed hair from out of her face, threw back her shoulders and took a stance that let him know she was ready for round two. "I am thinking about the baby. This is my fight as well as yours and there is no way you can keep me out of it."

"Wanna bet?"

She glared at him. "But what you're asking is unfair. Why do I have to be the one to stay behind and man the security room? I want to be part of the action."

"Listen, Tori, your job will be an important one. With the remote controls Trev, Ashton, and I will be carrying, I need you watching the monitors, being our eyes, so we don't walk into an ambush or something."

"But that's not what I want to do."

"And like I said, you don't have a choice."

"And if I refuse to cooperate?"

He crossed his arms over his chest after thumping the back pocket of his jeans. "I have keys to the basement, Tori. It has a steel door with a state-of-the-art lock. Don't tempt me to use it. It should hold you rather nicely until we're through dealing with Cross. Like I said, you're staying behind."

"Like hell I will."

He smiled. "It doesn't matter to me if you consider it hell or heaven. You will not be leaving this house."

"And I'm supposed to stay here, paint my nails while you, Trevor, and Ashton are getting shot at? If you think that then you have another thought coming, Drake Warren."

"Then I have another thought coming and here it is, Tori: I told you what I need you to do. Ashton, Trevor, and I will be too busy with Cross to have time to worry about you, and—"

"Worry about me! I know how to take care of myself, Drake. I'm an ex-marine, a self-defense expert. I can shoot better than—"

"I've heard enough," he growled, coming after her, catching her off-guard. His hands closed around her wrist and his legs blocked hers so she couldn't try a karate maneuver on him. He lifted her, pinning her smaller body under his muscled one to the wall. His control had snapped. He had to keep her safe. He had to. He would die if anything happened to her.

"Dammit, listen to me, Tori," his growl going deeper. "I love that baby you're carrying and I love you. I love you so damn much that if anything were to happen to you, sweetheart, I couldn't make it. I couldn't stand to lose you twice. Do you understand what I'm saying?"

Tori heard the anguish in his voice and saw the turmoil in his gaze, stark fear that if he didn't take such drastic measures to protect her that history would be repeating itself.

She also saw the love shining in the depths of his eyes and a shudder ran through her. He loved her. He'd told her that he loved her.

"Drake."

The soundless whisper of his name from her lips only pushed him even more over the edge. His hips pushed against hers and she gasped at the hardness, the thickness and the size of the erection that was pressing into her stomach. Automatically she opened her legs, needing him inside of her; needing the assurance that everything would be all right and this would not be the end for them.

Drake inhaled deeply and she knew he'd caught the scent of her arousal, of her panties suddenly becoming drenched. A curse hissed from his clenched teeth as he adjusted her position against the wall to gain access to what he wanted beneath her skirt. He pushed her outfit out of the way, nearly tore her panties off at the same time she felt him tearing at the zipper of his pants to release himself. And then he thrust against her, easily entering her, his hips moving rhythmically back and forth inside of her. His mouth took hers, fiercely, hungrily, as his tongue mated greedily with hers, matching the same pace of his body as it pumped into her.

Delirious with the passion that Drake had stroked inside of her, Tori wrapped her arms around his neck at the same time she wrapped her legs around his hips, locking him inside of her while he rocked her to sweet oblivion. Pleasure, profound, unadulterated, ripped through her the moment she felt his climax, the moment she felt him shoot his release inside of her. He kissed the scream of an orgasm off her lips and from the feel of his hips undulating against her, trying to push deeper, they both soared over the edge, beyond the stars and straight to heaven.

For a long moment after they had returned to earth, he

kept her pinned against the wall, stayed inside of her while she continued to let her inner muscles milk him greedily, even when he thought he had nothing left to give. Then slowly, he unlocked her legs from around him and let her slide to the floor. His breathing was just as irregular as hers and she marveled at his momentary loss of control.

She also gloried in the words he had said. He loved her. "Drake . . ."

He lifted a finger to her lips to silence whatever words she was about to say. "Promise me that you will do as I ask, Tori," he whispered, barely getting his breath out. "Promise me."

She opened her mouth, not to make the promise he was asking her to make, but to tell him why she couldn't make such a promise. However, before she could get the words out, someone pounded on the bedroom door. Drake quickly pulled down her skirt and tried to bring order to their clothing before crossing the room to open the door.

Trevor stood in the doorway with a huge smile on his face. "I hate to interrupt such a heated domestic argument, but I thought the two of you would want to know that Cross has made his move. We've been invaded."

When Drake quickly moved to get his gun off the nightstand, Trevor winked at Tori then chuckled and said, "Let's get this show on the road. It's time for a little action, Recon style."

CHAPTER 18

Tori watched as the three men prepared for what they considered an act of war. Their weapons and ammunition alluded to just what Trevor had said. They were ready for action, Recon style.

Seeing them get ready reminded her of the days when the four of them, known as "the Fearless Four" would go on missions for their country. And as she watched, she was becoming increasingly furious that they were leaving her behind.

"I want in, Drake," she implored again, although she knew her words were falling on deaf ears.

Drake stopped after strapping the extra bullets around his waist and met her gaze. Seeing the determined glint in her eyes, he sighed deeply and strode over to her.

She studied his features when he came to stand in front of her. He was combat-ready and it reflected in the hard, cold eyes that met hers as well as the impassiveness that lined his face. "I've told you, this isn't your fight. It's mine. You only became a victim because of me, Tori, and I need you here to man the security room. You'll know what's going on and can give us a heads-up as to what we're dealing with. I'll be at a disadvantage if I'm worrying about you."

She nodded, knowing to argue with him would be useless. She would do what he asked of her up to a point, but then . . .

"All right, Drake. I don't want you to worry about me. Please stay safe and come back to me and the baby."

A small smile fractured his rugged features. "I plan to."

She looked past him to Trevor and Ashton. She knew they read the plea in her eyes. Drake could get cocky at times and would be quick to take risks; she needed their assurance that they would rein him in when he did. He would be doing more than settling a score with Solomon Cross; he intended to bring an end to everything once and for all.

"I love you, Drake," she whispered softly. She still wasn't sure what the future held for them but she knew she had to let him know how she felt.

"And I love you," he said quietly. He leaned down and placed a kiss on her lips.

Tori wouldn't settle for just a small kiss and reached out and pulled him to her and took over the kiss, desperately mating her mouth with his. He returned her kiss, deepened it and would have extended it had Ashton not cleared his throat a few times.

"We have to go, sweetheart," Drake said, reluctantly pulling away from her. "Remember your promise."

She nodded. She would remind him later that she hadn't promised him anything. She watched as the three men headed for the stairs, then Drake hesitated briefly, glanced back at her, winked and then strode up the stairs. She wasn't surprised when she heard the click of the basement door when he locked it behind him. He wasn't taking any chances of her not following his orders.

She looked at the pistols he had left her that had enough ammunition to bring down an army. She walked over and saw the screen whose video scanned the north side of Drake's property, and then she saw the figures of several men, about eight of them, carrying heavy-duty weapons as they slithered determinately toward the wooded area of Drake's property, unaware they were being captured on film.

She switched her attention to another screen at the same time the video camera picked up a helicopter that was landing in a clearing. A few minutes later she watched as three men got out of the helicopter, each heavily armed. Although the thickness of the pine needles of the trees slightly impeded her vision, Tori immediately recognized one of the men from photographs she had seen of him.

Solomon Cross.

A cold chill went down her body. The man looked as demented as she'd heard he was. She sat down and leaned back in her chair, knowing she needed to contact Trevor, Ashton, and Drake to let them know what was going on and where the enemy was located.

She opened her hand and stared at what lay in the palm. She smiled with satisfaction when she gazed at the key she had slipped out of Drake's pocket when she had intentionally taken over their kiss.

If he actually thought she would be pushed to the sidelines while he risked his life for her, he had another thought coming.

Drake wiped his mouth with the back of his hand while his pulse pounded. He, Trevor, and Ashton had split up after receiving word from Tori that they were outnumbered three to one. He scanned the immediate area knowing that somewhere out there were men who meant to kill him and Tori, and he was intent on not giving them the chance.

He was about to make a move toward a group of trees when he heard a zing of bullets, a few coming close to his head. He had been spotted and someone was firing at him.

He quickly dropped to the ground, appreciating the bed of thick pine needles that cushioned his fall, and rolled his body into a massive cluster of pine trees that immediately swallowed him up. Heart beating fast, his Beretta clutched tight and drawn, he waited, steadying his breathing and squinting his eyes against the evening sun to make out the lone figure he saw and wondered where the other cutthroats were. Evidently the three men who had arrived in the copter had also split up.

In the distance he heard more gunfire and knew either Trevor or Ashton had found action. He shifted his body and eased his breathing when he heard not one but two male voices.

"What if Cross is wrong and the woman is not hiding in the big house? This entire valley will go up in smoke when he sets the place on fire."

Fire! Tori was in danger and he had locked her in the basement! With a curse Drake shifted his body once again and picked up a pinecone nearby. Throwing it in the direction opposite of him, he got just the reaction from the men he had expected. They began shooting where the pinecone had landed, and he used the time their attention had been drawn elsewhere to make his escape.

Running hard, he kept his gaze in front of him as more bullets flew past his head, some hitting nearby pine trees. *He had to get to Tori.* When he saw a clearing up ahead he knew he would become a sitting duck if he didn't take the two men chasing him out. He slowed down running and entered the safety of the tall pine trees. He waited. He didn't have to wait long and with two accurate shots he made direct hits.

He quickly pulled out his remote to contact Trevor and Ashton. "I'm on my way back to the house. Cross plans to torch it and I have to get Tori out."

He began running hard again, refusing to think he would not reach her in time. Suddenly he felt something graze his temple and he tripped and fell. He rolled and tried to get back on his feet but pain and dizziness set in. When he rolled again and tried making another attempt at standing, he glanced up and looked into the cold, dark eyes of Solomon Cross who stood only a few feet away, and the man had a pistol aimed directly at his head.

Trying to breathe through tightened lips, Tori aimed her pistol and shot the man who was coming at Trevor from behind while his attention was focused elsewhere, as he tangled on the ground with one of the cutthroats. The sharp sound of the gunshot so close to him made Trevor lose concentration, almost giving his opponent the upper hand until Trevor gave the man a hard blow to the face, knocking him unconscious.

He shook his head when Tori scrambled from out of the thicket of pine trees. He looked at the man she had just wasted and then shifted his attention to the still-smoking gun she held in her hand. "I see you haven't lost your touch," he said, smiling.

She returned his smile and glanced around. "Where's Ashton?"

"I talked to him a few minutes ago on the remote and he's holding his own, although I think I need to go check and make sure." He then frowned when something suddenly occurred to him. "How the hell did you get out of that locked basement?"

She shrugged. "A woman has her ways."

A flicker of amusement lightened Trevor's dark eyes. "Evidently. But Drake needs to know you're all right. He sent a message to Ash and me a few minutes ago that Cross was going to torch his house. He was trying to get back there to save you."

Tori immediately knew that something was wrong. "You go and check on Ashton and I'll find Drake."

Drake tried to ignore the pain that raced through his head. The wound he'd received was superficial but he was having a hell of a headache. The evening sun was peeking through the top of the trees, its rays hitting the metal of the gun still aimed at him.

He hissed a curse as he looked into Solomon Cross's face. The man was wearing an expensive double-breasted Italian silk suit and looked totally out of place in his surroundings. He was a muscular man and evidently in good physical shape since he hadn't worked up a sweat. And he had the audacity to smile as if he already tasted victory.

"We meet again, Warren. Over the past five years I've had several opportunities to kill you, but decided to let you live. I wanted you to go through each day knowing how it felt to have someone you loved brutally taken away from you."

Drake shook his head as he pulled himself up in a sitting position, fully aware that Cross had tightened his grip on the pistol when he reached up to touch his aching head. "You're a sick bastard, Cross."

"Yes, and you're going to find out just how sick I am. I don't like being made a fool of. So tell me, where is she? Only a cat has nine lives and she isn't one. This time I'm going to make sure she dies and you'll have the pleasure of watching."

Drake frowned. "Tori's not here. I sent her off the mountain before you arrived." He knew he had to keep the man talking while he tried working the bowie knife out of his shoe. Then he would take pleasure in cutting Cross's throat.

"I don't believe you, so tell me where she is."

Drake clenched his jaw tightly. "I'm not telling you a damn thing."

For one brief moment there was a flicker of some emotion in Cross's eyes, a dazed, crazed look. Then angrily, he raised the gun and aimed straight for Drake's head as a smile touched the man's lips. "Then you die first. Too bad you won't live to see what I'm going to do when I find her. It's going to be quite a show."

"You won't get away with it, Cross. We knew you were coming. Whether you realize it or not, by now all of your men are either dead or been captured. Both FBI and CIA agents will be swarming the place in a few minutes. If you're smart you would give up and turn yourself in."

"Never! I have to settle an old score. An eye for an eye." His hand tightened on the gun he held. "First you, then her, and don't think I won't find her. She's somewhere hidden on this mountain and I plan to find her or burn down every inch of this place. This time she won't escape."

Drake knew that although Cross had the advantage, he didn't plan to just sit and let the man coldly blow him away. He heard the cock of Cross's gun and knew he was about to pull the trigger. He clamped his jaw together hoping his reflexes would be faster than the bullet when he made his move. It was still a possibility he would get hit, but he refused to get his damn head blown off.

Then, as impossible as it seemed, Tori stepped out from behind a cluster of pine trees holding a black 9mm automatic aimed at Solomon Cross's head. Drake's heart contracted and he was too taken aback to figure out how the hell she had managed to get out of the locked basement.

He just stared at her, trying not to let Cross read his face to give away her presence. She was mad; her eyes were narrowing, her chin was tilted upward and her lips had curled in contempt. Her degree of anger was evident and he thought she was the most beautiful sight he had seen in a long time.

"Drop it, Cross!" she barked. The man gasped and whirled around, which gave Drake the advantage he needed, even with Cross's size. But Drake's earlier assumption about the man was right. He was in good physical shape and he also had a score he intended to settle. Although Drake did a quick maneuver and tried knocking the gun from Cross's hand and overtaking him, Cross held the gun tightly, jerked his body out of Drake's reach and with amazing speed, shifted his aim of the gun from Drake to Tori.

"Back off, Warren, or she dies!" he screamed as he scuttled farther away from Drake. "At this point I have nothing to lose, so go over there and join her or I'll blow her brains out now," he snarled. It was a standoff. Tori had her gun aimed for Cross and Cross had his gun aimed for her.

"Don't do what he asks, Drake. Don't do it!"

Drake stilled, his gaze on the scene before him. Deciding not to take any chances, refusing to put the woman he loved and the child she carried at risk, Drake slowly eased over to stand beside Tori.

"You bitch!" Cross screamed at Tori, almost beside himself in anger. "You were supposed to die in that explosion! I had planned it perfectly. You were supposed to die and now you will!"

He lifted his gun higher, aiming it straight for Tori's head. "Sandy Carroll, get ready to meet your maker."

Drake and Tori both noticed the movement in the woods out of the corners of their eyes and then, just seconds before Cross was about to pull the trigger, a shot rang out, hitting the man, the impact jabbing him full force and knocking his body sideways—but not before he raised his gun and tried taking another aim at Tori. Drake pushed Tori out the way at the same time another shot rang out, and then another. Blood gushed from the wound in Cross's chest and he stared over at Drake and Tori, looking at them in dazed disbelief before finally closing his eyes and slumping backward.

Hawk, Ashton, and Trevor stepped from behind a group of trees. Hawk was the one holding the still-smoking gun and the expression on his face was one of sheer satisfaction.

After approaching Cross to make sure the man would never be a bother to anyone again, Hawk turned and faced his two former agents. He shrugged when he saw them staring at him, speechless. "I thought the least I could do was join the fight, not as a law enforcement official, but as a friend."

Suddenly, in the distance, the sound of helicopters and the screeching of car tires caught everyone's attention. Hawk smiled faintly as he glanced over at Drake. "I also decided to take you up on your offer and come pick up the remains."

It was over an hour later before they got back to the house. Not only did the CIA arrive, but also the FBI and the DEA. Questions were asked and Tori, Drake, Ashton, and Trevor didn't have any problems letting Hawk provide all the answers.

And it had really helped matters that the ASI, in a surprising move—probably from feeling the heat of the South American government—had contacted the Justice Department earlier that day, denouncing its ties with Cross and claiming that Cross's personal vendetta against the two CIA operatives had not been sanctioned by them and there would not be any further attempts on their lives.

Trevor and Ashton took Hawk up on his offer to personally fly them back to Houston in his private plane. It was the midnight hour by the time everyone had left Warren Mountain. Tori held her breath as the last car drove off, leaving her and Drake alone. She knew they needed to talk but she wanted to take a shower first. She felt sweaty and dirty.

As soon as the door closed behind Drake, he turned and tried pulling her into his arms.

"Wait!" she said, pulling back from him. "I need to shower first, then we need to talk."

Drake's brow raised considerably when he sensed her nervousness. "All right," he said, taking a step back. "Talking isn't a bad idea since I'm dying to know how the hell you got of the basement."

He then reached out and lifted her chin with his finger. "Then after we talk, I'd like to pay our baby another visit."

Tori's heart fluttered with the feel of Drake touching her as well as the look of love and desire in his eyes. "Can I ask you a question?"

He smiled. "Sure, ask me anything."

"When there was a standoff between me and Cross and he ordered you to come stand next to me, why did you? Why didn't you take the chance and blow him away? You could have."

Drake shook his head. "No, I couldn't. He had a gun pointed at your head, Tori, and there was no way I was going to take a chance and risk losing you."

She looked up at him, confused. "But you take risks all the time, Drake. That's all you've done over the past five years is take risks."

He grimaced ruefully, knowing her words were true.

"Yes, but when it came to you and our child, I couldn't do it. I couldn't risk losing the two people that I love more than life itself. And because I love you, I don't want to take unnecessary risks with my life either. I want to be around to see our son or daughter grow up. I want to have other babies and watch them grow up here on our mountain, healthy, God-fearing, and strong." He smiled. "And all future marines."

Tori grinned. "Yes, future marines."

He looked down at her. "But speaking of risks, Tori, I haven't been the only person who's taken risks over the past five years. You nearly risked everything by coming to see me that night at the hospital. And later, when I needed you, you took a risk by opening your arms to me, taking my seed into your womb and binding us in the most primitive way." He lifted her chin to meet his gaze. "And let's not forget the risk you took by leaving that basement when I had locked you in it."

He leaned down and kissed her lips. "A woman's love for her man. I can't think of anything as powerful."

She smiled through the tears in her eyes. "And a man's love for his woman. I don't know of anything as compelling," she whispered.

He drew a deep breath, wanting her to know that he loved her. He had loved her as Sandy and now he loved her as Tori. And he needed to let her know how he felt, but first things first. "Come on, let's go take a shower."

When they got to the bathroom, he quickly removed their clothes and when he picked her up and placed her in the shower with him, under the warm, heated blast of water, he knew that more than dirt and grime were being washed from his body. His soul was also being cleansed. He was removing five years of pain and suffering, five years of not giving a damn and of taking risks no mortal man would take.

That part of his life was over. Now he had a lot to live for—Tori and their child. He pulled her into his arms and kissed her, needing to hold her while his soul became cleansed.

Moments later he picked her up and carried her out of the shower and began toweling her dry. Their gazes connected and she clung to his gaze as he crouched down and dried off her legs and her feet. When he stood back up, he whispered, tenderly, "I love you."

His three words, spoken in a heartfelt whisper, touched her, emotionally drawing her in. "And it doesn't matter to me if you're Sandy or Tori. What matters more than anything is that you're back in my life."

He inhaled deeply before continuing. "I am filled with so many imperfections that I can't name them all, yet someone up there looked beyond my faults and saw my needs, and knew I needed you. I have been given the most perfect gift and I will cherish it always. I will love you, honor you, and protect you. And I pledge to make you happy and live each and every day as if it were our last; enjoy every single moment and give thanks for every second. I love you, Tori, with all my heart and with all my soul."

Tears clouded Tori's eyes. "Oh, Drake, and I love you."

He wiped the tears from her cheeks with his fingers. "We've been through some rough times sweetheart; five years' worth," he said, his voice deep with his emotions. "But it's all behind us now. We'll look to the future and will tackle any problems that come our way. Together. I think anyone would agree that we're a good team."

She gave him a trembly smile and nodded. "Yes, the best."

And then he kissed her long and intimately hard in a way that intended to touch her the same way he was touched. And when he picked her up into his arms, she knew that everything would be all right. She had to concede that there were some risks that were worth taking.

They had gone through the storm together and there would be sunny days ahead. And when the rains came again they would find shelter in each other's arms and be protected by the love in their hearts.

They had solid history on their side. They also had time. Starting tonight, they would embark on a new beginning, one stronger, with deeper meaning and more powerful because of what they had endured.

"I want you in my life, Tori," Drake whispered. "Now. Tonight. Always. I love you and have always loved you. My life won't be complete until you agree to marry me. There's no way we can recapture the past but we can build a future. Together."

He took her lips hungrily again as he shifted her into his arms to open the door. Once they got to his bedroom, there were no words needed as he dropped the towels covering them.

"Do you still want to pay our baby a visit?" she asked as her arms wrapped around his neck, savoring the feel of him touching her everywhere.

"Always," he whispered, bending his head to take her mouth hungrily.

Drake's senses soared, they flew high, and a guttural sound was released from his throat as he gently placed her on the bed. This is what he had always wanted and desired but thought he would never have.

Peace.

His tongue made a path around her breasts, latching onto one nipple and then another, drawing moans after moans from her. She was his, had always been his and would always be his.

He took his time to enjoy the sight and taste of her, to

send heat sizzling through both of their bodies. The driving ache to bury himself inside of her was unbearable.

"Please, Drake."

She had begun begging for release from her sensual torment and he knew he would give her anything and everything that she wanted. He eased between her thighs and as he entered her with a single, hard thrust, he knew what it felt like to be high on the mountains, walking on clouds.

His movements quickened and he looked down at her. Their gazes connected. Held. And when he breathed in the sensual scent that clouded the room, he went up in flames and carried her with him. Shudders racked his body and went all the way through to hers, forcing a scream from her throat.

Moments later he collapsed on top of her, and then switched positions to pull her into his arms. He was still buried inside of her and wanted to stay that way forever. But it didn't take long before he felt himself get hard again and thought his desire for this woman was almost too much.

He appreciated every thing about her; including every single strand of hair on her head. "Tori."

Her only response was an exhausting moan that sounded sensual to his ears and made him even more aroused. And as he proceeded to mate with her again, he knew all his good fortune was a miracle; a special gift that could have only come from God.

And it had come to him, signed, sealed and delivered at . . . the midnight hour.

Epilogue

Tori glanced out of the window. It seemed that everyone was present for her and Drake's wedding and more people were arriving on Warren Mountains.

Over the past two months she had gotten to know all of Drake's new friends; the Madaris family; the Garwoods; and she had almost melted in a heap at Drake's feet when she had been introduced to Hollywood actor Sterling Hamilton, and his beautiful wife Colby.

Then there had been Trask Maxwell's wife, Felicia. Tori had also gotten to know Sterling's brother, Nicholas Chenault, and his wife, Shayla, and had renewed her acquaintance with Trevor's parents and his sister Gina, and had met Gina's husband Mitch as well as their newborn son Cameron.

She couldn't help but be in awe at the number of babies everyone had. Drake's friends either had babies or were having babies, and she felt right at home being included in that number.

"I hope you aren't getting nervous, Tori. Just consider everyone as family."

She turned from the window to smile at the two women in the room, Trevor's wife Corinthians and Ashton's wife Nettie. They had been wonderful and she enjoyed building a special relationship with them. They were exactly what she'd needed after having denied herself friendships with anyone over the past five years.

Everyone who had known of Sandy Carroll's death was thrilled to find out that she was alive. Hawk had told her that, with Solomon Cross eliminated, there was no reason she could not go back to being Sandy Carroll if that's what she wanted. But she and Drake had decided it would make things easier if they let Sandy Carroll remain at rest and everyone would continue to think of her as Tori.

"No, I'm not getting nervous, but I am rather anxious," she answered, smiling. She glanced down at the short gown she wore and thought it was beautiful. Even with the style of her dress, it was plain to see that she was pregnant. But she didn't mind who knew. She was marrying the man she loved and was having his baby and at the moment she couldn't be happier.

"I've heard from Ashton that Drake is rather anxious, too," Nettie Sinclair said, smiling. "I have a feeling if you weren't already pregnant then you would definitely get pregnant tonight."

The three women laughed and Tori glanced back out the window when another car pulled up. She watched as a beautiful young woman with a mass of reddish brown hair that flowed wildly across her shoulders and down her back, got out of a beautiful silver-gray Nissan 350Z. "Who's that?"

Corinthians and Nettie joined her at the window. "Oh, that's Christy Madaris, the youngest of the Madaris siblings," Corinthians said, smiling. "She just graduated from Howard University and that car was a gift from her brothers. I guess she decided to put it on the road and drive here from Houston instead of flying."

Nettie chuckled as she admired the vehicle Christy was driving. "I wonder if she got any tickets along the way."

"She is simply beautiful," Tori said as she watched Christy join her three brothers and, ignoring their frowns, she proceeded to give Justin, Dex, and Clayton hugs. Tori remembered the night she had met the brothers and was glad she had recently gotten the chance to meet their wives as well. She had found Lorren, Caitlin, and Syneda Madaris to be warm, loving, and caring women, and just what the three men needed. She could tell the Madaris family was a rather close one that extended the pinnacles of that closeness to include many friends, like Drake. She had even enjoyed her trip back to Houston where they had been the houseguests of Jake Madaris and his beautiful wife, movie star Diamond Swain-Madaris.

"Yes, Christy is beautiful and the brothers are very protective of her," Nettie whispered as if letting Tori in on a secret when it was a fact that everyone knew.

Corinthians Grant didn't say anything as a smile touched her lips. She gazed past where Christy was talking to her brothers to the man standing alone, off in the distance and watching Christy with keen eyes.

Alex Maxwell.

She knew that the Madaris brothers were clueless that their baby sister and Alex were attracted to each other. She wondered what would happen once they found out. She could tell by the way Alex was staring at Christy that all was not well between them. In fact, it seemed that Christy was deliberately ignoring him, something Corinthians had noticed her doing on a number of other occasions. But Alex was definitely not ignoring Christy and Corinthians had a feeling that as far as Alex was concerned, there was unfinished business between them.

"Well, I don't have too long to wait now," Tori said, breaking into Corinthians's thoughts.

Corinthians turned around. "No, you don't and you and

Sir Drake deserve to be happy. After all you have gone through, I don't know of any other couple who deserves happiness more," she said softly as tears clouded her eyes. She would always have deep love and affection for the man who had helped her husband rescue her from the clutches of a crazed kidnapper almost two years ago.

"And I agree," Nettie added. "Sir Drake was there for Ashton and almost single-handedly rescued him out of that forest fire when the park rangers had wanted to give up. But of course Sir Drake wouldn't let them." Nettie giggled. "He even threatened to blow off their heads with his Beretta if they tried."

Tori shook her head, smiling. She had heard the stories of those two incidents involving Corinthians and Ashton, as well as Drake's other escapades and how he took pride putting the fear of God into people and wouldn't hesitate carrying out any threat he'd made.

"Well, I plan to cool him down some," she said, smiling brightly. "He won't be taking unnecessary risks from now on. He'll be too busy playing the role of dad than of Rambo."

It seemed that nothing but blessings had been coming their way lately. Drake had made a decision to leave the Agency and start his own security company since he'd had such good success with the one he had installed.

"Is it true, Tori? Did you and Drake get a wedding gift from the president and first lady?" Nettie asked excitedly, as she stepped back from the window to adjust a curl that had fallen out of place atop Tori's head.

Tori smiled. "Yes, it's true." The president had been grateful for her and Drake's rescue of his niece.

"All right, ladies. It's time to go and you know how your father believes in things starting on time, Corinthians."

Everyone turned when Corinthians's mother, Maudlin

Avery, entered the room. Corinthians's father, the Reverend Nathan Avery, was ecstatic that Drake was giving up the cloak-and-dagger business and settling down and getting married. He had eagerly agreed to perform the ceremony.

Maudlin took one look at Tori and a huge smile touched her lips and tears formed in her eyes. "You look beautiful, dear, and I know Drake will thank God every day for bringing you back into his life."

Back into his life, Tori thought as a smile also touched her lips. "And I will thank God every day as well for bringing him back into mine."

It was a gorgeous day for a wedding, and a few minutes later, outside under the beauty of God's sky and surrounded by Warren Mountains, Tori walked down the aisle to Drake on Hawk's arms. Her old boss and good friend had been touched that she had asked him to do the honors.

She smiled when she looked ahead and saw Drake. His decision to have two best men didn't surprise her. It rounded things out perfectly since Corinthians and Nettie had agreed to stand beside her as her best ladies.

Once she reached Drake's side he took her hand from Hawk's and lifted it to his lips and kissed it with all the love he had shining in his eyes. Over the past two months he had proven to her in more ways than one that he loved her and that she and the child she carried were the most important things to him.

They had decided to keep the beach house in California and use it as a summer home. For their honeymoon they would be spending a month in the Caribbean, compliments of Drake's many friends.

The ceremony was memorable but brief, and when Reverend Avery said, "I now pronounce you man and wife and you may kiss your bride," Drake didn't hesitate to pull Tori into his arms and kissed her in front of all his guests with all the passion and love in his heart.

When he released her mouth, he whispered against her damp lips, "I love you, Mrs. Warren."

She smiled and said, "And I love you as well."

Later that night, after leaving the wedding reception and catching a flight that took them straight to the Cayman Islands, Tori lay naked in her husband's arms in the beautiful villa feeling completely satisfied and extremely happy. They had just finished making love and her body still glowed with passion.

She smiled. "I think our child is enjoying your visits more and more," she whispered.

Drake smoothed a hand over his wife's rounded stomach. "And I love those visits," he said huskily. It seemed she had started showing overnight and he would never forget the experience of their child's first movement. He and Tori had been in awe and had shared the moment together.

And seeing Tori naked and pregnant always did something to him. All he had to do was look at her and his sexual needs would become ferocious and all he could think about was burying himself deep inside her body.

"Do you want to make another visit?" she asked, gazing deep into his eyes.

Drake smiled. Her passionate appetite was just as fierce as his. "Are you sure you can handle it?" he asked. "I wouldn't want to wear out my welcome." Without waiting for her reply, he raised up and eased his body over hers.

"You could never wear out your welcome, Drake Warren," she said, knowing she loved her husband beyond reason.

He kissed her in a way that intended to give her pleasure,

immediately going after her tongue. She kissed him back and in that single kiss they shared, she knew love as she had never known it before.

And then he began making love to her again.

Slow, hot, intense, mind-whirling, earthshaking, bed-spinning lovemaking, and the last thought that came to her mind before a climax ripped through her and she felt a similar one rip through him was that Drake Warren was a man who was an ace when it came to passion.

As his arms closed about her, holding her tenderly to him, she knew this is where she would always want to be, close to his heart.

Carnival Cruise Line

New York Times and *USA Today* bestselling author BRENDA JACKSON lives in the city where she was born, Jacksonville, Florida. She is a graduate of William M. Raines High School, and has a bachelor of science degree in business administration from Jacksonville University.

Brenda is a retiree who worked thirty-seven years in management for a major insurance company. She is also a member of Romance Writers of America and Delta Sigma Theta Sorority, Inc. Brenda married her childhood sweetheart, Gerald, forty-seven years ago and they have two sons. She has more than 125 novels in print and many of her books have been adapted to movies. She is currently at work on her next novel.

More from Bestselling Author
BRENDA JACKSON

THE MADARIS FAMILY NOVELS

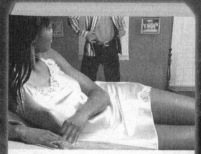

PLAYERS SERIES

Unfinished Business
Slow Burn
Taste of Passion

No More Playas
What a Woman Wants

STANDALONES

Ties That Bind - The Savvy Sistahs - A Family Reunion
Her Little Black Book - Some Like It Hot - Welcome to Leo's
The Best Man - Mr. Satisfaction - An All Night Man
Let's Get It On

AVAILABLE WHEREVER BOOKS ARE SOLD

brendajackson.net   ST. MARTIN'S PAPERBACKS